Praise for the Ivy Meadows Mystery Series

## MACDEATH (#1)

"Who cannot have fun with a disastrous (and murderous) production of *Macbeth*? Cindy Brown's first novel is a delicious romp with plenty of humor and suspense."

— Rhys Bowen,
*New York Times* Bestselling Author of the Royal Spyness Mysteries

"An easy read that will have you hooked from the first page...Cindy Brown uses what she knows from the theater life to give us an exciting mystery with all the suspense that keeps you holding on."

— *Fresh Fiction*

"A whodunit with a comic spirit, and Ivy Meadows has real heart. You'll never experience the Scottish play the same way again!"

— Ian Doescher,
Author of the William Shakespeare's Star Wars Series

"Funny and unexpectedly poignant, *Macdeath* is that rarest of creatures: a mystery that will make you laugh out loud. I loved it!"

— April Henry,
*New York Times* Bestselling Author

"Vivid characters, a wacky circus production of *Macbeth*, and a plot full of surprises make this a perfect read for a quiet evening. Pour a glass of wine, put your feet up, and enjoy! Bonus: it's really funny."

— Ann Littlewood,
Award-Winning Author of the Iris Oakley "Zoo-dunnit" Mysteries

"This gripping mystery is both satisfyingly clever and rich with unerring comedic timing. Without a doubt, *Macdeath* is one of the most entertaining debuts I've read in a very long time."

— Bill Cameron,
Spotted Owl Award-Winning Author of *County Line*

**The Ivy Meadows Mystery Series
by Cindy Brown**

MACDEATH (#1)
THE SOUND OF MURDER (#2)
(September 2015)

AN IVY MEADOWS MYSTERY

MACDEATH

*Cindy Brown*

To Breena,
Thanks for
supporting United Way
(& me!)

Cindy
Brown

HENERY PRESS

MACDEATH
An Ivy Meadows Mystery
Part of the Henery Press Mystery Collection

First Edition
Trade paperback edition | January 2015

Henery Press
www.henerypress.com

Copyright © 2014 by Cindy Brown
Cover art by Stephanie Chontos

ISBN-13: 978-1-940976-69-3

Printed in the United States of America

*For HHH, always*

# ACKNOWLEDGMENTS

Writing a first novel is tough. I never would have made it to the finish line without the feedback, advice, and support of an enormous number of people. Thank you to:

The wonderful folks at Henery Press, especially Kendel Lynn and Erin George, for believing in me (and Ivy), and for editing that felt generous and right and good.

The people who helped me get the details right: D.P. Lyle; the crimescenewriter listserv; and Roger I. Ideishi, JD, OT/L, FAOTA, Associate Professor, Dept. of Rehabilitation Sciences, Temple University. Any mistakes are my own.

Two workshops that especially helped me hone my craft: The Squaw Valley Writers Workshop, where I found great support from author Max Byrd and fellow writers Annam Manthiram and Emanuella Martin; and the Book Passage Mystery Writers Conference, where I met the gracious Rhys Bowen. I'd also like to thank the good people of Oregon Writers Colony, who have been fabulous guides and cheerleaders.

Portland mystery authors Bill Cameron, April Henry, and Ann Littlewood—wonderful writers, generous mentors, and good friends.

My early readers and writing friends, including Delia Booth, Randy Bonella, Jennie Bricker, Jane Carlsen, Pat Franko, Judy Hricko, Bernice Johnson, Suzanne LaGrande, Ruth Maionchi, Janice Maxson, Cynthia McGean, Emma Miles, Lindsay Nyre, Shauna Petchel, Rae Richen, Ed Sweet, and Autumn Trapani.

Barry "Victory Nipple" Siegwart, for several of the bad jokes.

Holly Franko, an extraordinary writer, editor, and friend who has been with Macdeath since the very beginning.

Hal, my first reader, first editor, first everything.

Thank you all. I feel incredibly lucky to have you as part of my life.

# CHAPTER 1

## *So Fair and Foul a Day*

Like every actor, I knew *Macbeth* was cursed, that death and destruction and all manner of bad things happen during the show. You'd think I would've remembered this the day of my audition.

"My name is Ivy Meadows, and I am an actress!" Yuck. I grimaced at myself in the rearview mirror and started up my car. I felt stupid doing these affirmations, and especially stupid when I did them badly. I was an actress, dammit, albeit one who didn't make a living at it, yet. Bob always says it's just a matter of time before someone recognizes my beauty, worth, and talent. Bob's my uncle, not my boyfriend. That's an affirmation for another day.

I put my little green Aspire in gear, pulled out of my apartment's parking lot, and headed for Phoenix Shakespeare Theater. I had scored a blue silk top off the sale rack at Re-Dud, and felt very elegant, very professional, very "classical"—for about three minutes. That's when I noticed my car's air conditioning was still blowing hot air. Which meant no air conditioning.

I took a deep breath. "My name is Ivy Meadows and *I* am an actress!"

The affirmation worked about as well as the air conditioning. The hundred-and-one degree day wasn't bad for August, but skyscraper-tall thunderheads made the air unusually muggy. My blouse was beginning to stick to my armpits.

"My name is Ivy Meadows and I *am* an actress!"

The car was heating up, but the affirmation was sounding better. I was getting used to my new name. It had taken me awhile to come up with it. I had tried what my drag queen friends do—that is, taking the name of your first pet and combining it with the name of the street where you grew up. They came up with great names like Mitzi Eldorado or Squeaky Dora, but mine ended up being Stubby Rural Route Number Two. So instead I took my name from a subdivision off the 51 that has neither ivy nor meadows, this being Phoenix and all.

Something tickled. I looked down. Sweat rivulets were streaking dark indigo stripes down my peacock-blue blouse. The dashboard clock showed just twenty minutes before my scheduled audition time. No time to go home and change. Dang, dang, dang! I really wanted this gig. Getting cast in this show could launch my career in acting.

I could do this. After all, "My name is Ivy Meadows and *I am an actress!*" I turned the fan on high, stepped on the gas, and zoomed toward the theater.

By the time I reached the theater parking lot, my top was soaked, stuck to me like Saran Wrap. But what could I do? I jogged to the stage door, heels sinking slightly into the melting asphalt of the parking lot, and shoved open the door. Inside, the blast of the air conditioning against my wet blouse gave me goose bumps, and nipples. It wasn't a look I was going for right then.

I ran into the hallway and tossed my headshot and résumé to a sturdy woman with close-cropped brown hair and a stick-on name tag that read "Linda, Stage Manager."

"Ivy Meadows," I yelled. "Two twenty. I'll be right back."

I turned around and ran right into Simon Black. Yes, *the* Simon Black. We'd worked together on an independent film a few months earlier—a film that never got made when Simon, its star, didn't show up on the final day of the shoot.

"Lovely to see you again." The aging star was looking a bit tarnished—dark circles under his brilliant blue eyes, a slight whiff of alcohol on his breath. It didn't matter. He still had the voice.

Deep and rumbling with a fabulous English accent, that voice had graced the stages of the Royal Shakespeare Company and thundered from movie screens in multiplexes. Only to wash up in Phoenix.

"I love you as a blonde, my dear, but..." He eyed my Saran Wrap blouse.

"I know. Gotta run." I headed for the restroom. As I skidded into the bathroom, Simon called, "Break a leg."

Instead I broke a heel. Right off. I'd just splurged twelve whole dollars at Payless for those piece-of-crap black vinyl pumps.

Soldiering on, I stuck my indigo-blue armpit under the hand dryer, then yelped as a gust of cold air shocked my system. I banged on the stupid thing and burst into tears.

A knock, and Simon poked his head in. "Everything alright?"

I looked at him with mascara-raccoon eyes, wearing one shoe, a wet blouse, and nipples.

"Ah," he said. "I see."

About a minute later, the stage manager pushed the door open and tossed me a leopard-spotted leotard. A hideous leopard-spotted leotard. "Simon said you needed this."

I tore off my top and skirt, kicked off my one good shoe, and pulled on the leotard. It fit, tightly, but off the shoulder—there was no way to wear my bra with it. I wriggled out of my bra and pulled my stretchy black skirt on over the leotard. I glanced in the mirror. Actually, it wasn't too bad, except for the mascara running down my...

"You're up." Linda pulled me out of the bathroom and into my new, very Shakespearean life, one full of love and betrayal—and murder.

# CHAPTER 2

## *Chance May Crown Me*

I ran down the hall to the audition room, pulled myself up to my full five foot two, and whispered under my breath, "My name is Ivy Meadows and I am an actress." I opened the door and strode into the room. Head held high, I focused on the director, who sat behind a table at the far end of the big, windowless space, chewing on a carrot. "Hi," I said, with my best smile, "My name is Ivy—oof!"

I fleetingly saw the cord snaked across the floor as I tumbled head over shoeless heels, pulled myself into a somersault, and landed at the feet of one of Phoenix's best directors. Edward Heath, a small thin man with a small thin mustache and a shirt unbuttoned one too many, stared at me, then slowly applauded. "Brilliant," he said, as I scrambled to my feet. "Perfect." A note of concern tugged at his mustache. "But the concept is supposed to be under wraps. Linda!"

The stage manager opened the door. A funky smell entered the room with her.

"It seems we have a leak," said Edward.

"That's just my shoes." Linda's white Nikes shone a slightly slimy green under the fluorescent lights. "Sorry."

"My concept. Someone must have leaked my concept."

Linda shrugged her flannel-shirted shoulders. "Don't know how." She turned to go.

"And the smell?" Edward wrinkled his nose at the odor, best described as eau d' dive bar bathroom.

"My old friend Simon." Linda's jaw clenched. "He threw up on my shoes."

Shaking his head, Edward dismissed Linda with a wave of his carrot and picked up my headshot and résumé from among the ones scattered on the table. "Ivy Meadows..." He looked up at me. "Aren't you Olive Ziegwart?"

He knew me! I nodded.

"Olive Zieg-*wart*. Ha! Smart to change *that* name."

My father used to tell us that Ziegwart meant "victory nipple" in German. I don't know why he thought that would make us feel better.

"So, Olive—*Ivy*—, how long have you been a gymnast?"

A what? Oh, the somersault. I punted. "Since I was little."

It was true. I did do gymnastics in school, and the occasional handstand on the front lawn if anyone interesting was watching.

"Good, good." He gnawed on the carrot. He had several more lined up like orange pens in his front shirt pocket.

"And how did you hear about," he lowered his voice, "the concept?"

I had no earthly idea what he was talking about. "Well, you know, your reputation for unusual..."

He raised an eyebrow.

"Unusual-ly intriguing..."

A smile. Phew.

"Adaptations..."

"I do not do adaptations! Every word belongs to the Bard." A fine spray of chewed-up carrot just missed me.

Dang. What word had he used earlier? Concept.

"I mean conceptualizations..."

His smile returned.

"Of Shakespeare's work fascinated me to the point where I did a little detective work, just to see how I could best fit into the world you have imagined." I was on a roll now. "Of course I can't reveal my sources, but I can promise you I won't breathe a word of this. It's a brilliant concept."

"Thank you. I don't believe it's been done before. Not many can say that. I did consider making our hero a pirate and setting the whole thing at sea, but I feel this is much more original, don't you?" he said, waving his carrot in the air.

I nodded.

"All right then. Based on your appearance and your entrance, you obviously had in mind one of the witches' roles."

I did?

Edward slid a "side"—several printed pages of the script—across the table. "Read the first witch in this scene."

Yikes. A cold reading of a Shakespearean tumbling witch. I really wanted to do the monologue I'd prepared, but I plunged into the part, starting off with another somersault. The side flew out of my hands. I scampered after it, and read, "Where hast thou been, sister?"

Edward, reading the second witch's part, replied in a squeaky voice, "Killing swine." Then, in a deep, raspy voice, he played the third witch, "Sister, where thou?"

Taking my cue from him, I squeaked and rasped, "A sailor's wife had carrots in her lap, And munch'd, and munch'd, and munch'd."

"Chestnuts!" Edward yelled. "She had chestnuts in her lap!"

"Chestnuts in her lap, And munch'd, and munch'd, and munch'd."

I threw in another somersault, hoping to distract him from my gaffe. "'Give me,' quoth I: 'Aroint thee, witch!' the rump-fed ronyon cries."

I didn't know what "rump-fed" actually meant, but slapped my ass as if I knew. Edward chuckled. Okay, then. I could do this.

"Her husband's to Aleppo gone, master o' the Tiger." I cracked an imaginary whip. "But in a sieve I'll thither sail, And, like a rat without a tail, I'll do, I'll do, and I'll do."

I chased my nonexistent rat tail and ended the scene with a triumphant cartwheel. I held a gymnast's victory pose while I waited for a response.

"Hmm," said Edward, worrying his carrot nub.

I tried to mask my heavy breathing. Who knew being a witch was such hard work?

"I see you're not especially modest," Edward said, eyeing my heaving breasts and bra-less perky nips. "That's good."

I found out two days later that I got the part. Victory nipple, indeed.

Too bad I'd forgotten about the curse.

# CHAPTER 3

## *Happy Prologues to the Swelling Act*

"Omigod, it's The Face of Channel 10," I whispered to my fellow witch.

"Quick, switch places with me." Candy MoonPie jumped up from the table in the rehearsal room where we sat waiting for the first read-through to begin. I obliged.

"Thanks, and watch out," Candy said as the overdressed newscaster zeroed in on the empty seat now next to me. "The man's a horndog. Last week on a commercial shoot, I had to 'accidentally' dump a soft drink in his lap just to get his hand off my knee."

I knew Candy MoonPie from theater parties. Candy was her real name, MoonPie wasn't. We called her that because of her affinity for the sticky sweet things and because her Louisiana accent was as thick as the marshmallow filling.

"Well, bless my socks!" she said. "If it isn't Bill Boxer. So nice to see you again. Can I get y'all something to drink? Maybe a Coke?"

The Face of Channel 10's smile froze in place. He ran a hand over his perfectly coiffed salt-and-pepper hair.

Candy gave me a conspiratorial smile. I'd always liked her. Everyone did. She literally bounced: a springy walk, lilting accent, and boing-y brown curls. I smiled back at her. This was going to be great. A cool castmate and my first show with a professional theater. I pulled my cotton cardigan tighter (damn air conditioning) and studied the people I'd be spending the next few months with. Lots of men—okay with me. Just four women: me, Candy, a freckly woman a little older than us, maybe early thirties, and Genevieve Fife. A thirty-something lithe brunette with pale skin and big dark eyes, Genevieve upstaged the rest of us just by walking into a room. I'd seen her onstage a number of times. She was an amazing actor, well-known for her Method acting. Once, in preparation for a role in Beckett's *Endgame*, she spent an entire day in a trashcan. She probably looked better in a trashcan than I looked at prom.

The smell of hairspray assaulted my nose as Bill sat down next to me. "Ivy Meadows," I said, sticking out my hand, just to be polite. "I'm playing the third witch."

The Face of Channel 10 shook my hand. "Bill Boxer. I'm reading Duncan." I could swear he was wearing bronzer.

Duncan. That was the role Simon would have played—if he hadn't thrown up on the stage manager's shoes.

Bill took something out of his briefcase, and settled it in his lap. I saw a yellow paperback cover. CliffsNotes for *Macbeth*. I nearly pointed it out to Candy, but took pity on the guy. "I'm so excited to be cast in *Macbeth*," I said. "What a great story."

"Er, right," said Bill, trying to sneak another look at his CliffsNotes.

"I mean, Macbeth kills his king and his best friend Banquo because he wants to believe a prediction by some so-called witches he meets at the beginning of the play."

"His king...Macbeth kills Duncan?" Bill tried hard to make his question sound like a statement. He had also tried hard to mask his bad breath with mouthwash. Neither trick was working.

"I know, right?" I said. "Imagine you're the king. You just rewarded Macbeth with a new title, so you think he's inviting you to his castle to thank you. Instead, he and his wife murder you in your sleep."

"Duncan dies?" Then to himself, "Ooh, maybe a death scene."

I was about to tell Bill that Duncan dies offstage when Edward entered, brandishing a carrot. A forty-ish blonde Amazon in four-inch heels followed close behind: Pamela, the executive director of the theater and Edward's wife.

"I don't get it," I whispered to Candy. "Isn't Edward gay?"

"So they say."

"But he's married?"

"It's a mystery," she said.

Edward and Pamela took their seats next to Linda at the top of the horseshoe of folding tables.

"Welcome all," Edward said. "Be prepared to make Shakespearean history with this production. Never before has the world, let alone Phoenix, seen the Scottish play like this."

It was bad luck to say "Macbeth" out loud in a theater, hence "the Scottish play." Part of the famous curse. The story goes like this: To impress King James I, who fancied himself an authority on demonology, Shakespeare included a real spell in the play. Ticked off that Will had spilled one of their secrets, witches cursed the play. As a result (or a coincidence), all sorts of people have been killed during runs of *Macbeth*.

I nearly slapped my forehead. I had said "Macbeth" several times during my conversation with Bill. The curse couldn't be real, right?

Edward continued, "Forsaking tradition, this production takes place in," he paused dramatically, carrot in the air, "a circus."

Of course. My acrobatic witch.

"Imagine a traveling circus from the 1930s. Mackers is the lion tamer, Lady M. is the aerialist, and Duncan the ringmaster."

As if on cue, Simon walked in. Pamela stiffened, Bill sighed, and Edward pointed his carrot at him. "Ah. Here you are. Cast, a bit of housekeeping first. I'd like to read my two potential Duncans before we get started."

That's why Bill had said he was *reading* Duncan. For whatever reason, Edward hadn't decided who to cast as Duncan. Now Bill and Simon were going to have to audition again in front of actors who were already cast. It was a sucky place to be.

"Everyone in Scene Four, please stay," said Linda. "The rest of you, take ten."

When we were all back in the room ten minutes later, the seat next to me was empty. Until Simon sat down.

I leaned over to hug him. "Congratulations."

"Better watch out for him, too," Candy whispered in my ear.

"Nearly didn't get the part." Simon hugged me back. Seemed like a perfectly friendly hug. "To begin with, Edward is not terribly fond of me. Then there was the, ah, incident with Linda's shoes, and..." He lowered his voice as a young bearded guy wearing a snug-fitting black T-shirt walked in. "Our Mac seems to have taken a dislike to me."

I surreptitiously checked out "our Mac," who had a broad, muscled chest and ocean-colored eyes that stood out against his dark hair and beard. Yowza.

Candy nudged me. "Hot, right?" Guess I need to work on my surreptitious skills.

"Ivy," Simon spoke quietly as I watched our hot Macbeth from under my eyelashes. "There's a bit of a favor I'd like to ask of you."

"Sure." Then I kicked myself inwardly. I always forgot to ask what the favor was before saying yes.

"I'd like you to witness my sobriety."

"What?" Simon had my full attention now.

"Yes, well, as you know, I'm a recovering alcoholic. I've started going to meetings again, but I have been down this road before." Simon set his mouth. "I've learned that it helps me to stay sober if someone watches over me. I do have a sponsor from A.A.—"

"Then don't you think he should—"

"But I find phone calls distract me during a play. I need it to be someone who's here, someone who's part of this world."

No, no, no. Not me.

My face must have betrayed my panic.

"It'll be easy," said Simon. "You won't have to take a bottle away from me, nothing like that. I just need to be responsible to someone."

He had no idea what he was asking, or what had happened to the last person I'd been responsible for. I looked around desperately. "Isn't there someone else?"

He shook his head. "I have a, ah, bit of history with much of the cast. You and I have no past and you're offstage much of the show. I know we haven't spent loads of time together, but I do consider you a friend."

Wow. Even my Uncle Bob had been impressed when I told him I knew Simon Black. "James Bomb?" he said, nearly choking on his coffee (Simon's spy parody was one of my uncle's favorite movies). And now the great Simon Black was my friend. I think I blushed. Then my past rushed back at me. I wasn't fit to watch over anyone.

Simon must have seen it in my eyes. "Please. I wouldn't ask if it wasn't so important. All you need to do is to check in on me every so often. When I'm offstage, I'll be in my dressing room. It won't be a problem, because I give you my word," he looked me solemnly in the eye, "that I will not drink. Will you be my witness?"

What could I do? I swallowed my past along with the lump in my throat. "I will."

# CHAPTER 4

## *Not Within the Prospects of Belief*

Simon was as good as his word. Three weeks of rehearsal flew past and I never once had to take a bottle away from him, never saw him drink, and never smelled booze on him. Which left me free to memorize my lines, work on my character, and ponder the important things, like the glory that was Jason in tights.

Tonight was our first rehearsal onstage. Until now, we'd been in the rehearsal room, working with an imaginary set marked out in masking tape on the floor. I wanted to check out the real (and as yet-unfinished) set, so I came early, right after work at the Olive Garden. Jason and Riley, the guy playing Macduff, were already onstage rehearsing the final swordfight. Even better. I made myself comfortable in the audience and settled in to watch. Riley, a curly-haired doofus who could act in spite of himself, wore torn sweats. Jason wore skin-tight Lycra that accentuated his, um, lower profile.

"I'm a lucky woman, aren't I?"

I turned to see Genevieve/Lady Macbeth, standing beside me.

"Sorry?"

"Being married to a specimen like that," she said, eyeing Jason. "Very lucky indeed."

I turned back to the stage. Jason's eyes flashed as he swung his sword. Even in rehearsal, he imbued Macbeth with a passion that made the Scottish murderer nearly sympathetic. The actors sparred their way into the wings. A loud clang and Macbeth's sword skittered onstage. "Arrrrrhh!" Riley shouted from the wings, as Macduff supposedly beheaded Macbeth.

"Nice," said the fight choreographer as the two sweaty actors returned to the stage. Jason bowed slightly and smiled into the audience at...who? Me? God, I hoped so.

Genevieve smiled back at Jason. Oh. Right. Genevieve wore a tight red leotard that showed off her breasts and made her look like a ripe tomato. I wore a white Oxford shirt and black pants with tomato sauce stains.

The two actors and the fight choreographer left the stage. Genevieve left, too. I made my way onto the empty stage.

Edward's circus concept was bizarre, but it did make for a great set. A striped awning hung from the proscenium (the frame around the stage), lending the feel of a big top. Flats painted to look like bleachers gave the illusion of an onstage audience—all the world's a stage, you know.

Edward walked onstage, omnipresent carrot in hand. Eli, our technical director, followed. "The cauldron will fly in, steam roiling from its innards," said Edward. "At first we'll just hear the witches, then see their faces, then like the steam, they'll slither out of the cauldron." He waved his carrot. "It'll be spectacular."

I looked up at the cauldron, which hung in the flyspace, the area above the stage where flats and set pieces that "flew in" during the show were secured by ropes out of sight of the audience.

"This is a bad idea," said Eli, staring at the swaying behemoth over our heads.

"It's fine," said Edward. "You did use fiberglass. It's lighter than the dozens of flats we've flown in before."

"I wouldn't call it light." Eli crossed tattooed arms. "And those flats weren't carrying actors."

"I've already cut Hecate's part," said Edward. "You should be pleased."

Since Edward (or maybe Eli) had decided that only three witches could fit in the cauldron, he'd cut the character of Hecate, the head witch. She only appeared for a few lines anyway.

"I'm not pleased," said Eli. "It's a bad idea—"

I must have made some noise of agreement, because Edward's eyes flicked toward me, and his face lit up.

"Witch." A carrot pointed at me. "Would you please do a demonstration for us?"

"No," said Eli, "Not yet. We're not ready."

"It's fine," said Edward. "She's non-union."

He directed his carrot at a couple of techies. "The cauldron, please."

Ropes and pullies lined the side walls backstage. One of the guys walked stage right and slowly pulled a lever, watching the mechanics as he did so. The rest of the crew, who had been chatty up until then, fell silent as they watched the cauldron descend like a monstrous alien from a sci-fi flick.

Edward pointed at the cauldron. "Witch, er...Holly."

"Ivy," I said.

"No," said Eli.

"Edward," said Jason, who had come up behind me. "Do you want me and Macduff to rehearse the fight scene onstage one more time while the fight choreographer's still here?"

Edward checked his watch. "Ah. Yes." He waved his carrot at Eli as he walked offstage. "We'll take care of this later."

Jason touched my shoulder. I turned around and looked into his eyes, those stormy, sea-colored eyes. He held my gaze and I felt my heart drop into the pit of my stomach.

"Everyone clear the stage." Linda shouted from the wings. Argh. Stage managers are such buzz-kills. "And places for the top of the show in five."

Jason walked into the wings to grab his sword. He didn't look back at me. My heart tried to return to its normal spot, but instead lodged itself at the base of my throat, like a goiter.

"I think he likes you," sang Candy, waiting for me offstage right.

"Really?" I watched Jason and Riley begin their fight onstage.

"Do you think there's anything going on between him and Genevieve?"

"Doubtful," she said, "Genevieve's crazy as a bedbug. Though I guess we should all give her a break. I heard her mama died recently."

Tyler, the third witch (Edward's one instance of gender-neutral casting), met us backstage. "Omigod," he said, "I heard they're going to put us in tutus. They wouldn't, would they?"

"Anyone seen Simon?" I asked as Linda shouted, "Places!" No one had. After we three witches opened the show (sans cauldron, for now), I walked offstage, spied Simon in his place waiting for the next scene, and breathed a sigh of relief.

"Lights up!" Linda yelled.

Simon strode onstage as Duncan, his retinue behind him. Another actor limped onstage, a wounded, bleeding soldier.

"Stop," Edward said from the audience. "Where is Duncan's hat? I want Simon to get used to wearing the hat."

All action stopped as a costume assistant scurried onstage and settled a ringmaster's hat on Simon's head.

"Again from the top," said Edward.

"What bloody man is that?" Duncan's voice boomed, the voice of a king. "He can report, As seemeth by his plight, of the revolt..." His voice changed: Simon's now. "Bloody hell. This is ridiculous. First of all, it makes no sense that Mac's castle and Duncan's palace are the same place. If Shakespeare had wanted—"

From his seat in the theater, Edward sounded edgy and weary at the same time. "Simon, we've been over this—"

"And now this bloody thing!" Simon tore off his ringmaster's top hat. "How am I supposed to act like a king with this god-awful thing on my head?"

He had a point. Overly large, and black and shiny like a cheap suit, the hat did him no favors.

"We've talked about this, too," said Edward. "The hat is an extension of your ego, of your insecurity. It's your mid-life crisis Corvette; helps you keep your pecker up."

"Duncan is not insecure!" Simon nearly roared. "And he's not impotent!"

He threw the hat into the theater, narrowly missing Edward.

Something changed in Edward's face. His voice was tight. "Simon, we will not discuss this now." He threw the hat back onstage. "Put on the goddamn hat." It sat there, at the lip of the stage. Simon did not move to pick it up.

"Simon." The threat in Edward's voice was thinly veiled.

The actor playing Malcolm quietly picked up the hat and held it out to Simon like a peace offering. Simon finally took the hat in a grand ceremonious gesture, slowly raised it toward his head, then threw it to the ground. He stomped on it, violently, crushing it beyond repair. No one breathed. "That's for Shakespeare."

"Simon!" Edward thundered from his seat in the audience.

Simon stopped. He took a few deep breaths, then shook off his rage as if it were a coat. Now hatless, he took a deep breath, turned back to his retinue and began again: "What bloody man is that?" Simon was gone; Duncan the king was back. Simon could slip back into character at the drop of a, well, hat.

Beside me, Candy let out a breath. "Whoa, doggy. If that don't beat all."

"Yeah," I said. "He really gave it to Edward, huh?"

"Darlin', that's not what I meant." She looked at me sadly. "The man is drunk."

# CHAPTER 5

## Something Wicked This Way Comes

I fought my way through a gaggle of actors to the greenroom's one full-length mirror.

"You look stunning," Simon said, appearing behind me.

It was opening night, over a week later, and I still hadn't asked him about the hat incident. I had been afraid to ask.

"Really?" I gazed at my reflection. It's one of the nice things about theater, you can look at yourself, really look at yourself, without anyone thinking you're vain or self-absorbed. It's understood that since the audience will be looking at you for hours, it's okay, imperative even, to check yourself out pretty thoroughly. Plus we all tend to be vain and self-absorbed.

"The green matches your eyes." He smiled at my reflection in the mirror.

I was costumed as a sexy serpent in a painted leotard with undulating stripes of iridescent, venomous green, and a long matted wig. Simon's ringmaster costume showed off his still-fine physique, and his hair was swept back from his forehead in a dashing 1930s film star look. He was right not to wear the hat.

"You're looking well yourself," I said.

"Wonderful what sobriety will do for you."

"Yeah. I've been meaning to ask...When you stomped on the hat, were you...?"

Simon met my eyes in the mirror. "I was not drunk. I have...an anger management problem. One of the reasons I drank. Now I act to stay sober. But thank you for checking." He gave me a slight bow and drifted away to a corner of the room, repeating, "I act to stay sober."

"A toast to the cast of *Macbeth*." A tuxedoed Bill Boxer stood inside the stage door holding a bottle of champagne aloft. A few actors groaned.

"Great. Thanks for ruining the show," Riley said.

Bill's smile slipped from his face. His brows knit together. I recognized his "breaking news face" from TV. I'd always thought it signified concern, but now I wondered if it just meant he was confused.

"The name of the Scottish play is not to be said in a theater." Genevieve had ice in her voice. "It brings bad luck. You know that."

"Oh right. I'm not supposed to say 'Macbeth.'" Either Bill didn't believe in the curse, or he was an idiot. Probably both.

"Right," Riley said, grabbing the bottle. He forcibly steered Bill toward the door. "Now go outside, turn around three times, and come back in." That was one of the supposed antidotes to the curse.

Bill shrugged off Riley's hands. "If you don't want me, all you have to do is say so. I was just being nice." He strode out the door.

Riley tore the foil off the champagne. "At least he brought something to drink."

"I'll take that." Pamela entered, her gray silk ensemble flowing. She looked like a thundercloud pushing her way into the room. "I will keep all alcohol in my office until after curtain. We don't want anyone getting drunk during the show." She made a show of looking at Simon. "Please bring any and all bottles to my office. Thank you."

She started to walk off, then stopped, "And break a leg, all." She left, gray silk trailing behind.

Jason smiled at Simon, but it wasn't a nice smile. His attitude toward Simon had soured even more since a preview article in last Sunday's paper. It had featured a large color photograph of Simon, and not one mention of the play's titular character. The article, which had been posted on a bulletin board in the greenroom, somehow disappeared after Monday night.

I punched Jason on the arm. "Stop it," I whispered. "It's not fair. You know he hasn't been drinking."

"You think he was sober when he stomped on his top hat?"

"Yes. He has an anger management problem."

"Ivy." Jason shook his head. "You're too sweet for your own good."

I started to protest.

Jason put a finger to my lips. "But not for mine." He trailed his finger down my neck.

"Five minutes to places," Linda's voice floated over the speaker.

Jason leaned in, his breath warm in my ear. "Meet me after the murder at the bucket of blood." He threw me a wicked smile over his shoulder as he strode backstage.

"Better watch out, Ivy, he's a married man," said Kaitlin, who played Lady Macduff.

"Married?"

"Yeah, Lady Macbeth might kick your ass," Riley said. "She's in my taekwondo class."

"Hon." Candy frowned at me. "Your lipstick is smeared. You better go fix your face."

Dang. I ran back to the dressing room I shared with Candy and yanked open the door. An exquisite, voluptuous white orchid stood on the counter near my makeup kit. I stepped closer to read the note tucked under its pot. "Nearly as beautiful as you."

"Witch," said a voice from the hall, "you'd better get into place." Genevieve wore a low-cut crimson leotard and brief skirt of blood-colored chiffon.

"I can't tell who this is from," I said, motioning to the orchid. "It's signed 'your king.' I mean, Simon is Duncan the king, but Jason is later crowned king..."

Genevieve stared at me.

"Right. Sorry. Getting into place and into character." I left the dressing room, followed Genevieve backstage, tumbled into the cauldron next to Candy and Tyler, and turned into a witch.

After Duncan's murder, I waited for Jason near the "bucket of blood," a tub of water the Macbeths used to wash the stage blood from their hands. Genevieve walked offstage, dipped her hands in the water and scrubbed. Even in the dim light backstage, I could see the water turn red.

Jason followed her. When he saw me, he held up his gore-covered hands. "Some say blood can be an aphrodisiac."

"Yeah, some vampires," I said. "But then, vampires can be pretty hot."

"I'm more into witches," he said, moving closer.

I glanced at his fictional wife, but Genevieve had turned her back to us. Probably to keep herself in character.

Jason traced a finger on my lips. A bloody finger. "Taste."

I did, hesitantly, licking the sticky stage blood off my lips. It was surprisingly sweet. A burst of laughter from the audience drew my attention. It was the beginning of the porter scene, the one bit of comic relief in the play.

"Distracted, are we?" whispered Jason. He pulled me into a big black velvet curtain, one of the legs (that's what we theater folk call side curtains) just offstage, and wrapped us in the soft darkness. "That was my plan," he said. And then he kissed me—a deep, longing, let's-never-come-up-for-air-again kiss. He pulled me close, really close, so close that through our flimsy costumes I could feel...

"Is thy master stirring?" said Macduff, onstage.

"How did he guess?" Jason smiled at me, arranged his cloak over the aforementioned stirring bit, and strode onstage.

I stood there for a moment, eyes closed in a haze of lustful anticipation. I floated to my dressing room, fixed my makeup (again), and headed out to the greenroom in time for intermission.

The name "greenroom" came from Shakespeare's time, when all the actors hung out in the nicest room backstage, the room where they stored all the plants. Our greenroom was pink, supposedly painted that color because it was soothing. I suspected it was because it was flattering. We theater folk are all about good lighting.

All the actors did look fabulous as they swarmed around a long table filled with potluck dishes. "Dibs on the sausage!" said Riley, behind me. He was one of the reasons we had all decided to bring food in lieu of opening night presents. He'd been living off a box of Bisquick for the past week. He squeezed past me and planted himself in front of an enormous antipasto plate full of expensive sausages, cheeses and pâtés, good stuff way beyond the means of most of us actors.

"Who brought that?" I said.

"Genevieve." Riley piled food onto his plate. "Aren't you glad she didn't bring sheep stomach?" We'd all been afraid Lady Macbeth might honor us all with haggis, a traditional Scottish dish.

Simon entered from backstage looking perturbed, but upon seeing the buffet the look of concern slipped from his face. He might have been a famous Shakespearean actor, but he was still a guy who liked free food.

"How are you doing?" I asked.

"I am wonderful. Stupendous. I have been sober for thirty-eight days and have never felt better. Or hungrier." He began filling a paper plate.

"Great."

"And thank you for inquiring, my secret, black, and midnight hag," he said, blowing me a kiss.

I breathed a sigh of relief and looked around.

"Have you seen Jason?" I asked Simon.

His face clouded. "Why?"

"Oh, he and I..." I trailed off as I noticed Genevieve watching us. Fictional wife or not, she made me nervous.

Simon motioned to me to come closer. "Ivy," he said, his voice low and serious. "I think we should talk after the show."

"Oh. Ah, I hope to have a date."

"With the aforementioned gentleman?"

"Um, yeah."

"Let's talk," said Simon. "Before your date. Come to my dressing room?"

"Sure."

He smiled and turned back to the food. I kept looking for Jason.

No such luck. Intermission was almost over. I wondered where Jason was, and what Simon wanted to talk about. The tension between the two men was palpable. I had put it down to old-fashioned stage rivalry, but could it be more? It couldn't be about me, could it?

Nah.

I didn't see Simon. Must have taken his food back to his dressing room. I was about to go there and find out what he had to say when I heard, "Places" over the speaker.

I hoped I'd run into Jason backstage, but I climbed into the cauldron disappointed. When I finally did see him, we were onstage: not Ivy and Jason, but a witch and a murderer. After the scene ended, there was a quick blackout, just enough time to let us witches scramble out of the cauldron.

As I stood to get out, I felt strong arms lift me. Jason smiled as he pulled me close and slid me down the length of his body until my feet touched the stage. "Soon," he breathed into my ear. My worries evaporated. Once offstage, Jason headed for a dark backstage area, probably to prepare for his next entrance. I drifted back to the greenroom, tingling and happy. *Soon.* I passed Genevieve, who was getting into character for the sleepwalking scene by rocking herself into some sort of hypnotic trance. I smiled as I passed her, feeling that wonderful nasty sort of victory when you get the prize everyone wants.

I nearly skipped as I headed to Simon's dressing room. His door was ajar, light spilling into the darkened hallway. "My dear Duncan, your witch is here. Which witch, you ask?" I knocked, just to be polite. "Your witness witch, of course."

I knocked again. He had to be there. His scenes were over and he wasn't in the greenroom.

"Simon?" I pushed open the unlocked door. It didn't budge, like something was jammed up against it. I pushed harder, trying to shove whatever it was away from the door. I got it open a crack, just enough that I could see what blocked it.

A body.

# CHAPTER 6

## *The Battle's Lost*

"Simon?" My voice sounded strangled.

No answer.

I pushed, cringing as the door jammed against the body. The smell hit me then—acrid, stomach-churning. Oh God.

"Simon?!"

Using all my strength, I opened the door enough to squeeze my shoulders into the brightly lit room. It was Simon who blocked my entrance, an overturned chair behind him. I couldn't tell if he was breathing. He had to be breathing. He had to.

I stretched a leg over him and leapt. As I did, I saw several things in a flash: a half-drunk cup of coffee on the counter, the squashed top hat next to it, a spreading pool of vomit on the floor. I touched down too late to catch myself. My foot slipped on the slick floor and I landed hard on my hip, several feet away from Simon. He lay on his side facing the door, an empty bottle a few feet from his outstretched arm. I couldn't see his face.

"Help!" I yelled. Someone would hear me. Someone would do something.

My hip aching from the fall, I inched across the floor on my knees, holding my breath against the smell of puke and alcohol. I fought the rising wave of panic that threatened to capsize me, tried to ignore the pre-digested food I crawled through. I drew near Simon. He must have fallen over, hit the floor, and crawled toward the door for help. I reached for his head and turned it so he faced upward. It was going to be okay. Everything was going to be okay.

Then I saw his face. Simon's eyes were open, staring at nothing. Chunks of vomit covered his mouth and nose, stuck to his beard.

I started to gag, but swallowed my nausea. I needed to do something: CPR, mouth-to-mouth, something. I tried to force my face close to his, but the smell hit again. I jerked back and my hand slipped on the slick floor. I fell, right on top of Simon's still-warm body. He didn't move.

Or breathe.

# CHAPTER 7

## *This Filthy Witness*

My teeth chattered. The greenroom was freezing. God.

I sat on one of the old couches, huddled in its corner, my arms wrapped around my knees for warmth. I concentrated on following the sofa's worn pattern with my eyes, blocking out everything but its faded orange swirls. Jason sat down next to me and draped someone's robe across my shaking shoulders.

"Can I get you something? A drink? Maybe some brandy?"

I nearly bit his head off. "No."

He backed off. Even in my state, I could see a bit of hurt in his eyes.

"Sorry, it's just that...Simon...there was brandy."

I saw the bottle again in my mind's eye. Brandy. Empty.

Just the thought of it brought back the smell of alcohol mixed with vomit. I swallowed hard, trying to keep down the bile that rose in my throat.

"Oh, God. Sorry, Ivy," Jason said. "I was trying to think of what people brought in situations like this. It sprang to mind. That and St. Bernards. Can I get you a St. Bernard?"

I nearly smiled. "You've been great. I just want to go home."

"Let me check on that."

He got up and walked toward the knot of police choking the hall to the dressing rooms.

I glanced toward them, just for a moment. A flash went off within Simon's dressing room. I knew what they were photographing. I forced my mind away from the scene, but one image was imprinted on the inside of my eyelids. Simon, on his back on the floor, eyes open. Eyes dead.

I hadn't done shit. I didn't try to help him, or go for help, or anything. I'd failed Simon and now he was dead.

"Ivy? Ivy." It was Jason. "Hey, hey, don't cry."

Was I crying? I wiped at my face. Wet.

"Hey, he did it to himself."

"No. *No.* I was supposed to watch him, I was supposed to help him."

I really was crying now, huge gulping sobs. Jason sat next to me and wrapped me in his arms. I was covered in vomit, but he held me tight. "Sometimes you can't help. Sometimes people do what they will," he said, rocking me.

"But I...it's happened..."

I nearly told him then. Told him it had happened before, that I was supposed to watch over someone and...something in my brain stopped me from saying it, protected the both of us. Instead I just cried louder.

Through my tears I saw Linda approach, trailed by a big, rumpled-looking guy and a young guy with red ears—cops, I guessed. "This is her," said Linda, "the girl who found him." She stood in between the cops and me, a bulldog guarding a toddler. Jason gently disentangled himself from me and stood nearby.

I tore my eyes away from him, from the sofa's swirls, from the safe space I'd created. I saw my fellow actors huddling in groups, heard the buzz of voices from the lobby down the hall, and felt the hole in the room that Simon had left.

"Miss?" said the red-eared cop. "We'd like to ask you a few questions, beginning with your name."

"My name is Ivy Meadows, and I am an actress." It just came out.

"Ivy Meadows?" The big guy gave a slight frown. "That a stage name?"

"Oh. Yeah. Legally, it's Olive Ziegwart."

"Olive Ziegwart?" Oh no, not now. "Are you Bob Duda's niece?" The frown on the guy's face faded.

It took me a second to process, but I nodded. He sat down next to me.

"Bob talks about you all the time." Then to the young cop, "Bob's a private investigator, one of the best in town." He turned back to me, raising his voice above the mounting noise from down the hall. "Tell you what. Why don't you..."

Bill Boxer rushed into the room, nearly tripping over Genevieve, who sat in the middle of the floor keening.

"Sorry." He flashed an insincere and inappropriate smile and bounded down the hall toward the hubbub. Edward's voice rose above the rest: "The show will be back on its feet day after tomorrow," he said.

The older cop raised an eyebrow at Linda. She shrugged. "Probably talking to the press. Critics must have called their newsrooms."

"Luckily, we have an understudy who can step into Duncan's role right away." Edward's voice again.

Linda and I exchanged looks. We didn't have any understudies.

"Bill Boxer," Edward said.

"The Face of Channel 10," said the young cop. A sharp look from the older guy turned his ears even redder.

"Like I was saying," the cop in charge said to me. "Why don't you go home, maybe even over to your uncle's house. We can talk tomorrow morning. You need a ride?"

"I'll take her," said Jason.

"Alright with you?" the cop asked. I nodded. "I'll call your uncle. Let him know you guys are on your way."

I nodded again. Jason gently pulled me to my feet. The cops nodded to me and walked away. Linda followed them.

"Ivy?" said Jason. "You want to, uh, change before we go?"

I nodded. I'd discarded my wig at some point, but was still in costume. I looked down at myself, saw the mess covering my leotard and tights. Simon's vomit. My own, too. I had thrown up after I fell on Simon. I almost heaved again but grit my teeth and started toward the restroom. And stopped. It was on the other side of Simon's dressing room.

Jason saw the dread in my eyes. "Never mind. A shower at home—at your uncle's house—that'll feel better."

"Can I let the rest of the actors go, too?" I heard Linda ask as Jason steered me toward the door.

"Yeah. Sure," the older cop replied. "It's not like it's a suspicious death or anything. This rookie here," he jerked a thumb at the red-eared cop, "interrupted my Friday night for nothing. If he'd looked closer," he said loudly, looking at the other cop, "he would have seen that the guy downed a bottle of Rémy Martin. If he'd really done his job, he would have noticed the medic alert bracelet lying on the guy's dressing room counter. The one that said 'heart patient.'"

"But sir," said the young cop, "It was Simon Black."

Was.

Past tense.

# CHAPTER 8

## The Pitiful Eye of Day

"Ivy?" I heard the voice as if from far away. I decided to ignore it.

Then I smelled coffee.

I cracked one eye open.

"Morning, you." Jason stood by my bed, holding a steaming cup of coffee. How did he look so good this early in the morning? And what did I look like? I wondered if I was wearing pajamas, but felt too sleepy to check.

"You gotta get up now."

I looked around me through half-open eyes. I was in my Uncle Bob's guest room, tucked into a twin bed. I didn't remember getting there. I did remember being carried from the car to the house. I remembered a soft couch and hushed voices, ginger ale and a pill, and a warm washcloth on my face.

A window air conditioner was blowing full blast. It sounded like the roar of the sea. Jason smiled and held out the cup of coffee. His eyes were gentle, warm, and that incredible ocean green-blue. Ocean...warm water...mmm. I felt myself drift along with some invisible current. It felt good to be buoyed along by something bigger than me.

At first. Then I realized the current was pulling me further and further from shore, dragging me out to sea. I suddenly sensed the unseen danger beneath the surface, the fathoms of water underneath me, the black depths that waited...

"Olive?" A different voice, familiar.

The sea turned dark and turbulent. It rushed around me, pulling me from side to side.

"Olive. Come on." I could somehow see the voice as a big bubble hovering above the surface of the water I swam in. I kicked toward the surface and grabbed at the bubble, hoping it would save me.

"Ow!"

I opened my eyes to see Uncle Bob standing over me, rubbing his nose. His bubble-shaped nose.

"Man, kiddo, you are one deep sleeper."

I shook my head, trying to shake off the water from my dream. Dream Jason was nowhere to be seen. I didn't care. I was glad to be awake.

"Olive, sweetheart, I wish I could let you sleep, but Pink— Detective Pinkstaff—is coming over pretty soon." My uncle pulled me to a sitting position and gave me a gentle smile, double chins tripling under a day-old beard. A cold cup of coffee sat on the bedside table. Coffee?

"Was Jason really here?" I asked my uncle. I was wearing pajamas, or at least a faded soft blue T-shirt—Uncle Bob's? The inside of my mouth felt like it was covered in stale cotton candy.

"Yeah, I thought you'd wake up for him," he said, crossing to the window. "If you were Snow White, you'd still be in the glass coffin. Guess those sleeping pills really hit ya." He twisted the blinds open. Light spilled into the room and bounced off my uncle's orange Hawaiian shirt.

I struggled to my feet, confused, but motivated by the thought of those sea-colored eyes. Jason was here. Wow.

Why? Something knocked on the door of my subconscious.

"There's still some hot water," said Uncle Bob, steering me toward the bathroom. "You got fifteen minutes before Pink shows up. Jason's on a bagel run."

That was all the incentive I needed. I shut the door to the bathroom, and started to strip. What was that smell? Maybe Uncle

Bob had burritos last night. Geez. I turned on the fan, but the smell remained. Oh well. I started toward the shower, then caught sight of myself in the mirror. The hair around my face was all matted with...Oh God. Not again.

I sat down hard on the toilet seat. My stomach started to churn. I leaned down, put my head between my knees, and tried not to think.

"Olive?" Uncle Bob tapped on the door. "Pink will be here soon. You gotta get in the shower, hon."

I sat still on the toilet, not moving, and trying not to breathe.

"C'mon. You'll feel better after you do something."

He was right. I needed to do something. I didn't do shit last night. I didn't do mouth-to-mouth or CPR. I didn't call 911. I just threw up, curled up, and cried like a baby. The least I could do now was talk to the police. I made myself get up and turn on the shower.

"That's the way, kiddo," Uncle Bob said from the other side of the door. "See you in a few."

I was still in the shower, letting the now-cool water wash over my shoulders, when I heard Uncle Bob again. "Olive? You got five minutes, tops."

Shit. I turned off the water and toweled off. I scrounged through Uncle Bob's medicine cabinet, used his Old Spice deodorant, ran a comb through my hair, put some toothpaste on my finger, and scrubbed my teeth. No time to do much else.

I saw a bundle of clothes laid on the counter—a way-too-big pair of drawstring sweats and an XXL T-shirt. I pulled them on, yanking the drawstring as tight as it would go, and stepped out into the hall where Uncle Bob waited.

"I dreamt about water," I said.

"Water." Realization dawned on my uncle's face, "Oh, hon. This is nothing like your brother. This thing with Simon was an accident."

His eyes knew it was a mistake as soon as his mouth spoke it.

"I mean, Simon was an adult..." he said, digging himself deeper.

He must have seen the tears threatening me, because his eyes grew wet, too.

"It's okay," I said, and meant it, at least as far as Uncle Bob was concerned.

"Thanks," he said.

He put his arm around my shoulders as we walked down the hall and into the kitchen. Sitting at the table was the detective from last night, recognizable by his broad back and rumpled shirt. I dug in my heels.

"Olive, hon," Uncle Bob whispered. "Don't worry about this too much. The police just want to wrap up a few details. They don't ask much when it's something like alcohol poisoning."

"But why is he here?" This was my safe space, this outdated kitchen with its scratched vinyl floor. Where I had pancakes and coffee at the formica table. Where I felt like family.

"We thought it was better than having you go down to the station."

The policeman must have heard us. He stood up and turned. His short-sleeved shirt had an ink stain on the front pocket. "Mornin'," he said as we walked into the kitchen.

I wasn't expecting his voice to be so gentle, or for his eyes to light up when he saw me. "Hey, you like Hap's too?" He chuckled. "You don't need no teeth to eat our meat."

I followed his gaze to my chest. It was kinda hard to read upside down, but I guessed I wore a T-shirt from Hap's Pit Barbecue.

My uncle gave the guy a sideways look. The detective rewound: "Uh, really sorry you had to go through all that last night." He pulled out a chair for me. I sat, and Uncle Bob appeared at my elbow with a fresh cup of coffee. I sipped it gratefully.

"So, is it Ivy or Olive?" The policeman pulled out a pen and a small black notebook from the stained pocket. My uncle drifted out of the room.

"My stage name is Ivy Meadows," I answered, "but legally, it's Olive. Olive Ziegwart."

He wrote that, or maybe something else, in his notebook.

"And you found the body?"

I sat up on the edge of my chair. "I found *Simon.*"

"Tell me about it." He leaned toward me across the table, like he was taking me seriously.

"It was after intermission, nearly the end of the show. I went to go check on Simon."

"Why?"

I heard the door to the carport open behind me.

"He'd asked me to keep an eye on him, make sure he didn't drink," I said.

A noise—a snort?—made me turn around. Jason walked in carrying two white paper bags.

The cop—had Uncle Bob called him Pink?—cleared his throat. "Why you?" he asked me. "What was your relationship with Simon?"

Jason handed me a toasted bagel, already schmeared, wrapped in a square of waxed paper. I felt his eyes on me.

"We were friends, that's all."

"I see."

Jason tore open the two bags to reveal more bagels and little tubs of cream cheese. The detective flipped through his notebook. "When you went to Simon's dressing room, were there people around?"

I nodded, wondering if the cop had changed subjects because of the waves of tension coming off Jason, who carefully placed the split open bags in the center of the table.

"Who was there?" asked the detective. Jason grabbed a bagel and stood behind me.

God. I tried to remember. "Genevieve and most of the guy actors were in the greenroom."

"I wasn't there," said Jason, his mouth full of bagel. "I was onstage when it happened."

The detective turned his attention to Jason. "When what happened?"

Jason swallowed. "The death. When Ivy found him. You know." He shrugged. "I'm onstage or backstage the entire show. I'm the lead."

Pink did not seem impressed.

"Is she almost done?" Jason looked at his watch. "We need to go to rehearsal."

The cop looked at him levelly. "Why don't you go ahead and tell them she'll be right along."

Jason took the hint. "I'll see you at the theater, Ivy." He left through the carport door.

The cop took a seeded bagel from the bag, and smeared a bit of cream cheese on it. "Simon Black had quite the reputation," he said. "But you were just friends?"

So I was right about the change of subject. And he was right about the reputation.

Simon had supposedly moved to Arizona because he didn't like life in L.A. "Boobs and beaches," he'd famously said in an interview. Phoenix was just an hour commute to Hollywood by plane, and had no beaches. Boobs we had plenty of, and his interview aside, that seemed to suit Simon just fine. Soon after he moved here, his photograph appeared regularly in the society section of the paper, always with a beautiful woman draped across his arm. After awhile though, the photos became less flattering: a glassy-eyed Simon drinking in a bar, brawling outside a nightclub, or breaking up very publicly with his latest conquest.

"I was just a friend," I said firmly.

The cop nodded. "So as a friend, Simon asked you to make sure he didn't drink." His voice was gentle again. "Did he? Drink?"

I thought about my conversation with Simon before the show: how good he looked, how steadfast he seemed, how proud he had been of his sobriety.

"No. He did not."

And as I said the words, I knew they were true.

# CHAPTER 9

## *Lay It to Thy Heart, and Farewell*

They were already rehearsing by the time I got to the theater. I sat down in a seat in the audience, next to Candy. "Glad you made it," she whispered, giving my arm a squeeze.

It was the top of Scene IV and The Face of Channel 10 was onstage. "Is execution done on Cawdor? Are not those in commission yet returned?"

"Got those lines right," Candy said.

Now, though, as Malcolm replied, you could see Bill's wheels turning. He was obviously trying to remember his upcoming speech instead of listening to Malcolm, which could have actually helped him to remember those lines.

"There's no art..." said Bill, "To find the mind's..." He scratched his head and looked up into the flyspace, as if his lines were hanging on a scroll up there.

A stage whisper from Seth, who played Malcolm: "The mind's construction in the face..."

"The mind's construction in the face," Bill said, repeating the words exactly the way Seth had said them.

"Needs some construction on his brain," Candy said under her breath. "But I guess he finally got what he wanted."

"What?"

"Being cast. You know."

"Omigod, I forgot." Before he realized Edward hadn't decided whether to cast him or Simon, Bill had actually announced on the nightly news that he'd be playing Duncan. The station had forced him to make an on-air apology.

Bill stumbled through the rest of the scene. At the end of it, Edward shouted from his seat in the audience. "Stop! Again from the top of the show. Maybe this time Bill will remember he's a king, not a newscaster."

"Ouch," I said as Candy and I made our way backstage.

"He's out of carrots and a mite testy," Candy said. "You shoulda seen him when he realized you weren't here. He asked Genevieve to read your part. She started in with the whole 'I'm Lady Macbeth' thing and Edward 'bout had a hissy fit. He flat out ordered her to read it and she said," Candy put on a snooty voice that sounded only slightly like Genevieve's, "'I believe my contract lists my role as Lady Macbeth.'"

"Wow."

"Yeah. Linda read your part. Now we know why she's a stage manager, not an actor."

We got into the cauldron next to Tyler, and the stagehands hauled us up into the flyspace. I was relieved to be onstage where I could concentrate on being a witch. The theater was a magical place for me, and not just because of the lights and costumes and glitter. I could lose myself in whatever world we had created, which helped me get through the world that had been thrust upon me. My childhood therapist called it "denial." I called it "survival."

We ran the show from the top through Duncan's last scene, then took a break. Candy went out to the loading dock for a smoke and I headed to the greenroom. Riley, aka Macduff the sword swallower, ran up to me, the scent of his drugstore cologne following a step behind. "Hey, Ivy. You feeling better?"

I nodded. I did feel better, being here.

"Great. Hey, I like Hap's, too," he said, pointing a finger at my T-shirt. "See you." Riley bounded away again, happy. He was a big sweetie, good-natured and good-looking, but he wasn't much for conversation. Not a lot upstairs, if you know what I mean. Candy variously described Riley as "dumb as a box of rocks," "two sandwiches shy of a picnic," and (my personal favorite) "one fry short of a Happy Meal."

I scanned the room. Ah. Jason stood in front of the room's three vending machines, lined up at one end of the room like guardians of bad food. One held month-old snacks. Another was a Coke machine that was always out of Diet Coke. Jason put a dollar into the third machine, which dispensed coffee and other lukewarm beverages.

I made my way to the beverage machine. "Hi." I said to Jason, whose cardboard cup was now full of cocoa. I suddenly felt shy.

"Hey, you." He smiled down at me and my shyness slipped away.

"I wanted to say thanks for last night," I said, pressing the button for the cocoa. Weak coffee poured into my cup. "Dang it."

"Did you want cocoa?" asked Jason,

I nodded. "I'm just distracted." I knew, like everyone else, that you had to push the coffee with cream button to get cocoa.

Jason smiled down at me. "You like café mocha?"

I nodded.

"We'll share." Jason took my cup from me, poured some of my coffee into his cocoa, and blended the two until both cups were full of milky tan liquid. He presented my cup with a flourish.

"Milady."

He leaned in close enough I could smell masculinity and romance and hope, or maybe just shaving cream. "I was happy to be there for you last night," he said. "Though I had planned a different sort of evening." He brushed a bit of hair off my cheek.

"Places for Act One," said Linda over the loud speaker. I was beginning to believe she was a romance-hating psychic.

"Catch you later," Jason said, taking off for backstage. I followed him and tumbled into place in the cauldron beside Candy and Tyler.

\* \* \*

We ran the first half of the show again for Bill's benefit. After the witches' scenes were done, I snagged Candy backstage. "Can we talk?"

"As long as you don't mind the loading dock," she said. "I am dying for a ciggie."

Candy grabbed a pack of cigarettes from a hiding space on top of an unused flat and opened the loading dock door. A wave of heat nearly pushed me over, but I followed her outside and watched her light up.

"So, you okay?" She exhaled a stream of smoke like a contented sigh.

"Yeah." I sat down on the dusty stairs that led from the theater to the driveway. I was sure Uncle Bob's sweats had seen worse. "But I was wondering, did they say anything about Simon?"

"When?"

"Before rehearsal."

"Um..."

"I mean, was there a moment of silence or anything?" I had thought they'd say something at break, but no one said a word.

"No," said Candy.

"I can't believe it." I stood up. "I don't think I even heard his name today. It's like saying 'Macbeth' in the theater or something."

Candy's eyes got big. "Omigod, the curse."

"Don't worry about the curse," I said, "We're outside the theater, not in it."

"No, I meant—"

"How in the world can they ignore Simon?" I was hot now and not just because of the 103-degree day. "He was one of us."

"But Edward's in charge."

"So?"

"So Edward hated Simon."

"Because of the hat?" I knew Edward was pretty pissed about that. I had heard them arguing about it one night in the greenroom.

"You are ruining my concept," Edward had said. "Without the hat, no one will understand you are the ringmaster. They will be thoroughly confused."

"And you believe that's for lack of a hat?" replied Simon. "Not because you costumed the wounded sergeant as a bloody tiger? Or because your soldiers are clowns? Or because Lady Macduff is a big bird?" Edward, taking the bird imagery surrounding Lady Macduff very literally, had costumed her entirely in feathers. A bit wide in the hips, Kaitlin looked like a large duck.

"Yeah, the hat," Candy said, pulling me back to the here and now. "But mostly that thing between Simon and Pamela."

"Oh. Right." I shook my head. "Simon and Pamela. I just can't see them together." I once saw a statue of the goddess Athena, suited up in armor and ready for battle, a haughty smile on her lips. Pamela to a T.

"I don't know what happened, but I guess it involved handcuffs."

That I could see.

Candy pinched out the end of her half-done cigarette, stuck it back into her pack, and opened the door, holding it for me. I scrambled to my feet and we walked into the cool dark theater.

"And there was *Streetcar*, of course," she said, stashing her pack away again.

When Simon first arrived in Phoenix, the theater community couldn't believe its luck—a marvelous actor whose fame guaranteed a full house. But when he drank, Simon screwed up royally, and often.

Like the time he forgot his lines in the middle of a performance, and improvised by saying, "Fuck" over and over (luckily, since it was a David Mamet play, no one noticed). Or the time when the Ghost of Christmas Present got a little too jolly and regaled Scrooge with stories of Christmas debauchery that had mothers grabbing their tots and running from the theater. But the topper came during *Streetcar Named Desire*. Simon's Stanley was fabulous, filled with booze and angst. "Stella!" he roared in the famous scene. "Stella!" Then "Stell—aaah!" as he fell off the stage into the orchestra pit.

"Yeah." I'd forgotten Edward had directed that show. We walked through the greenroom and into the hall where the dressing rooms were.

"Simon." Candy shook her head. "It's too bad he was such a drunk."

"But he wasn't any more," I said. "He was in recovery."

"But hon..." She opened the dressing room door, then stopped, effectively blocking my entrance. She turned to me, her eyes wide.

"Have you been in here today?"

"What? No. I came straight into rehearsal. I knew I was late."

"And you didn't come in here last night after..."

Had it only been last night? I shook my head. "Why are you..." I trailed off as Candy opened the door wide, and pointed to something sitting on top of my makeup kit.

A note.

# CHAPTER 10

## I' the Name of Truth

A slip of stationery, torn at the top and at the bottom, sat on top of my makeup kit. I sank down into my chair and picked it up. *"I am so sorry I caused you pain."* It was the same handwriting I'd seen on the note for my orchid. The one signed *"Your King."*

My king.

Simon.

Candy touched my shoulder. "It was here when I came into the dressing room last night after, well, after everything. You were already gone." She sat down in a chair next to me. "I am so sorry."

The same words Simon had written.

"Me, too," I said. So he had done it. Somehow slipped past all my best intentions.

"You want to talk about it? Maybe over a strong drink? Oh, shoot." Candy grimaced. "That was the wrong thing to say."

I shook my head. "Don't worry. But I have to work a shift at the Garden tonight. Thanks anyway."

"Alright, hon. Take care of yourself." She blew a kiss to me as she left.

I stared at the note. *I'm sorry.* Was that all Simon could say? I fingered the torn edges of the note. Maybe he had written more. He had to have written more.

I stayed in the dressing room for a few more minutes, waiting until I couldn't hear any sound from the hall. Once I was pretty sure everyone had left the area, I opened the door, double-checked to make sure the coast was clear, and tiptoed down the hall. Upon reaching my destination, I stopped. Could I really do this? Yes. If there were more to the note, it would be here at the theater. I couldn't imagine him writing the note at home and bringing it with him. I turned the handle to Simon's dressing room, stepped inside and shut the door.

Though the mess had been cleaned up, the smell of death still hung heavy in the air. Luckily, I had anticipated this. I remembered that people used to sniff at perfumed handkerchiefs to keep bad smells away. I'd searched through my stuff in the dressing room for anything scented. Though some of my makeup was slightly perfumed, my tin of Altoids won out as strongest-smelling. Now, I popped open the lid and stuck my nose inside. It worked. All I could smell was peppermint.

I mentally patted myself on the back and looked around the room. Bill wasn't using this dressing room. No one blamed him for wanting a different one.

Though the floor had been cleaned, the rest of the room was just as Simon had left it. The tackle box he used as a makeup kit was still on the counter. His script lay next to it, dog-eared from use. Tacked up on the mirror was the preview article with a color photo of Simon. In the picture, he was laughing, head thrown back, clearly delighted by whatever the interviewer had said. Oh, Simon...The grief I had swallowed threatened to reassert itself, so I took another big sniff of Altoids, pushing my nose deep into the tin. The shock to my sinuses pushed the lump of grief back down, and I looked at the room with more analytical eyes.

Next to the article, another piece of paper was taped to the mirror, this one with numbers written across it. I had Simon's note with me. I compared it to the paper with the numbers. Not the same. The paper he had written "*I'm sorry*" on was good stationery, heavy and cream-colored. The paper taped to the mirror was lined notebook paper. The numbers were written in pen and began at 6. They were all in order and they were all crossed out except for the last number, 38. Interesting, but not what I was looking for.

I checked the clock on the dressing room wall. I should be leaving for work, but I really wanted to find the stationery, to see if I could tell what else Simon had written. It had to be here. Ah. Another piece of paper peeped out from underneath Simon's ruined ringmaster's hat. Maybe this was it. I didn't have gloves, but Simon had left a pencil near his copy of the script. I used the eraser to pull the note out from under the hat, just in case there were fingerprints. I saw it on CSI once.

This note was on a plain white copy paper, the kind you use in a printer. In block letters was written, "You WILL wear the hat." Didn't seem to be the same penmanship as the note on the mirror as the lettering was much bigger. Pretty sure it was Edward's. Underneath the note was a doodle: Shakespeare wearing a top hat, but with a big circle around it and diagonal line through it, the universal symbol for "no" like you see on "No Smoking" signs. Simon had been quite the artist.

I searched the rest of the room thoroughly, even going through Simon's makeup case. No stationery. No more paper at all. Nothing he could have written a note on.

# CHAPTER 11

## The Milk of Human Kindness

Being late to work meant fewer tables and less money. I tried to make up for it by being especially perky, an attribute that often resulted in bigger tips. "Here you are, milady." I gave a little curtsey to my Olive Garden customers before moving the gigantic bowl of salad to make room for their gigantic plates of food.

"Mi-who?" my customer said, blinking up at me. Her eyes were heavily lined in navy blue. Her mascara matched.

"Hey, you callin' my girlfriend names?"

That from the guy across from her whose T-shirt and gut spoke of his affection for Pabst Blue Ribbon.

"Honey, it ended with lady. I think it was a compliment," she said.

Her companion poked me with an enormous breadstick. "You complimentin' my girlfriend? You like girls or somethin'?"

"No. Sorry. I'm in a play, *Macbeth*, and..."

"Mac-who? MacGyver? They bringin' him back on TV?"

"She said, 'Macbeth,' honey. It's Shakespeare, I think." His date smiled at me, her eyes crinkling up like navy blue spiders.

I nodded at her as I backed away from the table.

"Oh, Shakespeare," Mr. PBR said. "Awfully fancy for a waitress, aren't ya?"

"Olive." Sue, my manager, had come up behind me.

Everyone here still used my old name. It amused them to tell people I was the original Olive. Sometimes they made jokes about playing in my garden, too, but usually not in front of the customers.

"I need to speak to you," Sue said. "Now."

"Enjoy your Garlic-Herb Mediterranean Chicken and Five-Cheese Lasagna." I smiled at my customers and followed Sue into the kitchen, my sneakers squeaking on the linoleum.

Once through the swinging doors, Sue turned to me. Uh oh. She had a frownie crease between her eyes. "You were late."

I stayed in Simon's dressing room too long. "I know, but—"

She held up a hand. "I wasn't finished. You were late *again*. And this theater schedule of yours." Sue shook her head. I had needed to take off most evenings and weekends during the rehearsal period, and still needed dinners off most nights through the end of the run.

"I won't be late again." I crossed my heart. "And I could really help out once the show's over. I could cover every vacation, every single one, and..." I stopped. Sue was staring hard at my face, her frownie crease deepened to a trench. "Olive," she said, "What's that white powder on your nose?"

Damn Altoid dust.

So. It won't be Olive's Garden any longer. I unlocked my car in the parking lot, careful not to touch any sun-heated metal. I needed to figure out my next step, but I didn't want to think while driving, and I didn't want to go home. I couldn't think in my apartment, too many dishes and phone calls and half-read books calling to me. And it was hot. My last electric bill was a hundred and fifty bucks—a hundred and fifty bucks—for my dollhouse-sized apartment. I kept the thermostat at ninety now and hoped for a monsoon or a miracle to cool things down.

I ended up at Toyko Express. It was cool, pretty quiet, and they piped in classical music, which helps you to think clearly, or so I read in a doctor's office magazine. I ordered a fish sushi tray and a cup of green tea, took it to an empty booth, and thought about my predicament. I would get paid for the play, but how far does $500 get you? That's right, five hundred bucks for four weeks of rehearsal and a four-week run. And that's not atypical for a non-union actor. Except for the big stars, we actors are a pretty poor lot.

I looked into my cup and swirled around the tea dust, hoping for a tealeaf reading or something. I wondered if I should have talked Sue into letting me stay on, if I'd made a mistake, choosing theater over a paying job with good tips. I wondered for all of five seconds. I loved the theater, had ever since I saw my first show, a children's theater production of Dracula. I didn't care that the bats were rubber and the accents fake, because it was happening, right then, right in front of me. I could touch Dracula if I wanted to. In fact I did; my mother should never have let me sit in the first row. No, I had definitely made the right choice to feed my soul. Now if I could just feed the rest of me.

"Olive? Got your message."

Uncle Bob stood next to my table, balancing a tray with two steaming rice bowls and a super-sized soft drink crowded onto it. I'd texted him before I left the Garden. With everything going on, I wanted to be with someone who loved me.

"You doin' okay?"

"Better now." I was. My uncle always made me feel better. Even his Hawaiian shirts made me smile.

"You wanna talk about it? About Simon?"

I shook my head. I didn't want to go there. I wanted to sit and eat with family.

My uncle sat down heavily opposite me and immediately started tucking into his dinner. He took a bite from one rice bowl, then took a bite from the other. I didn't have to ask why. He had a teriyaki beef bowl, and a teriyaki salmon bowl. Bob's a big guy with a family history of bad tickers. His doctor told him to eat less beef and more fish. Bob couldn't give up the cow, so he decided that eating this way counterbalanced things. Only once did I try to talk to him about it. He just pointed at my Diet Coke and three slices of Meat-Lover's pizza.

"Hey," I said. "Did you know pandas do an average of eight handstands a day?"

"Ha!" Uncle Bob's eyes lit up. He loved trivia. "I just heard about a dog who can read."

"Really?"

"Yep. Print and cursive." He chuckled. "Panda handstands. Ha!"

He smiled at me. He was grizzled and gray and not a little overweight, but he had a killer smile. When he didn't have food stuck in his teeth.

"Thought you had a shift at the Garden," he said between bites, dropping a bit of rice from his chopsticks. That was another weight-loss strategy of his. He read somewhere that people who use chopsticks eat less. Judging from the amount of rice on the table, I'd say that was correct.

"Olive's Garden is no longer."

"Somebody finally torch the damn place?"

Bob was no fan of Americanized Italian food. Americanized Japanese food seemed to be okay.

"I got fired."

"Want me to torch the place?"

I loved this man. "It's tempting, but they'd probably just rebuild it bigger."

Both our faces fell at the idea of an even larger Olive Garden.

"So, your job at the theater?"

I recognized this as one of my uncle's PI tricks. Ask an open-ended question and see what you get. My uncle watched me, a question in his eyes and teriyaki sauce on his chin.

I wasn't giving in. "It's a great theater company."

"So it pays pretty good?"

Hoping to distract him, I pointed to the sauce on his chin. He wiped it and continued.

"Olive..."

No distracting Bob when he was on the scent. He was a private detective, after all. "You know your folks would help you out."

"No."

My parents lived in Prescott, a mountain town about two

hours away. I wasn't really on speaking terms with them. Oh, I let them know I was alive and well, but that was about it.

"Olive, I know how you feel. Your mom sometimes just says things."

Things that cut me to the quick. Neither Mom nor Dad could talk to me without bringing up Cody, even though it'd been more than ten years since the accident. No. I wouldn't ask them for help. Ever.

"Not going there, Uncle Bob. Discussion closed." I started stacking empty containers on my tray.

"Hey, hey, hey, no need to rush off." He threw his hands in the air, as if to say, "I surrender." "Sit," he said. "I'll buy you some more raw fish."

I sat.

"I'll sit, but I'm full." I folded my napkin. I folded it again. And again. It was beginning to look like origami. I wondered if there was any money in origami.

"You know, I thought you were pretty good in that last show I saw. What was it called? The one where you got married and died?"

"Steel Magnolias."

"Yeah. You were good."

I shrugged a modest thanks.

"You know, I could use someone with your acting skills."

I didn't follow.

"You know, sometimes it's easier to get people to talk to you if you can fit in, seem like their kind of people."

Still not following.

"And sometimes I need to get information outta someone. It'd be great to have a cute blonde..."

I loved Uncle Bob.

"To get them talking. All aboveboard, though. You see what I mean?"

"Not really."

"What I'm sayin' is I could use some help with the business, my PI business. I'd pay."

Now I did see. I saw through the loud shirt and teriyaki-ed chin to see a big beautiful guy who cared about me. I stood up. Uncle Bob looked a little worried he'd somehow offended me. I walked around the booth to stand beside him. I put my arm around his neck and kissed him on his stubbly gray cheek.

"When do you want me to start work?"

# CHAPTER 12

## A Peerless Kinsman

I was really happy to have the new job, for several reasons:

1. I needed money.
2. Uncle Bob said he could work around my schedule.
3. I loved my uncle. Not only would it be great to work with him, but I really wanted to help him out however I could.
4. Something about Simon's death was bothering me. By working with a PI, maybe I could figure out how to investigate what really happened.

This last reason I kept to myself.

The next day, Uncle Bob and I met at his house to talk about my new responsibilities over a late breakfast of chili dog nachos. The thought of Simon, which had been lodged somewhere between my gut and my throat, had moved up to my head, rattling around like a small pea where my brain used to be.

I decided to see if I could talk away the clattering in my head. "Could someone commit suicide by drinking himself to death?"

"It could happen." Uncle Bob expertly segmented a grapefruit with a small knife—the diet portion of his meal. "Though most people who kill themselves with alcohol combine it with drugs." He slid me a look. "What's more likely is the drinking led to impulsive behavior, like taking a few more drinks and then a few more, until it was too many."

I shook my head. "I just don't think Simon would do that."

"Your boyfriend told me Simon was drunk at rehearsal one night."

"He was not drun—" Wait. Boyfriend? Boyfriend!

Trying to act casual, I wiped my chin and belched. That seemed casual enough. "Drunk. So, you and Jason talk much that night I was here?"

"Yeah, some." Bob licked the chili juice off his fingers and pushed himself away from the kitchen table.

I reached for a toothpick from the shot glass in the middle of the table, even though nothing was stuck in my teeth. "What about?"

"You know, stuff. The D-backs, the Suns, you."

"Really?" The toothpick actually flew from my mouth.

"Gotcha." Uncle Bob smiled a gentle smile. "No, hon. Not really. Guys don't talk about that stuff. You ever heard me talk about a woman?"

"No."

"You think I don't like women?"

I didn't even have to think about it. Uncle Bob's favorite place to eat was Hooters.

"You think I never had a girlfriend?"

Now here was something interesting. I considered my uncle, dressed in a green Hawaiian shirt with palm trees scattered across it. "I don't know," I said finally.

"Well, maybe someday you'll find out." He rose and took his plate to the sink. "But it won't be from me talking about it."

He patted me on the head as he passed, something he'd been doing since I was a kid. I had never been able to get him to stop. I knew he meant well. "How long can you work today?"

"Pretty much the whole day. Call for the show isn't until 6:30."

The theater had changed today's scheduled matinee to an evening performance to give Edward time to work with Bill. I hoped it would help. It was an enormous amount of work for the box office.

"I'll take you down to the office and get you set up. I got some photos I need downloaded and filed," said Uncle Bob. "Plus a bunch of reports I need written up."

Uncle Bob washed the breakfast dishes. He really was a catch, in spite of his outward appearance. A lot of women would probably overlook his stubbly face and fifty extra pounds as long as he cooked breakfast and cleaned up after himself. Maybe he did have a girlfriend somewhere.

"Hey," I said, standing up suddenly. "You distracted me."

"Yeah?" said Uncle Bob, not turning around from the sink full of soapy water.

"Yeah. You got me thinking about work instead of the women in your life, and..."

I wracked my brain. What had we been talking about before that?

"And...Jason." Score one for my pea-sized brain.

"That," said Bob, "is a PI trick. Distraction. You'll be using that someday."

"What for?"

"Sometimes it's to have a chance to look around—you know, to see if somebody has anything in their office or on their person that tells us something. Sometimes, it's to get them talking, so we can find out what they know without them realizing it."

"Yeah, that makes sense." The pea snapped to attention. "Hey, you just did it again."

"And sometimes," said Uncle Bob, "it's useful when you want your niece to stop thinking and start working." He walked over and patted me on the head again, depositing a few soap bubbles on my hair. "Time to get going."

Hmm. I got up, poured myself a cup of coffee for the road, and reached inside the fridge for the milk carton. "Hey," I said. "Did you hear that cows with names give more milk than cows without?"

"Really?" said my uncle, drying his hands.

Score.

"Yeah," I said, sitting back down at the table. "They found that—"

"Good try," said my uncle. "But you can't distract me. Let's get to work." He grabbed his keys off a hook near the door.

"Just wanted to give it a try." I followed my uncle into the hundred-degree October day, wondering how I could use this PI trick to investigate Simon's death, sort out my unnamed fears, and calm my little pea brain.

# CHAPTER 13

## *The Heat-Oppressed Brain*

After an hour at Uncle Bob's office, I was done. Not as in "done with my work," or even "done with this job," but done as in "stick a fork in me, I'm done." Cooked. I was used to the heat (keeping your apartment at ninety degrees will do that for you), but boy oh boy.

Uncle Bob's office was on the second floor of an old converted warehouse overlooking the jail. He had furnished it himself with a couple of plaid easy chairs, a metal government-issue desk and filing cabinet, a brown carpet remnant whose original color may have been white, and a non-functioning swamp cooler. I guess it had broken a few days before I started work. Uncle Bob was probably the nicest man on earth, but he was also a proud penny pincher. "Since cool weather's coming," he told me, "I figured I'd wait to fix it." He went on to explain that he usually got a coupon in the mail around April.

April. It was October. The temperature today had already climbed to 100. Yeah, it'd cool down sometime this month, but today the office was suffocating. I couldn't even open the window because the swamp cooler was jammed into it.

I sat in my office chair and closed my eyes. The sweat beaded on my upper lip. Instead of fighting it, I imagined myself in a tropical paradise. I could feel myself relaxing. I added to my waking dream—bird calls, chattering monkeys, and Jason. Shirtless.

My imagination rescued me. I spent the day sweating and

working and pretending a dip in the sea and a tropical drink were waiting for me. Then I got into my hot little car, grabbed a burrito from Filiberto's drive-through window, and headed to the theater. Upon arriving, the air conditioning I'd been complaining about for weeks almost made me swoon with delight.

I headed straight for the theater shower, set in the hall in the midst of all the dressing rooms. I rinsed off, threw on a big T-shirt and panties from my duffle bag, and dashed across the hall to our dressing room. Candy was in costume and headed out the door on her way to the greenroom where she would probably flirt outrageously with one of the soldier actors. I undressed again, did my hair and makeup, pulled on my footless tights and reached for the paper bag my uncle had given me before breakfast that morning. "Your leotard," he said. "When you came here from the theater that night it was...kind of a mess. I washed it for you." He was a big sweetie, I thought as I pulled my leotard out of the bag.

Oh no.

He was a big sweetie who didn't know that you didn't put leotards in the dryer. I stared at my Barbie-sized costume. Okay, I'm exaggerating; it was more of a baby doll size. Maybe an American Girl doll size. Just not Ivy-sized anymore.

It was also my only costume. But leotards stretch, right? I stepped into the leotard and pulled it up over my hips—so far, so good—and then tugged to get it up onto on my shoulders, the way you do when you're trying to get a tight fitted sheet on a bed. There. I looked in the mirror. Not too bad. Squashed me a bit, but I still looked like a sexy serpent, the emerald stripes running from my breasts right down to...

Oh shit. I checked again, hoping against hope. Nope, there it was. A camel toe. I tugged at my leotard, hoping it would stretch back into a more modest shape, but no. It was there to stay, and was nicely accentuated by a big green splotch right near my crotch. Great, an iridescent camel toe.

"Places." Linda's voice came over the small speaker mounted in the corner of the dressing room.

I clasped my hands in front of my crotch and ran backstage. I tried to tell myself that maybe no one would notice the unfortunate fit of my leotard. After all, the green really did make my eyes pop, just like Simon said.

Simon. I had hoped the day's work would get my mind off his death. But even in my imaginary world of tropical drinks and half-naked Jason, the thought had surfaced from time to time. Working at Uncle Bob's reminded me that the world was not all rosy, and that people—at least some of them—were cruel. It wasn't just the air conditioning at the theater that was a relief. After a day of filing bad photographs of bad people doing bad things, I was glad to sink into the world of *Macbeth*—where not-so-bad people did unspeakable things.

Huh. I hadn't thought of it that way before.

I stopped to ponder this idea when Candy ran into the back of me. Probably because I had literally stopped to think in the middle of clambering into the cauldron.

"Darlin', the curtain is going up shortly and I don't want my ass hangin' out of this cauldron in front of God and everyone," said Candy.

"Sorry. I was thinking. I can't really move and think at the same time," I said, shifting gears back to the present moment. "Except when I dance, which makes me wonder if, when I dance, maybe I kind of turn off my brain or something."

Tyler sniggered as he pushed past me into the cauldron. I would have socked him, except I opened myself up for that one. I let it pass.

Candy climbed into the cauldron ahead of me and pulled me in.

"Maybe it's like really good sex," she said.

Tyler stopped sniggering.

"You know, how during it your mind goes away? You become all body and no mind?"

I nodded, though I was beginning to wonder if I'd ever had really good sex.

The techies, using a set of pulleys and strong ropes, hauled the cauldron into the fly space. As always, I felt slightly queasy, huddling with two other sweaty bodies in the swaying darkness. I wondered if a fall from this height would kill me or just maim me. I wondered if I should try to jump clear of the cauldron if it fell. I wondered if that thing about jumping up and down in a falling elevator was really true. I wondered...

"Oh! Did you see the article in *The Republic*?" Candy said.

"No," I said.

"Shhh!" Tyler said.

"I guess Simon was Jewish."

"Oh. And?"

"Would you two shut up?"

"No funeral."

"Why? That's not a Jewish—"

"For God's sake, the show's about to start—"

"And he was married."

Tyler didn't have to shush me anymore. I was speechless.

# CHAPTER 14

## *Guardian of His Bones*

At intermission, perched on the ratty old greenroom couch, I perused the profile of Simon on the front page of the Arts and Entertainment section of *The Arizona Republic.* The article explored his theater and film background, noted that he was born to a Jewish mother in Manchester, England, and said he was survived by his wife Nuala Colmekill of Galway, Ireland, whom he had married in 1986.

"But why didn't he get divorced?" I thought out loud, in case any of the actors gathered around had an idea.

"Turn the page," said Candy, at the same moment Riley grabbed the paper out of my hands. I shrugged.

"The paper said they got married in Ireland." Candy paused, waiting for me to take the bait.

I bit. "And?"

"And it was illegal to get divorced in Ireland 'til the mid-nineties. Even after that, it was pretty tough to undo an Irish marriage, especially a Catholic one."

Jason sat down on the couch next to me. I nearly purred.

"Sounds kind of like Spencer Tracy," he said.

"Does not," said Candy.

"Sure," he said. "You know he was married the whole time he was with Katherine Hepburn. Stayed with his wife out of Irish-Catholic guilt."

"That's the part that doesn't sound like Simon," said Candy. "The guilt part."

"So instead of divorcing his wife," I said. "He just carries on publicly with other women? Nice."

"Are we talking about Simon or Spencer?" said Candy.

"Both," I said.

"Come on, isn't it kind of romantic?" said Jason. "The whole star-crossed lovers thing." He slid closer to me.

"Ha! Star-crossed lovers." Bill Boxer's breath announced his presence behind the couch. That and his hand on my shoulder. "That's Shakespeare, right?"

Bill's first performance had been cringe-worthy. He skipped several lines, welcomed Macbeth "thither" (there) instead of "hither" (here), and sounded as if he were reading off a teleprompter that scrolled across the inside of his forehead. Though he did wear the hat. A new one that fit his big head.

Linda's voice floated across the room, "Places in ten."

Everyone started to disperse.

"Wait," I said. "I'm still confused. Why doesn't Simon get a funeral? And why did you just say 'a Catholic marriage?' I thought Simon was Jewish."

"He converted in order to get married," said Riley, who was moving his lips slightly as he read the paper. "But his wife decided Simon should be buried early according to Jewish custom. No Catholic services will be held."

"Thus increasing his chances of being damned to hell for all eternity," said Jason.

Both Candy and I looked at him.

He shrugged. "I'm Catholic, too. Was. Lapsed."

A sense of outrage bubbled up in me. Simon had turned his life around. He deserved better. I stood up and said in my loudest actor voice. "Excuse me, all. I have an announcement." A few cast members turned around. When they saw it was just me, they resumed their trek toward backstage. Ouch. I sat back down.

"What did you want to say, Ivy?" asked Jason.

"I think we should have a memorial service for Simon."

Jason considered it, nodded slowly, and rose to his feet.

"Everyone!" he said. The whole cast turned. They waited. The power of his role, I guess. "Wednesday, after the show, we'll have a brief memorial service for Simon." He turned to me, "Would you like to add anything?"

I stood. "I'll be taking up a memorial contribution. Please make the checks out to Alcoholics Anonymous."

I nearly sat down, until I noticed the expectant looks on the actors' faces. "And like any good memorial service," I continued, "there will be food." That was the ticket. A buzz went around the room.

"Can you bake?" I whispered to Candy.

"Girl, I'm Southern. I was born with a wooden spoon in my hand."

"I'll make banana bread," said Jason.

He baked. Wow. He seemed almost too good to be true.

# CHAPTER 15

## Show'd Some Truth

I was at the computer in Uncle Bob's still-sweltering office when I heard him coming down the outer hallway, whistling something someone else might have called a tune. Needing to get off the webpage I was visiting, I quickly clicked on the little house icon at the top of the screen. The screen now displayed Uncle Bob's home page, a trivia site. Just in time, too. My uncle opened the door and walked in as I perused the page. He wore his typical cargo shorts and Hawaiian shirt. This particular shirt featured drinks with pink umbrellas in them.

"Good afternoon," I said. "Hey, did you know you can make dynamite out of peanuts?"

"Yep," he said, tossing his keys on top of the file cabinet. "George Washington Carver discovered you could make nitroglycerin out of them. Also figured out how to make peanut paint, tuberculosis medicine, and just about everything you can imagine, except peanut butter. Aztecs beat to him to that."

I'd learned that Uncle Bob used trivia in his work, said it got people talking. I wondered where a conversation about peanuts might fit in. Bob came over to the desk we shared and peered over my shoulder at the computer monitor. "Are you hard at work or hardly working?"

Uncle Bob had given me a bunch of internet research to do. I liked it. I like checking the different databases, following little clues, trailing people in cyberspace. I felt like a spy.

"Got it all done," I said. "Want the dirt on William Nottingham?"

One of my uncle's big clients, Franko, Hricko, and Maionchi, was a law firm that specialized in family law—divorces, wills, prenups. The daughter of a wealthy aging socialite had requested a background check on her mother's considerably younger fiancé, the aforementioned Willy. The law firm had obtained the basic info and passed the case on to Uncle Bob.

It seems the mother and daughter had met William at a country club where they played doubles regularly. He showed up one day from Palm Beach and swept the older woman off her feet. "An abominable tennis player," she'd admitted to her daughter, "but so adorable in his tennis whites." His abominable tennis playing had raised the daughter's antennae. He'd told her he'd been a member of the Palm Country Country Club for years. The horrible redundancy of the club name, she said, was another clue that something was dirty beneath those tennis whites.

"So," said Uncle Bob, "is there a Palm Country Country Club in Palm Beach?"

"Nope," I said. "There is a Palm Beach Country Club, a North Palm Beach Country Club, a Palm Beach Polo and Country Club, and a Palm Beach National Golf and Country Club. I called them all, asking for him, just in case he misspoke. No William Nottingham."

"Good," said my uncle.

"Why do people lie about things that are so easy to check out?" I asked.

"Don't know." He shrugged. "But it happens all the time and it keeps us in business. Had a guy once say he'd been mayor of Why, Arizona. But Why's never had a mayor. It's not incorporated. Want to know why?"

I nodded.

"Then you gotta live there for awhile." He chuckled. "Get it? To know Why, you gotta live there."

I shook my head. Didn't want to encourage him.

"What else you got?" he asked.

"Aliases," I said with a grin. "A ton of them. His real name is not William Nottingham, it's Billy Bob Nuttin. He has been Bill Nettham, B. McNaughton, and Will Nott. He was billed as 'Naughty Willy' in a racy British film and had a brief career as a hip hop singer by the name of B.B. Nuthin."

"Never heard of him."

"He had a single that got a bit of airplay, 'Nuthin's Good Enough for You.'"

"Are you making this shit up?"

I crossed my heart. "Swear to God."

"Nice work," said my uncle, patting me on the head. I really wished he wouldn't do that. "Ready to lock up?" he asked.

"Almost," I said. "Just need to finish up a few things. See you in the morning?" I was learning that my uncle often spent most of the day out of the office doing PI-type stuff like surveillance.

"Yep," said my uncle, picking up his keys. "See you later, alligator."

"In a while, crocodile."

Uncle Bob left, whistling whatever tune he'd begun earlier. Once it had faded away down the hall, I quickly went back to the web page I'd been looking at before he came in.

"Alcohol poisoning," read the medical info page I'd pulled up, "can be deadly." I quickly scanned the information. Most people who die of alcohol poisoning, it said, either lapse into a coma and stop breathing or pass out and aspirate on their own vomit. When I found him, Simon was definitely unconscious and he had certainly thrown up. But did he really die from drinking one bottle of brandy? I kept reading until I found what I was hoping for—the information that convinced me Simon did not die from alcohol poisoning.

# CHAPTER 16

## Ere the Set of Sun

"HONK!"

"Oh my gosh, I'm sorry," I shouted out the open window of my car. I'd almost made a left turn into an SUV. "Sorry!" I yelled again to the woman behind the wheel, who shook her head at me.

I was on my way home from Uncle Bob's and thinking about Simon. Not only could I not think and move at the same time, it seemed I couldn't drive and think either. Luckily, I was nearly at my destination. I focused on the road until I got to my apartment complex, pulled into my reserved space, locked my car, and resumed thinking again.

It wasn't the new information I had about alcohol poisoning that was bothering me. It was the note. And the fact that Simon was Jewish. My brain had decided there was a connection, but couldn't quite make sense of it, like when you see the shape of a missing piece in a jigsaw puzzle, but none of the ones that look right actually fit.

I climbed the exterior stairs to my second-floor apartment, went in, and wanted to leave immediately. I had prepared myself for the 90-degree interior, but not for the smell. While grocery shopping after the show last night, I bought some "discounted for quick sale" chicken breasts, brought them home and skinned and cooked them. I had thought losing a few pounds might help me fit better into my XXS leotard (which the costumers had deemed okay, probably because they were already building costumes for the next show). I had also left raw chicken skin in a 90-degree apartment all day. I grabbed the offending trash bag, scuttled down the stairs, and threw it in the dumpster.

Back in the apartment, I used up a whole can of Dollar Store air freshener. It didn't get rid of the stink, just layered a grape juice-like scent on top of it. I turned off the air conditioner and opened all the windows. A hot breeze wafted through the screens. It would raise the temperature inside a few degrees, but it should also take care of the smell.

I changed into a tank top and pair of shorts and headed out toward the canal. Maybe a walk would clear my head while the breeze cleared out my apartment.

The canal was just a few blocks from my apartment. Part of an irrigation system that zigzagged across the Valley, it had gravel walking/biking paths along each side and a slightly cooler air temperature, thanks to the water. The coolness was what drew me, not the water. I made sure to stay a good fifteen feet away from the canal's steep concrete edges.

I walked at a good clip (fitting into that leotard was never far from my mind), my jigsaw puzzle mind still sorting pieces. What was it about the note? The words "*I am so sorry I caused you pain*" did sound like they came from someone who knew he was doing harm, but they weren't specific. Was that what was bothering me?

I heard a crack under my feet and looked down. Just an old bit of sun-bleached plastic trash. A scrap of paper fluttered nearby.

A scrap. Huh.

I stopped, that "not being able to move and think" issue kicking in. A scrap. My brain tried to fit this piece into the puzzle. Simon's note had been torn—at the top *and* the bottom. Even if he had decided to not give me the first part of the note, why tear off the bottom?

A duck landed with a splash in the canal, which shone orange with the setting sun. I turned to go home. One of Arizona's superlative sunsets stretched across the western sky. Sunset.

"Sunrise, Sunset..." The tune from *Fiddler on the Roof* ran through my head. My mind picked up the Jewish piece of the puzzle.

A few weeks ago, I was in the greenroom with all of the other actors when we heard shouting down the hall. The typical pre-rehearsal hubbub stopped as we all tried to eavesdrop.

"You've got to be kidding." Pamela, her voice loud and uncharacteristically screechy.

A murmur from a male voice.

Riley poked his head into the hall. "It's Pamela," he said, stating the obvious. "And Simon."

"Your behavior?" Pamela sounded a bit unhinged. "Your treachery, you mean? Your betrayal? Your—" We all heard what sounded like a slap, followed by a door slam.

I waited a few minutes then knocked on Simon's dressing room door.

"Come in."

Simon sat in front of the mirror staring at a red slap mark on his face.

"I heard," I said.

"I just wanted to talk to her. To apologize." He shook his head at himself. "This step, I thought it would be like the Day of Atonement, but I'm afraid for me it may turn out to be a Lifetime of Atonement."

I was confused by what Simon meant, but it didn't seem a good time to ask about it. I patted him on the shoulder and left him alone. Now, thanks to *Fiddler on the Roof* and the strange way my brain made connections, I recognized the Day of Atonement as something from Simon's Jewish past. But what did the rest mean?

I had stopped walking again. Not good, as I wanted to be off the canal by dark. I stepped up my pace and walked toward the sunset, now fading into violet.

By the time I reached my still-smelly but bearable apartment, my brain had fit the puzzle together. "This step," Simon had said. He was in A.A., a twelve-step program. Atonement must be one of the steps.

# CHAPTER 17

## Commencing in a Truth

I tried out my new theory on my uncle the next day at the office. He was working on the computer at his desk, so I had set up my laptop on a wooden TV tray facing the window. "So when he said 'atonement,'" I said, "I figure he must have been talking about..." I consulted my computer screen. "'Making direct amends to such people wherever possible, except when to do so would injure them or others.'"

Uncle Bob had moved the swamp cooler to his garage for the season so I could see out the window. It was a nice idea, but all I could really see was the jail across the street. Bet some of those folks could have used a Day of Atonement.

"Olive." The look my uncle gave me was tinged with sympathy.

I ignored it. "So I'm thinking maybe he wrote that note to make amends, as an apology."

"Olive—"

"Not to *me*," I charged ahead, "but to someone else, for something in his past. I mean, he had quite the past."

"*Olive!*"

I stopped. My uncle rarely raised his voice.

"I think you're going to be disappointed in your theory," he said.

"Why?"

"Look at your screen."

I did.

"That step you just read to me—it's one of the Twelve Steps. Right?"

"Right."

"What number?"

I looked. "Step Number Nine."

"And how long had Simon been in A.A.?"

I stopped to think. He'd started going to meetings right before the read-through and we had four weeks of rehearsal. "A little over a month." As I said it, my heart sunk a little. "Does it take longer than that to get to Step Nine?"

"Yeah," my uncle said. "Usually a lot longer."

I'm sure he saw the way my face fell, because he decided to put it in a professional light. "If you're going to work in a detective agency, you're going to have to remember you can't stop investigating when you find the answer you want. You have to follow any ideas all the way through."

So I did. After work, I used my budding investigative skills to find Simon's former A.A. meeting. Actually, it was pretty simple. Simon had told me he attended meetings at "the Cupcake Church." I Googled that, found out the real name of the church was Asbury United Methodist, and with another click of my mouse discovered that an A.A. chapter met there on Tuesdays at 6 p.m. I felt inordinately proud of myself.

I spotted the church a block before I reached it. Its nickname served it well—the stand-alone concrete building looked like, yep, a giant cupcake, with several slender crosses where birthday candles might be.

My dashboard clock said six on the dot when I turned into the parking lot. I jogged to the cupcake and pulled on the door, but it didn't give. I looked at my watch. Just a few minutes past six. I was sure this was the right time and place.

"You looking for the A.A. meeting?" A fiftyish man wearing a shirt and tie called to me from the parking lot.

"Yeah."

"Over here." He pointed toward a low cinderblock building. "That's just the chapel," he said, nodding at the building I'd come from. "We meet in the Fellowship Hall."

I followed the nice man, who held the door for me as we entered the building. The utilitarian-looking room was brightened up by a colorful mural of a desert scene on one wall. I smelled cigarette smoke and coffee, though I couldn't see anyone smoking.

The meeting was already in session. A small group of people sat in a circle near the mural. They were a real mixed bag: from a young guy with a shaved head and tats to a sweet-faced woman with a long gray braid.

"I'm Tammy and I'm an alcoholic," said the woman with the braid.

"Hi Tammy," everyone said. My new friend grabbed two more folding chairs from a rack. A few people scooted to make room for us.

"Want a Big Book?" The guy I'd followed in grabbed a blue book from a stack on the table and handed it to me. I sat down and flipped through the book, which had Alcoholics Anonymous written on the cover. Inside, passages were underlined and circled, and in the front of the book someone had written "Sober for 17 days."

I heard Simon's voice in my head: "I have been sober for thirty-eight days." Thirty-eight. That was the last number on the notepaper taped to the mirror. Simon was keeping track of his days of sobriety. One item crossed off my investigative checklist and one more reason to think he hadn't been drinking.

I noticed it had gone quiet.

"It's your turn," said my new friend.

I stood up. "My name is Ivy Meadows and I am an actress."

"No last names," the woman with the gray braid said kindly. "And it's 'alcoholic,' not 'actress.' Though some of us are pretty good at acting." A few chuckles from the group.

I felt my face flush. I hadn't thought this all the way through. "But I'm not," I said. "An alcoholic, I mean." Sympathetic eyes looked at me. "Wait, let me start again. I'm a friend of Simon Black—"

"No last names," someone said.

"Right. Sorry." I fumbled for the words. "I'm here because they say Simon died of alcohol poisoning. But I don't think he relapsed. I just don't believe it. I guess I'm here to see what you think. Oh! And to find out what step he was working on."

My new friend in the shirt and tie shook his head slowly. "Ivy, there's a reason it's called Alcoholics *Anonymous*."

Oh. Duh. I shut my eyes. "I am so sorry," I said. I sat down.

"It's okay," my friend said. "But we can't help you." Then he said, "I'm Rodney and I'm an alcoholic."

"Hi Rodney," said the group.

I was getting ready to sneak out of there when Rodney said, "I used to go to a regular A.A. meeting..."

A regular meeting? Then what was this? I sat back down and listened. People shared their experiences and their struggles. They took turns reading from the Big Book, passages of which were also projected on a screen. Every so often, someone would read a question and the entire group would respond affirmatively. The experience felt a bit like going to a very accepting church. In fact, they closed the meeting with the Serenity Prayer: "God grant me the serenity to accept the things I cannot change; courage to change the things I can; and wisdom to know the difference." I prayed it along with them.

When the meeting broke up, most of the group ambled over to a table where coffee and cupcakes waited. "In honor of the church," Rodney said, handing me a pink frosted beauty with red sprinkles. I wasn't planning to eat one (that leotard again), but I took the cupcake, just to be polite. "Listen, if you ever want to know more about A.A.," he said, "just give me a call." He handed me a business card. It had only his first name, a phone number, and "A.A. Back to Basics" written on it.

I put the card in my purse. "I'd like to apologize for the way I barged in here tonight."

He waved away my apology, no big deal. "You were just trying to help your friend," he said. Then, as I opened my mouth, "But we really can't talk about that."

"No, no, I understand. I wanted to ask what you meant when you said 'a regular meeting.' Isn't this a regular meeting?" I nibbled at my cupcake. It was moist and tender and really, really good.

"Well, it's a regular meeting of Back to Basics."

"Back to Basics?" I took a bigger bite of the cupcake. Calories be damned.

"Yeah," he said, warming to the subject. "We work on the Twelve Steps the way the original founders of A.A. did back in the 1940s. Back then, people who came to A.A. had a 50-75% rate of recovery. The success rates in regular groups have gone down since then."

"But what's the difference?" I said, trying not to lick my empty cupcake wrapper.

"Sorry." Rodney smiled with all his teeth. "I do get on a roll. It's just that this program has worked so well for me. The difference between a regular A.A. group and Back to Basics," he said, "is that we complete all of the Twelve Steps in one month."

# CHAPTER 18

## *Worth More Sorrow*

After the show on Wednesday, the greenroom was full of people waiting for Simon's memorial. Everyone was in attendance: Pamela, Edward, Linda, the entire cast and crew. I snaked my way through them, an enormous plate of Candy's homemade Pecan Sandies in one hand and a pitcher of punch in the other. I tried to focus on handling the very full pitcher and the plate stacked high with cookies, but my mind kept circling a new idea: If Simon didn't drink himself to death, something else killed him. Or someone else. I considered each person I passed. Did Simon write one of them a note of apology? A note that ended up in my dressing room, intended to convince me Simon's death was suicide?

"Witch!" I jumped at Bill Boxer's voice, too close. One of the Sandies slid off the plate onto the floor. Riley nabbed it. "Five second rule!" Right. Riley's rule was probably more like five months.

"May I carry that for you?" asked Bill. Unusual. No one would call Bill gracious.

"Thanks." I handed him the pitcher.

"And may I say how devastating you look in that costume. Rarrr." He gave what was supposed to be a sexy growl.

I thought about grabbing back the pitcher, but continued toward the table where we'd laid out all the food. Bill followed me. I breathed through my mouth. The Face of Channel 10 and the breath of hell.

"So, Witchie..." said Bill.

"Ivy."

"Ivy." Bill wore his fake-looking acting smile. "What exactly is going on here?"

"Oh, sorry," I said. "You must have been out when we made the announcement. It's a memorial service for Simon."

The smile slipped off his face. His brows knit together in confusion. That face was quickly replaced by his "earthquake in South America" serious newscaster face.

"Oh," said Bill. "Of course."

Still holding the pitcher, he trailed me toward the food table. Behind the piles of snacks and baked goods, people had tacked up photos of Simon. Simon in theater, Simon in film, snapshots of Simon. Bill plunked the pitcher down on the table, harder than he needed to. "Witch?"

I didn't turn around. He tapped me on the shoulder. "I really don't like being called a witch offstage," I said.

"Sorry, um...Lily?"

I sighed. "Close enough. Yes?"

"Are you sure you didn't invite me because you didn't want me to know?"

"Double negative, Bill," Tyler said.

"Why wouldn't I want you to know?" I asked Bill, who wore his real face for a change. An unhappy face. A guilty looking face?

Next to me, Candy rapped a spoon against a glass. "Come on, y'all. This memorial is about to begin." Everyone ignored her.

"People!" Jason said. The room hushed. Jason commanded respect, even in his silly (but kinda sexy) lion tamer unitard.

Bill rolled his eyes at Jason. "Socks," he said to me and Candy in a stage whisper. "Socks, stuffed down his dance belt. Doesn't he think we can tell?"

"Yeah, Bill, you're just jealous," Candy said under her breath.

"No need for me to be jealous. They don't call me 'Big Boxer' for nothing." His left eye scrunched up. I think he was trying to wink but his facelift was too tight.

I grabbed a Pecan Sandie and stuffed it in his mouth. "This is a memorial service." I pointed to a corner.

Bill had the good grace to look embarrassed. He slunk over to where I had pointed and leaned against the wall, looking at the floor.

Jason had been watching us. I nodded at him to begin.

"Duncan is in his grave," he said, quoting Macbeth. "After life's fitful fever he sleeps well. In honor of our departed king, we'd like to say a few words in Simon's memory." He turned to me. "Ivy? Would you like to begin?"

I'd have to think about Bill later. I stepped forward. "Simon was a kind, generous man..."

A loud snort from someone in the crowd.

No. No one would be that unfeeling. I gathered my thoughts and continued, "A kind, generous man who was just getting his life back together..."

Another snort. This was pissing me off. "Listen, if one of you has something to say—"

"I do," said Genevieve. "I could say something." She looked at me levelly, and I realized I should shut up. I'd nearly ruined Simon's memorial. I stepped back into the crowd.

Genevieve had brought a sheaf of paper with her. "Duncan's scenes from *Macbeth*," she said, holding the papers aloft. "Every service needs some sort of ritual." She paused dramatically and flicked a silver lighter. She held the script above the lighter's flame. "In Simon's honor, I burn these pages, knowing that no one else will ever play Duncan as he did."

Snort. Bill. It was definitely Bill.

"Remove the pig." Genevieve pointed at Bill with the still-flaming pages. Two of the bigger soldier actors rumbled toward him.

"But...snort!" Bill waved his half-eaten cookie as the actors advanced on him.

"Hold it," said Linda, stepping forward. "We can't afford to lose another Duncan. Besides," she said, "he's not the pig. I am."

She stared at Genevieve and smiled a tight smile, "Post-nasal drip." She tapped the side of her nose and snorted, an exact copy of the earlier snorts.

Bill drew himself up. "Thank you," he said in a raspy voice. "I am not a pig. I am choking on a cookie." He snort-coughed a few times for good measure and left the room, head held high.

I went to my dressing room a few minutes later. The service was still winding down, but I couldn't hack it. I was afraid I'd say something I shouldn't. I was so angry for Simon. I could still hear the snorts.

I shut my eyes and tried to think good thoughts, like...what? Puppies. I tried puppies. Didn't work. I imagined pug puppies, who wiggled—and snorted. Try something else. Flowers? No. Made me think of funerals.

I heard the door open quietly behind me. In the mirror's reflection I saw Jason. Yes, that would work. Jason.

He carried a plate of banana bread and a cup of coffee. I was now having very happy thoughts.

"Thought you'd want to try some of this before it's all gone," he said. "And I made you a mocha."

He sat the paper cup and plate down in front of me. The bread was studded with chocolate chips. Mmm, chocolate. I filed that away as another happy thought for the future.

Jason stood behind me and began to gently massage my shoulders. Our eyes met in the mirror.

"Sorry," he said, glancing toward the greenroom. "I know you wanted it to be nice for Simon."

I shook my head. "I can't believe them."

My head kept shaking, as if anger had taken over my neck muscles. I squeezed my eyes shut, then felt Jason's lips on the back of my neck. I let out a breath I didn't know I'd been holding. It came out as a sigh.

One of Jason's hands kept massaging my shoulder, while the other slipped inside the neck of my leotard, pulling it off my shoulder. I opened my eyes and met Jason's glance in the mirror. I felt my heart drop, and a tingling start low within me. I nodded slightly at him, and he kissed my neck again, his hand reaching for...

"Woo hoo!" Candy skidded into the dressing room, displaying a plastic bucket like a game show hostess. I quickly pulled my leotard back onto my shoulder. She grinned at us. "Ya'll, if you're going to make whoopee, you at least need to close the door."

Now I was really red. Even Jason looked a little embarrassed.

"The service was a hit after all," said Candy. "We made $500!"

"Really?" Jason and I spoke at the same time.

I pushed back my chair and frowned. "Isn't this the same cast that eats Bisquick for days?"

"Well." Candy fished around in the bucket. "They are mostly fives and ones." She pulled out a dollar bill, then a couple of checks. "But Pamela wrote a check for a hundred and fifty dollars, and someone put in a check from Actors' Equity for fifty bucks."

"Great," I said.

"And..." Candy paused for dramatic effect. After all, she was an actress. "Someone dropped two hundred dollar bills in the bucket. Doesn't that just dill your pickle?" She waved two crisp one hundred dollar bills in the air.

She whooped again, then caught sight of my face.

"Why Ivy, darlin', I thought you'd be pleased. It'll make a nice gift in honor of Simon. Might even get a mention in the paper."

Something wasn't right. "Who donated two hundred dollars?"

Candy shrugged. "Didn't see."

The gears in my mind were grinding slowly, like they were rusty. I took one of the bills from Candy's hand and examined it, even though I didn't know what I was looking for. I sniffed it. Did the bill have a scent? Perfume? Aftershave? Or was I just smelling nearby Candy or Jason?

"I think it's nice," said Candy. She looked to Jason for support. He shrugged his agreement. She went on. "Especially since none of us knew Simon all that well. Heck, some folks didn't even like him and they contributed."

That was it. "Right," I said. "Most of the cast didn't really know him. The ones who did, didn't really like him."

"Except you," interrupted Candy.

"And all of us are strapped for cash. So why?"

"Maybe they felt guilty," said Candy, her hand sliding toward my banana bread.

I snatched it away from her. "Uh, uh, uh."

Jason suddenly stood up. "I'll see you ladies later." He left.

I stared after him. What the hell?

Candy shrugged. "Sorry to ruin your party."

I pouted at Candy in the mirror, then shoved the entire piece of banana bread in my mouth as a consolation prize. The bread was chocolaty and fabulous, but something still bugged me. "Ffff guh ee," I said.

"Swallow first," said Candy. "Then talk."

I did as told. "Felt guilty," I said. "Guilty about what?"

"Got me. Maybe about not liking him."

I shook my head. Two hundred dollars was a lot of money for any struggling actor. Too much to fork over for not liking Simon. But not enough for killing him.

# CHAPTER 19

## *If You Would Grant the Time*

"I want you to take the case," I said as my uncle steered his Mustang down Indian School Road. The seriousness of my request was undercut by a rumble from my stomach. We'd picked up some Mongolian Beef and vegetarian eggrolls for lunch en route to Uncle Bob's office and the smell was driving me crazy.

As we slowed for a yellow light, the car next to us sped up and zoomed through the intersection. "Did you know Phoenix is the red-light running capital of the U.S.?" said Uncle Bob, looking at me out of the corner of his eye.

I nodded, my eyes drawn to a young woman standing in the middle of the road.

Phoenix not only has an inordinate amount of red-light runners, but a lot of pedestrians with death wishes. Walking in Phoenix gets really uncomfortable with the heat reflected off the asphalt. Intersections and crosswalks are about a quarter mile apart, so impatient pedestrians with heat-addled brains often cross in the middle of the blocks, even busy six-lane thoroughfares like Indian School. They run across two or three lanes, then stand in the middle turn lane waiting for a break in the traffic, while cars whiz around them going 50 miles an hour.

We passed the young woman, still standing in traffic. She held a baby in her arms. I wished I could keep her safe. I wished I could keep the whole world safe.

My stomach growled again. The smell of the Chinese food proved too much for me. I grabbed an eggroll out of the bag, tore open the accompanying little packet with my teeth, and squirted soy sauce onto the tasty treat.

"Olive! No eating in the car." My uncle snatched the eggroll and the grease-stained bag from my hand without ever taking his eyes off the road.

Uncle Bob was not exactly a fastidious guy, except when it came to his baby, his red 1969 Mustang. It was his pride and joy, and I suddenly noticed a splotch of soy sauce on the custom white leather upholstery. Ack! Did leather stain? I really hoped not. I surreptitiously dabbed at it with a napkin, then scooted over it, hoping my pants would blot up any remaining sauce.

"Sorry," I said, meaning it more than he knew, and thinking about places to buy leather cleaner. "So will you take the case? I want you to figure out what killed Simon. With everything I know now, I really don't think he died from alcohol poisoning."

My uncle sighed. "Let's look at this logically. Why do you think it wasn't an alcohol overdose?"

"Because he died so quickly and—"

"What's quickly?" asked my uncle.

I frowned. "I checked on him at intermission. I guess maybe forty-five minutes had passed before I found him."

"Actually that could be enough time. How do you know he hadn't been drinking when you saw him at intermission?"

"Because he had just come into the greenroom from backstage."

"Where he could have stashed a bottle."

I shook my head. Simon had seemed completely sober when we were at the buffet talking about Jason.

Hey, that was another reason. "Simon was at the buffet during intermission. He had food in his stomach. That would have slowed the alcohol absorption."

"And also caused him to vomit," said my uncle. "What did you see him eat?"

I saw Simon in my mind, a full paper plate in his hand. "Oh. I guess I saw him with food. I didn't see him eating."

My uncle stopped for a red light and turned to look at me. "The brain tends to make those leaps. One reason eyewitnesses are notoriously unreliable."

This was not going the way I'd planned. "But what about the amount of alcohol? It was just one bottle of brandy."

"A: brandy is pretty high proof. B: you don't know it was just one bottle. C: he was an older guy, probably on some other meds, ones that could have interacted with alcohol."

"But..." I knew my uncle was being logical, like the detective he was, but I was beginning to feel defensive.

"And D: Pink told me Simon had a bad heart. The doctor who signed the death certificate said it was a heart attack, probably brought on by all that booze in such a short time. Didn't even require an autopsy."

"I thought that was because his wife didn't want—"

"It was because Simon's death wasn't suspicious. Hell, it wasn't even considered an accident."

"But—"

"Olive. Honey. Simon's heart gave out because he drank too much. It's not your fault."

Not your fault. Uncle Bob had said those words to me before. Many times.

No. Not going down that road again. I grabbed my mind's wheel and jerked myself back into the present. "There was also the note. And the memorial I told you about. Don't those facts make you suspicious?"

"What facts?" said Uncle Bob. "The fact that Simon apologized for something? Or that someone put a few hundred bucks into a memorial kitty?"

"And there were the pig snorts during the service."

"A pig snort does not a murder make."

"Fine." I stared out the car window. I couldn't help being pissed, even if I knew it was unreasonable. Uncle Bob's argument sounded logical, but I knew in my gut that I was right. Simon did not kill himself, even accidentally. I decided then and there to prove it, with or without my uncle's help.

My uncle pulled into the parking lot of our office building. "Olive," he said quietly. I didn't turn. He pulled the Mustang into his reserved spot and turned off the engine. "I'm so sorry this happened," he continued, "but I think we both know where this is coming from. Simon's death is not your fault, just like your brother's..."

I jumped out of the car. Now I was pissed off with reason. I slammed the door. How dare he bring up Cody? This wasn't like that at all. It wasn't.

I stood there in the parking lot clenching my fists. I could feel the heat from the asphalt through my shoes, but it had nothing on the fire burning in my chest. Shit. I was afraid my uncle was right. I didn't want him to be right.

He had gotten out of the car and walked around to me. I still wouldn't look at him.

"Olive, listen, if it means that much to you, I'll do it. I'll 'take the case.' Okay?"

I nodded, met his eyes, but didn't move. My uncle could be a big softie, but he didn't usually agree so quickly. There had to be a catch. I waited.

"But I want you to do something for me."

Please, please, please, let it not be about Mom and Dad.

"I want you to go see..."

No, no, no. I held my breath.

"A counselor. To help you get past your, uh, past."

I could breathe again. A counselor. I could do that. "Can I wait until the show closes?"

"Sure." Uncle Bob extended his hand and I took it. We sealed the bargain with a handshake.

I heard my cell phone ring from inside Bob's car. I opened the door and grabbed my purse from the passenger side floor. My phone stopped ringing, but still I rummaged in my bag trying to find it. Instead my hand touched a slick square of paper I didn't recognize. I pulled it out.

"Scoot, hon," said Uncle Bob as he reached around me and grabbed our lunch out of the car.

I stared at the photo I'd taken out of my purse. It was one of the pictures we'd used at the service: Simon with donkey ears on his head. There were pine trees behind him, and he had his arm around someone who'd been cut out of the picture. Tiny pinholes were scattered across the surface. Where was this taken and who had been cut away? How did it get in my bag? And why was Uncle Bob glaring at me?

"Olive?" said my uncle, his voice no longer gentle. "Is that soy sauce on my seat?"

# CHAPTER 20

## Bear Welcome in Your Eye

My uncle must really love me. He agreed to check out the cast for me and forgave me for the soy sauce stain. I'd taken the Mustang to the carwash, where the expert cleaning guy just shook his head sadly and pointed me toward the seat covers. I found a Hawaiian-themed pair. Uncle Bob nearly smiled when I presented them to him. Nearly.

We drove to the theater for the Sunday matinee. Uncle Bob always handled his car like a skilled cowboy rode his favorite horse. A nudge here, a flick of the wrist there, and the Mustang obeyed. I wouldn't have been surprised to find out the car had a soul and that it loved my uncle.

"Park over there, at the far end," I said as we pulled into the theater parking lot. "We're supposed to leave the good spots for the audience."

My leg jiggled as Uncle Bob maneuvered through the lot. I was excited he had agreed to look into Simon's death, but nervous about what he might find. I mean, I knew all of the suspects. Someone I knew was a murderer. I shivered.

But only for a moment. The Phoenix heat invaded the car as soon as Uncle Bob turned off the engine and the AC. Didn't matter that it was early October. Too hot to shiver, even at the thought of a real murderer in *Macbeth*.

"Thank God for the sixty-four-ounce Big Gulp." Uncle Bob took a swig from his Diet Coke. He wiped his brow with the back of his hand and opened the car door. "Let's walk and talk."

We crossed the sizzling asphalt toward the theater. "Here's the deal," he said. "If anyone asks, your car wouldn't start, so I drove you here."

"They'll certainly believe that."

"I know. Always make up believable shit. We'll say I didn't want to watch the show 'cause Shakespeare makes me fall asleep."

"More believable shit."

"Right. So that's why I'm hanging out in the break room."

"Greenroom," I said.

"This is the room where I met you after rehearsal that one time, right? The one painted pink?"

I nodded.

"Anyway, that's why I'm hanging out in the greenroom." We were almost at the theater now, so he spoke softly. "Because I don't want to fall asleep and make an ass of myself."

"Got it," I said as we went through the stage door. Then, "Oh." Uncle Bob had just punched the right code into my brain. "That photo of Simon with the donkey ears—he must've been playing Bottom. In *A Midsummer Night's Dream*."

"Yeah, he looked like a real ass." My uncle chuckled. "Bottom, ass—get it?"

"Yeah, Shakespeare loved those double entendres," I said. I'd actually never made the connection before. Duh.

We walked into the greenroom, which was full of actors warming up, swinging their arms, humming to themselves, walking and talking in various stages of undress. Not my uncle's typical world. I snuck a look at him. His jaw looked a little tight, but he caught my eye and winked at me before sinking down onto one of the ratty sofas. He started to set his Big Gulp down on a table next to it, but stopped mid-air. He stared at the table.

"It's an old prop from Sweeney Todd," I explained. "Mrs. Lovett made her meat pies there."

My uncle just shook his head—"theater folk"—as he set his drink on the fake-blood-stained table. He looked up at me and I caught my breath. I'd never noticed how much his eyes looked like my brother's.

"Olive, it wasn't your fault," he said quietly. "Either time."

"How could you know what I was thinking?" I whispered.

"I'm pretty sure you think about Cody a lot."

"Hey, Bob." Jason sat down on the couch next to my uncle, giving me a brief smile but nothing more.

I hadn't seen him alone since the time in my dressing room after Simon's service. He hadn't called either. I couldn't figure it out. I looked around the greenroom for Mrs. Macbeth. Nope, just a bunch of guy actors and Edward, who was talking to Bill but looking our way.

"Jason." Uncle Bob nodded in greeting, while obviously giving him the once over. Jason was in his lion tamer's costume, a tight black unitard with dark red sequins splashed across it like splatters of blood. Uncle Bob kept nodding, a "well, well, well, what have we here?" sort of nod.

Jason nodded too. "I know. I'm playing Shakespeare's most manly man, and I'm dressed like Siegfried or Roy or somebody. At least it doesn't chafe like armor."

"Done a lot of Shakespeare?" my uncle asked.

"It's my forte. That and pirates. I'm quite the swashbuckler."

"That you are, my dear," said Edward, walking past.

Jason reddened. Uncle Bob persisted. "I hear Simon was a swashbuckler, too."

Jason's eyes followed Edward as he made the rounds, checking in with the actors. "Was he? I didn't know him very well," he said. "Just by reputation."

"This was your first time acting with him?"

Uncle Bob knew Jason hadn't worked with Simon before. He must be asking in order to get more information. I was catching on to this detective stuff.

"First and last." Jason stood as Genevieve entered the room.

"Sorry, maybe that was rude. It's just that I need to get into character."

"Yeah, sure. Hey, you got a script I could look at?" asked Uncle Bob. "Maybe if I read Shakespeare I'd get it better."

Jason looked at him, amused. "That's not the way it usually works, but sure, let me get mine."

I waited for Jason to say something to me. He didn't, just walked off toward the dressing rooms.

Genevieve came over and perched on the edge of the couch. "He means that most people understand Shakespeare better when they see it performed," she said. "That's why Shakespearean actors are so revered. We help the audience understand the language."

Genevieve didn't speak to me either, but then she usually ignored me. I didn't take it personally. She usually ignored everyone except for "her husband." We all put it down to her adherence to the Method. She even stayed in character the one time she joined us for drinks after rehearsal. We'd ordered her Bloody Brains (a nasty concoction of grenadine, Irish cream, and peach schnapps) hoping she'd launch into Lady M's "Dashed the baby's brains out" speech. She didn't disappoint.

But my uncle seemed to be an exception to her rule. She leaned closer to him, putting her breasts right in his line of vision. I was pretty sure she put them there on purpose.

"Nice to meet you," Uncle Bob said, sticking out his hand. "You must be..."

"Lady M," she said. "I heard you asking about Simon, our Duncan. He was a master, a legend among Shakespearean actors. He could make the language sing."

"Then what was he doing here?" he said. "No offense, but this isn't Broadway or anything."

"He was a drunk. Highly unstable." Her eyes filled with tears. "And it killed him in the end. Excuse me." She rose dramatically and walked off toward backstage, dabbing her eyes. Uncle Bob rolled his eyes at me. He was no fan of drama queens.

"Ivy." Riley, who had obviously been eavesdropping, bounded

over like a birddog. "Did I tell you I know why Simon died?"

I shook my head and glanced at my uncle, who looked more amused than intrigued.

"It's Bill's fault," said Riley. "'Cause he said 'Macbeth' in the theater."

I should have known better.

"So did you," said my uncle. "Right now."

"What? Oh. I'll fix it." Riley ran outside.

"I'd better get in costume," I told Uncle Bob. I turned to go. Jason walked toward us. I decided to stay. I took Genevieve's spot on the arm of the sofa.

"Heads up." Jason tossed a well-used script to Uncle Bob. "Read it and weep." He grinned at my uncle. "It is a tragedy."

Through the glass stage door, I could see Riley turning around, working off the curse.

Uncle Bob thumbed through the script. "Kinda long, huh?"

"Not for Shakespeare," said Jason.

"What's it clock in at?"

"Haven't you seen it?"

He hadn't. I knew he would—he always saw my shows—but he hadn't got around to it yet.

"Yeah," my uncle lied. "But I fell asleep." He put on a sheepish look. I tried not to smile.

My uncle is, in fact, a pretty good actor. Not on the stage, not his style. But he's got the innocent friendly thing down. I call it his Santa Claus act, 'cause he seems like a jolly fat guy who'll buy you beer for presents. Don't get me wrong: he is a jolly fat guy, but a shrewd one, too. People tend to miss that.

Riley ran back in, panting a little. "We should be good now."

Jason looked at him.

"The curse, I mean," Riley said. "You weren't here, but I said 'Mac—'"

Jason jumped in. "Don't say it."

"Olive told me about the curse," said Uncle Bob. "So you guys believe in it?"

Riley nodded, his lips shut tight.

"I don't know," Jason said. "Better safe than sorry, I guess."

"I read about it. Pretty weird stuff. Did you know during its very first run, the boy playing Lady..." Uncle Bob stopped.

"Lady M," said Jason quickly.

"She...he...died?" my uncle said.

"Dude," Riley said.

Jason shook his head. I didn't know that little fact either. Uncle Bob must have looked it up. Oh, the trivia trick. I was learning.

"Yeah," he said. "Shakespeare had to play her instead. And then there was this opera version where an audience member killed himself by jumping off the balcony at the Met during the show."

"God." Jason's eyes widened.

"But the really creepy one was where Mac...Okay to call him Mac?"

Jason and Riley both nodded.

"Substituted a real knife for the prop and killed Duncan in front of the entire audience, who still thought it was all acting."

Jason stared at Uncle Bob. "That is creepy."

"Fifteen minutes 'til places," Linda's voice announced via a speaker mounted in the corner of the greenroom.

Riley sprinted toward the dressing rooms. "Gotta get dressed."

I jumped up and gave my uncle a quick kiss on the cheek. "Me, too." Uncle Bob didn't take his pseudo-friendly eyes off Jason, but he gave me a little wave.

Jason gave me nothing.

# CHAPTER 21

## *The Night Has Been Unruly*

Bummed about what wasn't happening with Jason, I threw myself into my role and had a pretty good first act. I was about the only actor who did. It was easily the worst show so far. Jason was stiff, Bill Boxer kept losing his ringmaster hat, and Genevieve actually said "Unfix me now" instead of "Unsex me here." Sunday matinees could be a little off, but not this off.

I trotted back to the greenroom at intermission. The atmosphere here was weird, too. Fewer actors than usual hung out, and the ones who did kept glancing at the couch where Uncle Bob sat talking to Bill. Only Riley seemed relaxed, standing nearby and scratching himself when he thought no one was looking. I felt a thrill of excitement. Uncle Bob must really be onto something. I walked over and perused the vending machines, close enough so I could hear the conversation on the couch.

"Champagne, huh?" said Uncle Bob "That was pretty nice of you, seeing as how you didn't get the part."

Bill's surgery-enhanced face looked tighter than usual. "I'm just that kind of guy."

I punched the coffee with cream button. Cocoa poured into the cardboard cup.

"Did you bring something else for Simon?" my uncle asked.

Bill's eyebrows shot up nearly to his hairline. I was afraid they might stay there. "No."

"I thought you mighta brought some of that sparkling cider crap, since he was a recovering alkie and all that."

I grabbed my cocoa and punched the hot chocolate button to get coffee.

"I...I didn't think of it," Bill said.

"Yeah, neither would I," said Uncle Bob, doing the buddy-buddy thing. "Gonna drink that stuff, you might as well have soda pop." He gave Bill a friendly nudge. "Know what else?" He leaned in. "Shakespeare puts me to sleep. Need to take a breather to stay awake. You?"

"No. I sat through the play." I couldn't tell if Bill sounded offended at the suggestion or proud that he had stayed awake. I poured my cups of steaming liquid back and forth to make mochas.

"Except for intermission," said Riley, who was now rearranging his unitard.

"Of course," said Bill. "I left my seat during intermission, to mingle and—"

"And come down here," said Riley, oblivious to the color that crept up Bill's neck. "I saw you at intermission, remember?"

"That's right. I'd forgotten." The flush reached Bill's face.

Linda strode across the greenroom. "Sir?" It wasn't really a question, more the beginning of a command. I hung back and sipped one of my mochas, watching.

Bill grabbed onto the interruption like it was a lifeline. "Oh," he said to Linda. "Have you met..."

"Bob." My uncle rose and extended a hand. "Olive...Ivy's uncle."

"And this is our stage manager," said Bill. "Um..."

"Linda," she said, shaking Bob's hand as Bill scuttled off. "The cop mentioned you. You're a PI, right?" Her words seemed cordial enough, but something in her stance made me think of a sheepdog checking her perimeter. "It's nice to meet you, but I'm afraid you'll have to leave. Only actors in the greenroom."

Yep, sheepdog.

"Really?" said Uncle Bob, keeping his eyes on Linda's. "Lotta these folks don't seem like actors."

Linda's eyes did a quick sweep of the room. Like always, there were a bunch of non-actors—roommates, girls keeping an eye on their actor boyfriends, boys keeping an eye on their actor boyfriends. "Guess I need to put my foot down. Starting now. With you."

"Harsh," said Riley. Linda ignored him. Bob nodded slowly at Linda.

"Oh, hey," I said. "Don't you want to finish this mocha I just made you?" Weak, but what else did I have?

"Nah, I'm good," said Uncle Bob, waving at his soda sitting on the table.

"I'll take it," said Riley, grabbing the cup out of my hands before I could respond.

"See ya," Uncle Bob said to Linda as he ambled down the hall toward the dressing rooms. I trailed behind.

"The door is this way." Linda pointed to the stage door.

"Yeah." He grinned at her. "Just need to take a leak. Got a Big Gulp habit."

Linda started to follow him, but checked her watch. "Five minutes 'til places!" she called out. She headed toward the lighting booth, with a glance over her shoulder at Uncle Bob.

"Doesn't she stay down here for the show?" he asked me, loudly enough that Linda could hear. She stopped.

"No," I said. "She has to call the cues for the show from the lighting booth."

"So why is she down here now?"

It was a good question. I didn't have an answer.

Linda turned slowly to face him, like a cowboy in a standoff, but Uncle Bob just smiled and walked into the men's room.

# CHAPTER 22

## *O, Treachery*

I was on autopilot as I made my way backstage for the top of Act Two. I wasn't thinking about my lines or my character. I was thinking about what Uncle Bob had told me right before he left.

"I started to read the play to see if I could figure out when people were onstage," he said to me after he came out of the bathroom. "Thought I could figure out who mighta had time to kill Simon. But I'd forgotten about that break."

"Intermission?"

"Yeah. After seeing that, I realized if Simon was murdered, everyone had opportunity."

He chucked me on the shoulder as we walked to the greenroom.

"And you heard, I'm being kicked out. So if you want to go ahead with this, you're going to have to figure out who had a motive. I'll help you take it from there."

He grabbed his Big Gulp off Mrs. Lovett's blood-stained table. "Not that I think there's any 'there' there." He waved to me over his shoulder and left by the stage door.

My autopilot clicked off as out-of-tune organ grinder music began to play, signaling the top of the act. Tyler, who had become so obnoxious we'd christened him "The Real Witch," was already in place. Candy sat on the lip of the cauldron, flirting with a buff stagehand. "You best be real nice to me," she said, "or I'll cast a spell on you." He didn't look like he'd mind.

I scrambled into the cauldron. Candy followed me, waving an imaginary wand at the stagehand, whose biceps pumped with the effort of working the ropes and pulleys that hauled us into the air. "Mmhmm," she said to me under her breath. "That boy is finer than a frog hair split four ways."

I wondered if frogs had hair, but a more important thought began to swim its way to the top of my murky mind. I helped it along by thinking out loud. "Wasn't it weird that Linda came down at break?"

"Um...yeah?" answered Candy, not knowing it was a rhetorical question.

"Shhh!" That was The Real Witch, of course.

"Has she ever come down at intermission before?" I didn't know if I was asking myself or Candy. I was just hoping for an answer.

"Darlin', I'm always so busy repairing my witchy makeup, I can't say I've noticed."

"Shhhhh!"

That elusive thought finally broke the surface. "Wait," I said. "She always gives us five minutes over the PA system, which means she's using the mike in the booth, which means she doesn't come down."

"SHHHHH!"

God, Tyler was annoying.

"Thrice the brinded cat had mew'd," I recited in my sultry witch voice, catching Candy's eye.

"Stop it," The Real Witch said through gritted teeth.

"Thrice and once the hedge-pig whined," said Candy.

"You know that confuses me," whined our own little hedge-pig.

We'd recently discovered the only thing that made The Real Witch crazier than talking in the cauldron was reciting his lines—it thoroughly flustered him. It was completely unprofessional, way too much fun, and harmless. The Real Witch never actually screwed up his lines, he was just a Nervous Nelly. This got him off our backs.

After our scene (which went perfectly), Candy and I headed back to our dressing room. No more scenes left, just curtain call. With the play done for the day, my mind turned back to motives.

I watched the rubber snake in Candy's brown hair bounce as I followed her into our dressing room. Did she have a motive? Not as far as I could see. Oh wait. Sheesh. Some detective I'd make. I was with Candy almost all the time. She's the one person who didn't have opportunity. Could I trust her with my suspicions about Simon's death?

I shut the door, turned to Candy, and took a leap of faith. "Help me figure out who might have wanted to kill Simon."

"Kill him?" She looked at me with something like pity in her eyes. "Hon, the man drank himself to death."

"Just play along with me for a minute."

She still had that look on her face

"And stop looking at me that way."

Candy nodded and settled back in her chair. She put her feet— her enormous feet—up on the dressing room counter. "Can't blow me over," she said, admiring her size twelves.

Oops, she was distracting me. That's not how it's supposed to work.

I reached into my purse, pulled out the photo of donkey-eared Simon in *A Midsummer Night's Dream*, and handed it to Candy. She examined it for a moment. I watched her carefully, for what, I wasn't sure.

"Nice ass," she said.

"Yeah, yeah. Have you seen this before?"

"Well, it was tacked up behind the table at the service. Can't remember who brought it. D'you think it was a statement or something? About Simon being an ass?"

Oh. I considered that for a minute. "Maybe. Have you seen it— this photo, I mean—since?" I didn't want to come right out and ask her if she'd put it in my purse.

"Since the service? No," she said, looking genuinely confused.

Good. One bit of detective work crossed off my list. "So who hated Simon?"

"Pretty much everyone except you."

I gave her a look.

"And me," Candy said. "I liked Simon just fine. But you know, Edward hated him, Bill hated him, Linda hated him—"

"Linda? What, because he threw up on her shoes?"

"You never heard the love triangle story?" Candy took her feet off the counter and sat up on the edge of her chair. "Ooh, this is a good one. Linda and Simon were both working some summer Shakespeare-in-the-Park type gig up in Flagstaff years ago. She'd gone up there with her girlfriend, Lucy."

"Wait, how do you know this?" I hoped it wasn't from a theater party, where the general motto is "Never ruin a good story with the truth."

"Lucy told me. She was the art director for a movie I did once," Candy said. "'Beaver Canyon.'"

"An indie film?"

"Sort of." She grinned, a little sheepishly. "Softcore lesbian porn."

I couldn't tell if she was kidding or not. I hopped down from my perch on the counter. "Really? You did porn?"

"Softcore, hon. Just nudity, really." Her smile faded into a serious face I'd never seen before. "I needed the money."

Candy was giving me her secret to hold. Our eyes held each others' for a moment. I nodded and her smile returned. "So Linda was the stage manager. She and Lucy had been doing this Flagstaff summer gig for years. They were real tight. Guess you rarely saw one without the other. Linda would help build sets, and Lucy would sit in on rehearsals. Then Simon came along."

"I thought Lucy was a lesbian." I turned to the mirror, where I could see Candy and repair my makeup. Had to look good for curtain call.

"So did everyone else. Even Genevieve—"

"Wait, Genevieve was there, too?"

"Yeah. Riley, too. And Edward. Anyway, Lucy was a looker. Tall, blonde, athletic type. Like a Scandinavian ski model."

"Huh," I said, imagining short, sturdy Linda with a Swedish skier. I could see it.

She went on. "I guess Simon swept her off her feet and away from Linda, all in the space of one..."

I heard a noise from the door, a sort of a choke or snort. I jumped off the counter. Linda was standing in the open doorway, watching us. Listening to us. How long had she been there?

"Ever heard of knocking?" said Candy.

"The door was open," Linda said, not looking at either of us. Had the door been open? I could have sworn I shut it.

Something wasn't right. I listened to the show over the dressing room speakers.

"Lay on, Macduff!" That was Jason, just about to get beheaded by Macduff. The show was nearly over, but not quite. Linda should have been up in the booth, calling the light cues.

"Better get into place for curtain call, Candy," she said, giving her a look that said she wanted some privacy. Candy ignored her.

"And Ivy, you might want to skip bows tonight. We...uh..." She looked at Candy again. No dice. Candy was not going anywhere. Linda gave up on that idea, straightened her shoulders, and finally looked me in the eye. "We just got a call about your uncle."

# CHAPTER 23

## *The Deed Confounds Us*

The curse of *Macbeth* was alive and well in the twenty-first century. My favorite person in the world was hurt and I couldn't get to him.

I couldn't get a ride to St. Joseph's right away because no one wanted to miss curtain call. I thought about taking a taxi, but it wouldn't have arrived at the theater before we'd wrapped up. So I waited impatiently, bowed, and ran back to my dressing room, where I pulled on a pair of shorts over my leotard. I'd hoped to catch a ride with Jason, but couldn't find him after curtain call. Candy wouldn't drive me because she had an audition.

"Now? On Sunday night?"

"They made a special arrangement for me 'cause of the show. That's why I have to go."

"Candy, the cops called. He's in the hospital. Do you know what that means?"

"No, hon, and neither do you. He could have had a little indigestion or something."

"Don't 'hon' me. I need you."

"And I need a job." Candy looked at me seriously. "It's a film audition, the job pays five hundred bucks, and I'm perfect for it. I need the cash."

"Whatever." I turned away from her. She sighed, walked over, and opened our dressing room door.

"Gentlemen?" she called out. "Who would like the honor of driving Miss Ivy home?"

"Not home, to the hospital," I hissed.

She shook her head. "Better chance for a ride if they think they might get invited in." She winked. I ignored it.

I heard running footsteps. Riley bounded up. "Sure, Ivy, I'll take you," he said. He was panting. I hoped it was from running.

I glared at Candy, slung my duffle bag over my shoulder, and left with Riley.

Riley was a nice guy. He was also one of those talking drivers who looks at you instead of watching the road. After three near-collisions, and one guy who yelled something about Riley's mother, I made it out of the car and into the hospital, only to hit a dead end at the information desk.

"Robert Duda," said the friendly, white-haired volunteer, staring at her computer screen. "There's no one here by that name."

"Please check again," I asked. "Maybe you mistyped it. It's D-U-D-A."

She typed the name again, slowly. She stared at the screen. "Nope. Sorry, dear."

"But the police called. They said he was here."

"The police? Did they now?" She screwed up her face, her wrinkles compounding. She sized me up with piercing blue eyes. I was wearing shorts over my too-tight leotard and tights, and lots of sparkly stage makeup. Whatever she was considering me for, I didn't pass muster. "No, I don't think—"

"Listen," I grabbed her hand. It was soft and powdery. "I know this looks weird. I'm an actress. I just came from a show, where I got this message that something had happened to my uncle." Tears threatened. "It must be serious, or the police wouldn't have called me at the theater." I wiped at my brimming eyes.

"Oh, honey," said the nice old lady, who stood and patted my shoulder awkwardly across her desk. "I really don't have him in my system." She pulled me closer and said in a whisper, "But one of the other volunteers said there's a policeman on guard at Room 607. Give that a try."

So I did. Outside Room 607, which I felt sure was my uncle's room, I pled my case to a cop whose head looked like a mottled bullet. "Please," I said. "What if he's dying? What if I never get a chance to see him alive again?" I encouraged the tears that still waited at the back of my eyes.

But the bullet-headed policeman was like one of those guards at Buckingham Palace. Not a word, not a ruffle, not a glimmer of humanity.

I parked my butt in a chair outside the room, figuring the guard would have to pee at some point. He didn't.

An hour passed. Two. No sound from inside the hospital room, but my stomach growled at me. Really growled, like it was mad it had been denied food. I gave in and headed to the cafeteria. I came back with some food and an idea.

"Here," I said to the cop. He looked down at the maple bar I offered. "I brought coffee, too."

"I find your assumption offensive," he said, but he did take the coffee and donut.

I sat down, tucked into my hamburger, and waited for the extra-large coffee I'd brought to take effect on the non-peeing policeman.

I must have fallen asleep. A slight squeak woke me—the policeman's shoes as he padded down the hall toward the restrooms. Success.

Silvery pre-dawn light spilled from the windows into the hallway. Must have slept longer than I thought. I opened the door to Uncle Bob's room and slipped into the dark room. I could just see Uncle Bob's bulk under the thin bed covers.

A shaft of light sliced the darkness as the door opened. I heard footsteps behind me. A hand grabbed me by the shoulder. "Hey!" The hand spun me around until I was face to face with—who? Not the bullet-headed policeman. I caught a whiff of menthol cigarettes as I peered at the vaguely familiar face in the dark. "Olive?" it said.

"Sir!" The policeman rushed in. "I just left for a moment and she was asleep and—"

"You're lucky she's his niece," said the guy, who I now

recognized as the detective who'd questioned me about Simon.

"His next of kin," I said to the bullet-headed policeman.

"Back to your post." The policeman skedaddled before the last word was even out of the detective's mouth.

"Is my uncle okay?" I whispered to the detective. "What happened?"

"Yes, and we're not sure. He hadn't regained consciousness when I called earlier, but..."

"Well, I have now, what with all this goddammed whispering and shit," came a scratchy voice from the bed.

Relief washed over me. He was okay. If he was that grouchy, he was okay. Uncle Bob fumbled for a cord and turned on a light. He had two black eyes, a splint over his nose, and tubes running in and out of the covers. His left leg was immobilized in a black contraption with lots of Velcro strips.

"Hey, Bob," said the detective, who looked like he'd slept in his clothes, too. "We wake you?"

"Nah, I've been awake for an hour or so," rasped Uncle Bob. He clutched his neck. "Damn, my throat hurts. What in the hell happened to me? I feel like someone rammed a sparkler down my throat."

"A what?"

"A sparkler. You know, from the Fourth of July. "

The detective chuckled. "A sparkler. That's cute. Sweet. The guys downtown will love that."

"Aw, give me a break. Something hot and fiery. Just say something hot and fiery."

"Something pretty and sparkly, you said?"

I watched the two of them, my mouth open. Until a few days ago, I had no idea they even knew each other. In that moment, I realized I knew very little about my uncle.

Uncle Bob saw me watching him and held out his arms. I went to him and hugged him hard, working around the tubes that ran out of him and connected to various blinking machines.

"Oh shit," he said. "I think you just unplugged something."

I jumped back, shouting, "Omigod! Call a nurse!"

I turned to the detective, who was holding his stomach, laughing. So was Uncle Bob.

"Ow," he said. "Ow, shit. Hurts to laugh."

"Serves you right," I said. "Not funny."

"Ow," he said again. "My throat hurts like a son-of-a-bitch. Why in the hell is that?"

His friend—Pink?—pulled up a chair and sat next to Uncle Bob's bed. "It looked like you'd OD'ed and passed out. I guess you didn't respond to the medications they gave you in the ER, so they pumped your stomach just to make sure."

"Ah." Uncle Bob nodded. "What was in it?"

"Some shit that nearly ate your stomach lining."

"Yeah?"

"Yeah. Diet Coke. You gotta stop drinking that shit. You know, you drop a nail in it, it'll dissolve in four days."

Uncle Bob chuckled appreciatively. I didn't. This little routine they had was cute, but I was scared and impatient. "I suppose the Coke broke his leg," I said.

Uncle Bob raised his head to peer at his leg. He squinted, or tried to. The splint on his nose didn't give much. "Ow! Damn." He felt his face. "Don't tell me someone's messed up my good looks."

"That would have been the light pole," said Pink. "And whatever or whoever made you pass out and crash into it."

"Crash?" My uncle looked upset for the first time. He swallowed audibly. "My car...is it...?"

Pink looked at the ground. "Yeah. Totaled," he said. "Sorry."

A tear leaked out of one of Uncle Bob's swollen eyes. "There's no justice in the world."

"Yeah there is," said the detective. "If some bastard did this to you, he's toast."

# CHAPTER 24

## Things without All Remedy

In the hospital parking lot, I climbed into the passenger side of the detective's car, over empty pop cans and Burger King bags. I rolled down the window, hoping to dissipate the stale smell of menthol cigarettes with fresh air. Nope, just a lot of other downtown-type smells—asphalt, exhaust, fast food grease—good stuff like that.

The detective hopped in and started up the car. We smiled at each other, both relieved, I think, that Uncle Bob was going to be fine.

"Thanks for driving me home," I said, "Mr., uh, Pink?"

"Pink's a nickname, but everybody calls me that. Short for Pinkstaff."

I knew a drag queen with that name. I decided not to mention it.

"And you," he said, "you like to be called Olive?"

"Olive or Ivy."

"Isn't that a Christmas song? The Olive and the Ivy?"

I looked at him out of the corner of my eye, to see if he was kidding. He chuckled. I was beginning to see why he and my uncle were friends.

We drove up Central Avenue to my apartment. "Oh crap," I blurted. Pinkstaff looked at me out of the corner of his eye. "Nothing. Don't worry. Just need to call my folks, that's all." Right: that's all. I dialed their number on my cell. It had been weeks since I'd talked to them. No, months.

My mom picked up. "Olive? You're not usually up this early."

I glanced at Pinkstaff's dashboard clock. 7:48 a.m. Not that early. But not too early for a jab at what she called my "bohemian lifestyle."

"I just wanted to tell you that Uncle Bob is in the hospital."

A pause. "And?"

"And?" I repeated.

"And is he going to be alright?"

"Oh. Yeah. He's going to be okay." I glanced at Pinkstaff, who was openly eavesdropping. "He was...in a car accident." The detective nodded in approval.

"But he'll be alright?"

"Yeah."

Another pause. I couldn't wait it out. "Are you going to come down?" Uncle Bob was her brother, after all.

"He'll probably be out of the hospital before we even get there." My folks lived two hours away, not twenty. "Give him our best. And thanks for calling." She hung up.

"Gee, thanks, Mom," I said to the dial tone. "Me? I'm okay, a little shook up about Uncle Bob. He looks pretty bad. Did you get the review I sent you of *Macbeth*? It would be great if you'd come see it. My first pro gig, you know. Yeah, love you, too."

I hung up. Pinkstaff stopped for a red light, looked at me and shook his head. "And I thought you were an actor."

"I'm better onstage."

"She hung up right before 'Gee, thanks.'"

I nodded.

"I am a detective, you know."

Pinkstaff looked at me before stepping on the gas, an awfully tender look from a middle-aged guy I didn't know well. It could have been because of my relationship with Bob, or my non-relationship with my folks, but just in case it was something else, I decided to preempt any romantic strike.

"I really appreciate the ride," I said. "My boyfriend had to..." Oops, hadn't thought that far ahead. Where was Jason anyway? "Go to an early morning commercial shoot." Maybe he did. We didn't have a show today. I'd texted him last night after getting to the hospital and again this morning, but hadn't heard back.

Pink shook a cigarette out of a pack of Kools stashed in the cup holder. "An actor, too, huh?"

"Yeah. You met him. In Uncle Bob's kitchen."

"That's your boyfriend?" He looked at me sideways.

"Yeah."

He rolled his window down an inch and lit his cigarette. "Huh," he said.

I was dying to know what he meant by that but didn't want to open the boyfriend can of worms again. Besides, I had a more important question to ask. "Do you think Uncle Bob was poisoned?"

Pink blew a stream of Kool air out the window. "I think he was damn lucky he crashed his car. Might not have gotten his stomach pumped in time otherwise." He jerked a thumb toward the window. "There's his light pole."

I twisted around in my seat as we passed. I wouldn't have known it if he hadn't pointed it out. Uncle Bob's car may have been totaled, but the light pole looked good as new.

"You never answered my question," I said. "About poison."

Pink sighed. "We know Bob passed out and hit a light pole. We think something he ingested made him pass out. We don't know what it was, or if someone gave it to him on purpose. We gotta wait 'til the toxicology report comes in."

"And that'll be?"

He shrugged and stubbed out the Kool in the near-to-overflowing ashtray. "Depends on what else is coming down the line. Bob's okay. We don't have any proof that anyone is out to get him. Probably won't be real high priority."

"Not high priority? But someone tried to..." I took a deep breath and tried to be rational. "But there was a cop outside his room. Someone must suspect foul play."

The detective slowed down, and turned into my apartment

house's parking lot. "Listen, Olive, Ivy, whatever I'm supposed to call you: that guy outside your uncle's door? He's a rent-a-cop I hired. It's just a precaution. Your uncle's a PI. Sometimes people get pissed at PIs. I like Bob, so I didn't want anything else to happen to him. That's it, okay? Just leave it."

I looked at him long and hard, hoping he'd tell me something else. He stared back. "Okay," I finally said. But I didn't mean it.

# CHAPTER 25

## *Angels Are Bright Still*

"How's your uncle?" Candy asked as she slipped out of her undies and pulled on her tights.

"He's okay, probably getting discharged today."

We were in our dressing room getting ready for the Thursday night show. Already in costume, I faced the mirror and slathered foundation on my face. I was still peeved at Candy for not giving me a ride on Sunday so I didn't ask how her audition went. Petty, I know.

"So what happened?" she asked, as she stepped into her leotard. Her brown and black costume had the diamondback markings of a rattlesnake and no camel toe. I'd stretched and stretched my leotard, hoping it would ease up a little. No dice.

"Ivy?" said Candy.

I'd thought about this, how to answer without letting anyone know I suspected Uncle Bob had been drugged. I'd decided to keep it simple. "He crashed his car into a light pole."

"Good lord! He just lost control or something?" She'd pulled her leotard up to her waist, and was unhooking her bra when there was a knock at the dressing room door. Riley stuck his head in. "How's your uncle?"

Sweet.

"He's okay," I said. "It was just an accident. He should be getting out..."

Riley stared at the mirror, trying to get a glimpse of Candy's half naked body. So much for sweet.

"Soon." I shut the door in Riley's face. He knocked again. I flung open the door. "Our bodies are not for public consumption."

Bill Boxer stood there, his mouth open. Probably didn't know what "consumption" meant.

"Oh, sorry Bill."

He stepped into the dressing room. "Just wanted to see if your uncle was okay," he said.

Bill? Really? How did he know about Uncle Bob? I slid a look at Candy, who was busy applying glittery gold eye shadow.

A sunglass-clad Jason stepped in behind Bill. "How's your uncle?"

This would have been getting weird, except that Jason knew about my uncle from the half dozen calls and texts I'd left—which he'd never returned.

"He's fine," I said, a bit tightly.

Jason took off his sunglasses. His eyes, those beautiful marine-blue eyes, were swollen and ringed with prune-colored bruises. A butterfly bandage held together a gash across the top of his nose.

Candy whistled. "Where's the mule that kicked ya?"

Bill and Jason exchanged glances. "Long story," said Jason. He shook a pill out of a bottle and swallowed it dry.

"Way too long," agreed Bill, too quickly. "Glad to hear your uncle's okay." He scurried out of the dressing room. Everyone seemed a bit too concerned about my uncle—my uncle who might have been poisoned at the theater. Huh.

I couldn't think about that now. Had to get ready for the show. I turned to the mirror and started putting on my eye makeup. Jason came and stood behind me as I drew thick black liner around my eyes. He was so close I could smell the shaving cream he used.

"It's gotten better," he said looking at his reflection. "The swelling's almost gone."

I could tell he was trying to meet my eyes in the mirror, but I was having none of it. Black eyes or no, he could've returned my calls.

He gave a small sigh, then kissed me on the top of my head, like I was a five-year-old. What the hell?

"Let me know if Bob needs anything, okay?"

Bob! What about me?

He took the butterfly bandage off the bridge of his nose and gingerly touched the cut. "I'd better go cover this up." He turned to leave. "Shit. I forgot to buy some pancake. Either of you have any?"

We shook our heads. Thick, heavy pancake makeup used to be the stage makeup of choice, but most of us don't use it anymore, unless...

"Any of the boys here do drag?" Candy asked. Pancake works great for covering up a stubbly face.

I shook my head. Most of our cast was straight. Maybe Shakespeare draws straight guys. They do get to play with swords and stuff.

Wait. Shakespeare...makeup...what idea was knocking at the back door of my brain?

Jason sighed. "Edward's going to kill me. Maybe they won't be able to see it from the audience."

Aha! The idea pushed its way into my mind. "Simon," I said. "He used pancake."

Linda stuck her head in the door. "Half hour 'til curtain— Man." Linda stared at Jason. Guess she hadn't seen him yet. "Better get to work covering that up." She started to leave.

"Linda," I said. "Is Simon's makeup still in his dressing room?"

"Yeah," she replied. "I wasn't going to do anything with it 'til strike."

"Brilliant, Ivy." Jason kissed me, this time on the lips. I tingled in spite of myself.

"You doing anything after the show?" he said. "Maybe we could go for a drink, just the two of us?"

I was confused as hell, and pissed off he hadn't returned my calls. I was also curious. Where the hell had he been these past few days? It seemed like he was always disappearing. Like during intermission on opening night—the intermission that Uncle Bob said gave everyone opportunity to do the dirty deed. Jason couldn't have anything to do with Simon's death or Uncle Bob's poisoning, could he?

I finally met Jason's eyes in the mirror and nodded. Curiosity got the better of me. And you know what happened to the cat.

# CHAPTER 26

## *Some Sweet, Oblivious Antidote*

Carved into the side of Camelback Mountain, The Spa at Sanctuary hid from the hoi polloi with discreet signage, a long drive up a desert lane and understated lighting along mesquite-lined paths. Burbling fountains and birdcalls replaced the sounds of sirens and car mufflers. In the middle of the city, the resort was a secret hideaway from the noisy world, designed to make the weary sink into a Jacuzzi and say, "Ahhhhhh."

But as I sat across from Jason at the outdoor bar my stomach was in knots, my face tight from fake smiling, my legs crossed so tightly I worried about my circulation. Jason still hadn't said a word about not returning my calls. I needed to know what was up, but I also knew from Uncle Bob that direct questioning rarely got you real answers. What was the right way to ask?

"Alone at last." Jason smiled and reached a hand across the table. "Feels great."

I didn't take his hand.

"Ah," he said, "I bet you're wondering about..."

You bet I'm wondering, buster.

"My face," he said.

Why did I like this self-centered guy?

A waiter wound his way through the tables toward us. I hadn't decided what to have yet, so I picked up the menu I'd set down earlier. I scanned it again. I flipped it over. Nope. No prices. I didn't know there were places where menus didn't have numbers. Didn't help the knot in my stomach. My credit card was maxed. I had twenty bucks in my wallet. I hoped Jason was paying.

I looked around to see if there were any other types of menus sitting on nearby tables. I didn't see any. I did see people dressed in designer wear I'd only seen in magazines. I saw slate and wood and good design. I saw a deceptively simple place where the décor was minimal but cost a fortune. I really hoped Jason was paying.

"Welcome to Sanctuary at Camelback," said the waiter. "How may I...Oh!" He smiled at Jason. "How are you this evening? I almost didn't recognize you."

Jason's eyes were still puffy, though the bruises were partially covered by the remains of his pancake makeup. "Yeah, hi." He didn't look at the waiter.

I looked at the waiter. He had perfectly white teeth, a trendy, expensive haircut, and waiter blacks that looked like they'd been custom tailored. I was suddenly conscious of my Target T-shirt and cotton skirt.

"Vodka martini with a twist?" the waiter asked. Jason nodded.

"And for you, Miss?" He emphasized the "Miss" and smiled at Jason. Huh.

"A margarita, on the rocks. Salt."

The waiter slipped away, but not without glancing again at us over his shoulder.

"You a regular here?" I asked, thinking of the price-less menu. Maybe Jason had a trust fund I didn't know about. He was dressed pretty nicely for an actor, in a fitted collared shirt and khakis that showed off his, um, assets.

"Been here with my agent, and with Edward. And my dad. In fact, my dad and I had an...exchange the last time we were here."

"You had a fight here?" I couldn't imagine people raising more than a glass in this environment.

"My dad hates that I'm an actor. Says it's for sissies."

Jason, a sissy? He swung a sword like he was born to it. "He might change his mind if he saw you play Macbeth."

"That's what we fought about. He said he would have seen the show if Simon was still in it." He shook his head at the memory. "Maybe my mom will sneak into one of the matinees. Your parents going to see the show?"

"My folks? No way. They haven't even come down to see Uncle Bob in the hospital." There it was—the elephant in the room.

"Ivy..." He took my hand.

I waited. That was another PI trick I'd learned from my uncle.

"He's okay, right?" Jason rubbed my fingertips absently.

That wasn't what I was waiting for.

A sigh. "I should have called you back. I'm sorry."

The waiter glided over and silently deposited our drinks. Jason dropped my unresponsive hand and thanked the waiter with a nod that told him nothing more was needed.

"'Sorry' isn't enough," I said once the waiter was out of earshot. "Unless there's a good reason behind it."

Jason leaned back on the banquette across from me. He looked at me, those beautiful turquoise eyes serious. "I am that rare animal," he said, "an introverted actor."

I was all ears. I had heard tell of such a creature.

"All the people and the attention and the activity—it overwhelms me sometimes. The only antidote is to hole up and hide out." Jason closed his eyes and put a hand to his forehead, like he had a headache. "I turn off my phone, don't look at the internet, don't do anything except eat and sleep and watch mindless movies."

So not really self-centered, just shy and in the wrong business. Jason was letting me see his vulnerable side. First his dad, now this. I was beginning to thaw.

"As you can imagine, these past few weeks put me over the edge. And once I turned my phone back on and saw all your messages, I felt so bad that I was overwhelmed again. Do you know what I mean?"

"It's like when your cousin calls and says he broke his arm, but stuff happens so a week passes and then it feels weird to call, so you put it off and then it's a month later and..." I trailed off. I did understand. Maybe because I wanted to, but still, it seemed plausible.

"Jason?" He still had his hand to his head, his eyes closed. "You okay?"

"My face hurts."

"Maybe you should take another pain pill?"

He nodded, shook a pill out of a bottle he'd had in his pocket, and downed it with a glass of water.

"And maybe you should tell me the long story of how your face got that way?"

Jason smiled then. Relaxing, I settled back on the pillows that lined the banquette. I took in our surroundings: the rising half-moon, the palm trees twinkling with white lights, the pool glowing behind Jason. I smiled back at him.

"Not such a long story," he said. "Bill talked me into playing in a squash tournament, a charity gig. Said it would be good PR." Behind him, the pool's underwater lights changed from blue to orange.

"I beat Bill, of course." No ego in his statement, it was a pretty foregone conclusion, a strapping guy like him beating a sixty-ish non-athlete. "After the game, he was pissed off and wound up. He decided to show off for the TV cameras, demonstrating his 'form.' Backhanded me in the face with his racket." He raised an eyebrow, amused. "He swore it wasn't on purpose."

A shadow crossed his face. "There was something weird, though. When we were alone, he asked me about my 'whereabouts' on opening night. Wanted to know if I'd seen anything. He say anything like that to you?"

"Don't think so, but then I try to forget everything Bill says to me." It was true. The Face of Channel 10 tried my last nerve. But what a perfect opening. "Speaking of opening night..." I really didn't believe Jason had anything to do with Uncle Bob or Simon, but I had to put that worry to bed. "I looked for you. At intermission."

"Oh, Ivy," he said, reaching for my hand again. This time I let him take it. "I'm so sorry." He twined his fingers through mine. "Opening night always undoes me. I just find a dark corner backstage, hide out and try to stay in character. I should have warned you." Jason let go of my hand, crossed to my side of the table and sat next to me on the banquette, his thigh touching mine. "Please forgive me. For everything."

My body, which had just been starting to relax, began to thrum. This particular brand of tension didn't bother me. In fact, it was fine. Very fine.

Jason brought my hand up to his lips, kissed it and held it against his cheek. His face was warm. "Do you? Forgive me?" He searched my eyes.

Candles flickered on the low table in front of us, the margarita's heat coursed pleasantly through my veins, and that thrumming was revving up.

"I'm not sure." My voice purred despite myself. "Maybe you need to convince me of your good intentions."

He kissed my hand again, his lips lingering. "Did I say they were good?"

# CHAPTER 27

## *Shake Off This Downy Sleep*

"Mmmph," I said to the waiter, biting down on my lip. I had to, or I would have made some embarrassing noise.

"No, that'll be all. I think we're ready for the check." Jason smiled at the waiter, but his hand stayed where it was, underneath the table, underneath my skirt, caressing my leg, inching upward along my thigh.

The waiter tore off a check and left it on the table. Jason glanced at it, pulled several twenties from his wallet, and left them on the table. His hand returned to my thigh, a little higher this time. With his other hand, he cupped my face and kissed me. "Shall we?" he said.

Oh boy, oh boy, we shall.

We left the bar. The winding path to the parking lot felt long and delicious. Every time a mesquite tree threw a shadow on the moonlit path, Jason caressed me, brushing my face, my arms, my breasts. Once we got to the dark lot, he lifted me onto the hood of his car and pressed himself against me, kissing me hard. I wondered if we were even going to make it out of the parking lot. A security guard with a flashlight answered that question.

Back at my place, Jason picked me up and carried me to the bedroom. We were all mouths and hands and hot breath. Somehow my blouse came unbuttoned, and my skirt, and his jeans.

"No socks," I gasped.

"What?" said Jason.

"No socks. In your dancebelt."

I couldn't believe I'd said it, wished I could put a sock in my mouth. I was sure I'd blown it. But Jason just laughed and said, "Nope. It's the real thing. Here, let me show you." And, boy, did he.

Later, he asked if he could sleep over. I couldn't believe my luck. He wanted to stay.

I opened my eyes to the morning light, stretched, and turned over to look at Jason. He was still sleeping soundly, snoring actually, his back toward me, a pillow pulled over his head. I closed my eyes again, luxuriating in the morning. That's one of the great things about being an actor, you never have to be anywhere before noon.

Except when you're supposed to pick up your uncle from the hospital.

My eyes flew open and searched for the clock, which wasn't in its typical spot on the bedside table. I spied it on its side on the floor. Must have knocked it off last night. I hung my head over the side of the bed to read it. Only eight-fifteen. Phew. I didn't have to be at the hospital until after ten.

I put the clock back where it belonged, then slipped out of bed, figuring I'd start some coffee and surprise Jason with a cup in bed. I grabbed a robe off the hook on the back of the bedroom door, padded into my kitchen, poured some beans into the coffee grinder, and stopped. The grinder would certainly wake Jason up. Did I have any ground coffee? I looked in my freezer and searched through a few cupboards. Nothing. I stood a moment and thought, my gears grinding slowly, as they always did in the mornings. I looked around my kitchen. The cupboards were painted a sunny yellow, to complement the yellow and baby blue 1940s-style tiled counters. I'd gone with the whole girly cottage-style look—lace curtains and embroidered thrift shop tea towels. Towels. Ha. I grabbed one with daffodils on it and wrapped it, swaddling-clothes-style, over the grinder. I pressed the button. Much less noise. Pretty smart. Maybe I was turning into a morning person. I yawned. Nah.

A few moments later, my ancient coffeemaker was huffing and wheezing along, when I heard a bigger wheeze. The refrigerator? It made odd noises on a regular basis. I cocked my head, listening. Not the fridge. The noise came from the bedroom. Oh. Jason. Snoring. I wasn't used to having anyone else in my apartment in the morning.

I tiptoed in to check on him, hoping he wouldn't wake before I could bring him coffee. He was making an awful racket. Was that a choking noise? I hurried around to his side of the bed. Shit! Jason's face was swollen three times as much as last night. Worse yet, it was turning blue.

"Jason." I shook him. "Jason! Wake up!"

He didn't.

# CHAPTER 28

## *Death's Counterfeit*

The light was yellow and I wasn't even near the intersection. I pushed the pedal to the floor and prayed as my Aspire whizzed through the obviously red light. One more for Phoenix's record.

I could see the ambulance, Jason's ambulance, a few cars in front of me. I followed it, maneuvering around execs in Beamers and moms in SUVs, until I skidded into St. Joe's ER loading zone.

I jumped out of my car and ran into the emergency room, on the heels of the EMTs pushing Jason's stretcher. I was relieved to see his face had gone from blue to purple, but still worried. He seemed to be pretty out of it, and the part of his face I could see under the oxygen mask was swollen beyond recognition.

Once inside, the EMTs propelled Jason through swinging double doors. I tried to follow, but a woman with gray hair and an official bearing stopped me. "Best if you stay here," she said.

"But—"

"You'll be in the way. And I need your help," she said. "Answering my questions is the best thing you can do for him."

I stamped my feet like an impatient horse, but did my best to answer her. What had Jason eaten? (martini olives), what had he drunk? (the martini), and what had he been doing last night? (having incredibly athletic sex with me). I left out the adjectives. I didn't want to appear smug.

After she realized I didn't know much and wasn't family, she directed me toward the ER waiting room. I told myself that the lady was right, I'd just be in the way. I made myself sit for a moment, but couldn't take it for very long. Too much misery in the room. The people with their broken arms I could handle; it was the morning TV news show that blared from each corner of the room that did me in. "Your drinking water could kill your dog," said Bill Boxer solemnly from behind his Channel 10 desk. "But first, is your neighborhood playground safe? Stay tuned, your child's life may depend on it."

I asked the lady again if I could see Jason. She shook her head. I asked if she could tell me anything about him. She shook her head. I asked her if she knew you could make tuberculosis medicine out of peanuts (trivia and distraction in one fell swoop). She shook her head and left the desk.

I paced under the fluorescent lights of the waiting room, in between crying kids and weary relatives. Most looked bleary-eyed, but one teenage boy slept soundly curled up on one of the couches. I rang Uncle Bob's hospital room on my cell phone, just to let him know what was going on.

"I'm sure he'll be all right, hon," said Uncle Bob, after I'd told him the whole story. "Oh, hey. Pinkstaff just walked in. Talk to you later." He hung up.

Turning my attention back to the waiting room, I noticed the gray-haired lady had been replaced by a new intake person. I sidled over to the desk, hoping to convince the new guy to let me see Jason.

"Hi," I said to the balding man behind the desk. I looked at the sun pouring through the windows. "Nice day, huh?"

"Yeah," he said. "It's nice."

I smiled.

"Nice here in the ER. Broken bones, ODs, gunshot wounds." Someone moaned as if on cue. "Yep," he said, "Sure is nice."

I turned away. I never was one to fight a losing battle. I decided to go see my uncle.

Twenty minutes later, after several wrong turns and dead

ends, I walked into Uncle Bob's hospital room. "You workin' for St. Joe's now?" asked Pink.

I sat down next to the bed in one of those wipe-clean vinyl chairs so ubiquitous to hospitals, and shook my head, confused.

"'Cause when you take one away," he said, "you bring one in. Keepin' the beds full."

Uncle Bob chuckled. I didn't think it was funny. I guess it showed. Pink shrugged and headed toward the door. "See ya, Bob, Olive."

Uncle Bob waved goodbye to Pinkstaff and poured milk onto a bowl of gloppy oatmeal. He looked at me with uncle-y concern.

"C'mon, Olive," he said. "Don't worry. I'm sure Jason's gonna be fine. You said he wasn't blue anymore. That's a good sign."

My uncle, who was supposed to be released at ten, didn't look like he was ready to go anywhere. It was now nine-thirty, and they'd just served him a tray full of hospital food: oatmeal, O.J., limp toast, and what Uncle Bob said was surprisingly good coffee.

"Isn't it late for breakfast?" I said. My mind wandered back to the breakfast in bed I'd planned with Jason. I told myself again that he was going to be fine.

"The aide likes me," said Uncle Bob. "I convinced her that nine-thirty was a much more civilized time for breakfast. Guess I still have my good looks."

He looked awful, but I wasn't going to tell him that. I looked at his leg, still encased in its medical casing. How was he going to fit in my little Aspire? "Can you bend that? So you can get into the car, I mean?"

"I thought I told you. They're taking me home in some sort of medical transport. Once I get there, they'll set me up. You got the hospital bed and wheelchair waiting for me at home, right?"

I nodded, then rose out of my chair, stretching. "Back in a sec. Have to pee." I started to walk out of the room.

"You can use the bathroom in here," said Uncle Bob, looking at me sideways. Dang. He knew.

"No, thanks. I'd prefer a little more privacy." I nearly ran out of the room. Did he tell me? How could I have forgotten?

I called Candy, who worked part-time as a nursing assistant at a care center. She was there when I called.

"Whoo. You are up shit creek without a paddle," she said.

I paced in the hospital hall, my shoes squeaking on the linoleum. "I know, I know. Just help."

"Let me think a sec, okay? It's not like I can just wheel them outta here...Oh, I know." I could almost hear her smiling over the phone. "I'll call Ray at Western Medical Supply. That's two birds with one stone."

"Two birds?"

"He's cute, and I am ready for cute. I'll handle this. Just get to your uncle's house PDQ, and have a check ready for Ray."

"Great. Thanks." I gave her Uncle Bob's address. "I really appreciate this. I know I've been a little pissy these last few days."

"Water under the bridge."

"And I was hoping your audition went well. The film audition. Did you get it?"

There was an uncharacteristic silence on the other end of the line, then, "Oops, got a call on the other line. See you at the show."

"Oh," I said. "I forgot to tell you—" She hung up. "Jason's in the hospital," I said to the dial tone. Oh well, she'd find out soon enough.

I ambled, maybe a bit too nonchalantly, back into Uncle Bob's room.

"Feel better now? Seems like you were gone awhile." He grinned at me, a bit of oatmeal stuck to the side of his lip. I nodded and decided not to tell him about the oatmeal. That's what he got for being a smart ass.

His grin faded suddenly, and he motioned me near. "Olive? I'm beginning to think you're right."

"About?"

I had an idea what he was going to say, but wanted the satisfaction of hearing him say it. I was also distracted by the glob of oatmeal waggling near his lip.

"Simon," he said. "Maybe there was some foul play." The few sticky oats wobbled, but hung on, stuck on a few stubble hairs. "Olive? Did you hear me?"

I grabbed a napkin, dunked it in his glass of water, and wiped his surprised face. "Better," I mumbled, then sat down in the orange vinyl chair. Now I could concentrate. "So now you believe me," I said. "Why?"

He looked at me seriously. "We can't prove anything yet."

"We?"

"Pink's looking into this, too, as a favor to me." He checked to make sure I was with him. I was. "We both think I was drugged, probably at the theater."

"How? By who? I mean, by whom?"

"Just hold your horses." He took a deep breath. "Makes us wonder whether Jason was poisoned, too."

"Poisoned?" I launched myself out of my chair. "What do you know that I don't?"

"Sit down, Olive. I told Pink about your boyfriend. He talked to the doc. Jason's going to be okay. Right now they don't know what caused him to—"

"Is it serious? Is he okay? He's not going to die, is he?"

"Sit, Olive."

It was a command. I sat.

"If you'd been listening, you would have heard me say he's going to be okay. Got that part?"

I nodded, but felt my face flush. I hated letting my emotions get the best of me. Uncle Bob must have noticed, because he softened his tone. "If Jason had been alone this morning when his throat started swelling, yeah, he mighta died. But he didn't."

Did that mean I saved his life?

"Listen, Olive."

I sat up straight, cleared my head, and looked him in the eye.

"I want you to quit—"

I jumped in. "Quit what? Quit looking into Simon's death? Simon's murder?" I liked emphasizing that I'd been right.

"Yes. And I want you to quit the show."

He took advantage of the fact that my mouth was open to keep talking.

"There's something going on there, and I don't want you to be a part of it. You can tell them you have to stay home and take care of me. There's your out."

He clearly didn't know what he was asking me. My career, my happiness, my promise to watch over Simon.

"But..."

"Pink and I'll take care of the investigation, all right?"

I didn't say anything.

"All right, Olive?" Uncle Bob sounded sterner than I'd ever heard him.

I nodded. I didn't say it out loud, so it wasn't really a lie.

# CHAPTER 29

## Can the Devil Speak True?

"Did you know that Louis the fourteenth used to hold court in bed?" said Uncle Bob. Thanks to Candy MoonPie, he was holding court from a rented medical bed. He wanted it in the living room so he could see out the front window and watch TV at the same time. I wouldn't be surprised if he kept it there.

"Did you know that Shakespeare, in his will, left his wife his second-best bed?" I replied.

"Ha!" said Uncle Bob, who was now playing with the bed's electronic adjustment. They must have doped him up pretty good for the ride home.

My cell rang. Uncle Bob lay back, grinning, as the head of his bed slowly dipped.

"Hello?"

"Is this Ivy Meadows?" The woman sounded like she was afraid someone was playing a joke on her.

"Yes."

"I'm a volunteer at St. Joseph's, calling for Jason Birnam."

"Yes?" I said. "Jason," I mouthed to Uncle Bob. He brought his bed upright.

"He asked if I could call you, to let you know he's all right."

"Oh." I hadn't realized how tense I was until all my muscles relaxed at the time. I sank into the kitchen chair I'd placed next to my uncle's bed. "Can I speak to him?"

"He's sleeping now, but he can receive visitors. Room 304."

"Thank you, thank you, thank you!" I said.

"You're welcome, dear. Goodbye."

"Bye." I hung up.

"He doin' okay?" asked Uncle Bob.

"Yeah. He can have visitors now."

My uncle looked me in the eye, his goofiness gone. "I wish you'd stop seeing him. I'm afraid he might be involved in whatever's going on."

I didn't reply.

"But, hey, who am I to mess with a budding romance?"

I hugged the old poop around his neck, careful to avoid his splinted nose.

"But," he said. "I want you to be careful. Something smells fishy and I want you to stay clear of it. Any funny business, you pull back, right?"

"Right. No fishy funny business."

He tried to hide a smile. "And I did mean it about the investigation. Pink and I'll take care of it. Not you. Got that?"

"Got it."

I didn't wait for him to mention quitting the play. "When's your aide coming?" I said.

Uncle Bob looked at the clock mounted on the wall above the TV. "In about an hour," he said.

This distraction thing did work.

"So..." I began.

"So go see your boyfriend," said my uncle. "Just bring me my phone first."

I grabbed his phone from its charger in the kitchen. "You sure you'll be alright?"

The bathroom and bedrooms in my uncle's 1940s house were situated off a hall two steps above the rest of the house, rendering them inaccessible for the six weeks he'd be using a wheelchair.

Uncle Bob took stock of the situation. The TV tray next to his bed held several bottles of pills, a water bottle, a package of Oreos, and the TV remote. A urinal was tucked in along his side, and a portable commode near his bed. "The key's in the mailbox?" he asked.

I nodded. The aide needed a key to get in. Per his instructions, I'd hidden it between a few folded pieces of paper, stuffed the whole thing into an envelope, and addressed it to Robert Duda. It was now in the mailbox by the front door, along with a few old pieces of mail I added for cover.

"I think I'm set," Uncle Bob said. I headed toward the door. "Except for one thing."

"Yeah?" I turned.

He pushed a button and the bed rose like a magic carpet. "Can I keep this?"

I drove back to the hospital. I made several wrong turns in St. Joe's maze of corridors before finding Jason's room. He was asleep. I was so relieved to see him breathing normally that I sat there and watched him sleep for awhile. When he finally awoke, he smiled groggily at me. I kissed him lightly on his swollen lips.

"How are you feeling?"

"Like someone hot-glued marshmallows to my face." He touched his face gingerly, swallowed and grimaced. "And to the inside of my throat."

I poured him a glass of water from the blue plastic pitcher that sat on his bedside table. He took it gratefully, though from the face he made, it didn't help that hot marshmallow feeling.

Jason squinted, looking around the room. I'd discovered last night that his beautiful blue-green eyes were the result of contacts. Without them, his eyes were mud-gray and myopic.

"You're in the hospital," I said helpfully.

"Yeah, I can see that," he snapped, then sighed. "Sorry, I'm just pissed off. It was stupid."

"What was?" Being an egocentric ninny, all I could think about was us.

"I forgot to check with the bar about peanuts. I'm allergic."

Peanuts? I searched my memory for peanuts. I remembered eating some sort of snack mix, but...

"I usually make sure to ask, but, well," he smiled at me as best he could, "I had other things on my mind."

I breathed a sigh of relief. It wasn't about us and he hadn't been poisoned.

Jason, still peering around the room, said, "What time is it?"

I glanced at the clock with its senior-sized numbers. He really needed those contacts. "Six-thirty. I'd better get going."

"What're they doing about the show? Going to cancel it?"

I froze. Omigod. I hadn't told anyone.

"Ivy?"

"Tell you later. Gotta run." I blew him a quick kiss (which he probably couldn't see), dashed out of the room, and pulled out my cell phone. Damn. Dead battery. I rushed to the nurses' station.

"Could I use your phone? It's an emergency."

A large nurse, stuffed into her uniform like a sausage, looked at me skeptically. "Why didn't you ring for a nurse?"

"It's not that kind of emergency."

"What kind is it?"

"A...uh...theatrical emergency."

She gave a little "phh" of disapproval. "There's a pay phone in the basement."

After spending fifteen minutes trying to find the damn pay phone, I gave up and ran to my car. When I got to the parking garage toll booth, the gum-chewing cashier said, "Five dollars, please."

"Five?" I hoped I'd heard wrong.

She didn't even look my way. "Yeah. Five dollars."

I looked in my wallet, even though I knew what I would find. Three one dollar bills and some change. I pulled out the bills, dumped the change into my palm, and shoved it at the cashier.

She looked at it. "You're a dollar forty short."

"It's all I have and I'm really late. It's an emergency."

"What kind of emergency?"

I wasn't about to go through that again. "Listen, can't you please just let me out?"

She chewed her gum lazily, like a cow who'd heard it all before. "This is my job, lady."

The car behind me honked. Like that was going to help. My air conditioning started blowing hot air. Damn. I'd just spent a couple hundred bucks on the stupid thing. The car behind me honked again. I looked pleadingly at the cashier. She seemed perfectly content to let us all stay in her garage forever. I reached into the back seat for my duffle bag, scrounged around through makeup and tights, and found four quarters. I held them out to the cow triumphantly.

"Good," she said.

I waited for the gate to go up.

"Now you're only forty cents short."

The driver behind me really laid on the horn. I was about to flip him off when I had a better idea. I yanked my scoop-neck T down to show some cleavage, hopped out of my car, and ran to the big black SUV behind me. A tinted window slid down, revealing a forty-something driver with enough product in his hair to withstand a hailstorm.

"I am so sorry," I said breathlessly, bending over and squeezing my arms together to ensure maximum cleavage. "But I'm a little short today." I watched his eyes go straight to my chest. "Could you possibly help me out? I just need three dollars." I wasn't going through this for forty cents, let me tell you.

"Um, sure." He said, fishing out his wallet, his eyes flickering to mine for a second. He pulled out a twenty, as I'd hoped he would, and handed it to me.

"Thank you so much!" I gushed, with a little wiggle. After all, he was paying for it.

I ran up to the attendant booth, gave her the twenty, and waved at the SUV driver, who was now staring at my ass. Staring so hard, in fact, that he nearly missed seeing the cashier give me change. But he did see. He honked as I hopped back into my car. I waved at him and hotfooted it to the theater with an extra nineteen dollars and sixty cents.

I squealed into the theater parking lot, jumped out of my car and ran toward the theater. I had just passed the guy we called Homeless Hank when I had an idea. I ran back, pulled the SUV driver's bills out of my shorts pocket and handed them to him.

"Just call me 'Robin Hood,'" I said.

Hank whistled in appreciation and attempted a bow, wobbling dangerously. I made sure he was steady, then hurried on my way.

I finally skidded into the theater. Linda was already there, prepping for the show. This was going to be bad. I flagged her down as she headed backstage to check on props.

"Linda? Can I talk to you a minute?"

"Only if you can walk and talk. I got business to take care of."

I trotted after her as she headed to the darkened backstage area, toward the butcher-paper-covered prop table. Each prop was outlined on the paper in bold black marker so that the table looked like the crime scene for lots of tiny dead bodies.

I couldn't figure out how to tell her about Jason without pissing her off, so I didn't say anything, just hovered. I watched her move Genevieve's dagger to its proper place on the prop table.

"What is it? Spit it out, Ivy."

"Jason's in the hospital. He can't do the show tonight." I spat it out, just as she requested.

Linda turned, squinting at me in the low light. I guess she was trying to see if I was kidding.

"I would have called earlier, but my cell battery ran out and I couldn't find a pay phone." I sounded lame, even to myself.

Linda looked at me a moment, her expression unreadable, then said, "I'll meet you in your dressing room in two minutes. Go, and do not tell anyone what you just told me." She pulled out her cell phone.

I walked to my dressing room, eyes to the ground, past the cast members who had arrived. I was afraid to make eye contact with anyone for fear I'd spill the beans. I felt bad letting all these people prep for a show that wasn't going to take place.

I sat in my dressing room, depressed. If I kept making mistakes like this, I was going to need another career. I caught sight of myself in the mirror. I didn't have any makeup on—my mad dash to the hospital had precluded that—and with my blonde hair, pale face and no visible eyelashes, I looked like someone out of a Vermeer painting. Maybe I could be an art school model. I wondered how much they paid. I wondered if I'd have to get naked.

Linda, true to her word, showed up in two minutes. She said, "Edward's on his way." And then didn't say anything more. She just stood behind me, flannel-ensconced arms crossed. How could she stand to wear flannel in this heat? I surreptitiously studied her in the mirror. Ah, she wore a white T-shirt under the flannel shirt. She probably wore that outside and put on the shirt to fight the air-conditioned chill indoors. Linda's hair was reddish-brown and cut in a severe, boyish style. She was fit, almost muscular. She didn't have on any makeup either, but she looked more Vin Diesel than Vermeer.

Candy swept into the room, taking in Linda as she did. "So how's our Diet Coke today?"

Linda squinted at her.

I looked at the plastic cup full of soda sitting on the dressing room counter. "Didn't check," I said. Candy came over to look for herself. Linda squinted again. Maybe she needed glasses.

I cleared my throat. "Someone told my uncle Diet Coke would dissolve a nail. We thought we'd test it for ourselves."

"And?" She looked interested. An image flashed into my mind: Linda at rehearsal with, yep, a Diet Coke in hand.

"Nail's still there," I said. We all peered intently into the cup, as if testing my veracity. The nail was still there and looked in good shape, no rust that I could see.

"Hmph," said Linda. "Looks like a waste of Diet Coke to me."

Edward knocked and entered. It was the first time I'd ever seen him without a carrot.

"Why do y'all knock if you're just gonna come in anyway?" said Candy, hands on her hips. Her outrage disappeared when Edward said, in a dangerously soft voice, "I need to speak to Ivy. Alone."

Candy huffed a bit under her breath as she went out into the hall. Edward jerked his head at Linda. "*Alone.*" I saw Linda's reflection. Her look of surprise mirrored mine. She left, pulling the door shut hard behind her, just short of a slam.

I faced the mirror. I could see Edward glaring at me, but I didn't turn around. It was easier to face him this way.

"Why in the name of God did you wait until an hour before curtain to tell us we have no lead?" he said. "Are you as stupid as you appear?"

Ouch. What do you say to that? I stayed silent.

"What do you expect us to do now?" Another angry rhetorical question. I wasn't biting.

Edward paced behind me. I could see his wheels turning, thoughts flitting one way and another. He was no actor. Everything showed on his face. I reminded myself to invite him to a poker game when he'd forgotten about all of this.

"Why you?" he asked, turning to face my reflection. I could feel his breath on my neck, smell a faint whiff of brandy. I'd heard Pamela was out of town, maybe he was living it up. "Why did Jason call you?"

Something hard and brilliant in his eyes gave me pause. It reminded me of the villains in the cartoons my brother used to love when we were kids. That—and the fact he hadn't asked what happened to Jason or if he was okay—influenced my answer.

"This whole thing was a big coincidence." I put on my dumb blonde face. If he thought I was stupid, I was going to use it. "I was there to pick up my uncle."

"Yeah, I heard about that. How is he?" Edward actually looked concerned. That was weird. Really weird. I filed it away for later.

"Fine. I was going to get him a pop from the cafeteria when I saw Jason being wheeled down the hall." I cringed inwardly. Even I wouldn't believe that.

"They were wheeling him to the cafeteria?"

"No, no, I was in the hall. They were taking him to his room. He was still unconscious."

"Unconscious." Did Edward smile? "So you haven't spoken to him?"

That glint was back in his eyes. "No," I lied, thinking I'd call Jason ASAP and let him in on my deception. "I came back later, but he was sleeping. I talked to a nurse. She said there was no way he'd be released today."

Edward's director face replaced his villain face. "Shit, shit, shit. We have a full house tonight." He glanced at his watch. "Shit." He yanked open the dressing room door, shouting "Linda!" He nearly ran into her. She must have been standing there the whole time. "Assemble the cast in the greenroom. Now."

Linda strode off immediately. I could hear her knocking on dressing room doors. I got up, meaning to join the rest of the cast. But Edward still stood in the doorway, blocking my way.

"Ivy?"

That soft voice again.

"I'd stay away from Jason if I were you. He's dangerous. Just ask his last girlfriend." He looked me in the eye. "Oh, that's right. You can't," he said. "She's dead."

# CHAPTER 30

## Saucy Doubts and Fears

Jason, Edward, Uncle Bob...My thoughts swirled like the fake mist onstage (I never could figure out what mist was doing in a circus, but that's neither here nor there). Still, being a consummate professional, I dove into my role.

The first scene went fine, because it was just us witches. Scene II was Duncan's introduction. Bill Boxer knew his lines now, but his acting hadn't improved. Then it was the top of Scene III. I tumbled out of the cauldron with the other witches to greet Banquo and Macbeth.

"All hail, Macbeth! Hail to thee, Thane of Glamis!" said Candy/First Witch.

The Real Witch was next: "All hail, Macbeth! Hail to thee, Thane of Cawdor!"

Then me: "All hail Macbeth! Hail to thee, thou shalt be king hereafter!"

A near-sob escaped my lips. I hoped the audience would interpret it as some sort of witchy noise, when in fact I was praying that this Macbeth would not be king hereafter. My true feelings came out along with the line. Guess I wasn't a consummate professional.

Edward was our new and, please God, temporary Macbeth. He'd only spoken a few lines so far, but, oh boy. His acting veered from wooden to flamboyant. It was as if he'd caught himself sleepwalking and then decided to make up for it with a burst of energy.

"Hail!" Candy said to Banquo.

"Hail!" said The Real Witch.

"Hail!" I said, a beat late. I had no business talking about sleepwalking. I'd nearly missed that cue.

We made it to the end of the short scene. "Stay you imperfect speakers," yelled Edward, in flamboyant phase. "Tell me more!" He wore Jason's lion-tamer costume. The tights hung loosely around his skinny legs, like the skin on a chicken drumstick.

We may have been imperfect speakers, but we didn't stay. The stagehands hauled our cauldron up into the fly space, where we were hidden from the audience. We had to wait there, huddled together in our human stockpot, until the techies could let us down in the blackout at the end of the scene.

"The audience is going to want their money back after this show," grumbled The Real Witch.

"If he can't run with the big dogs, he should stay on the porch," agreed Candy.

I couldn't get worked up about the show right then. I couldn't get Edward off my mind. He'd acted so...malevolent earlier. And there was that dead girlfriend thing. I shivered, not sure if it was from the air-conditioning or the thoughts that kept trying to invade my head.

"Have we eaten on the insane root, that takes the reason prisoner?" asked Banquo, onstage below us.

I needed to call Jason. I had to tell him I had lied about not talking to him in the hospital when I spoke with Edward. My cell phone was still out, though.

"Candy, I need to ask you something," I whispered. I knew she had her cell in the dressing room.

"Shh!" said The Real Witch.

"Hello? You just talked, witchie-poo." Candy poked The Real Witch with a finger. "You could start an argument in an empty house." Then to me, "Yeah, I need to talk to you, too."

At the blackout, we hurried back to our dressing room. Candy shut the door and leaned against it. She spoke before I had a chance to.

"I am so sorry about your uncle."

My jaw tightened. Uncle Bob. What had happened now?

Candy must have seen the look on my face, because she said, "Oh no, don't worry. There's nothing new. I'm just sorry about telling everyone. About your uncle."

I stared at her, trying to puzzle out what in the hell she was talking about.

"I mean, I just wasn't thinking, and people asked why you were at the hospital, and I told them and then they wanted to know what had happened to your uncle, so I told them he was poisoned and—"

"You told them he was poisoned?"

Candy cringed. "Yeah. I mean, when you told me, you didn't say it was a secret or anything, but now, well, you've been sorta distant these last few days and I thought maybe you were mad at me."

I was mad, but just at myself. I should have known better. Candy was sweet, but she had a mouth the size of Texas.

And had I told her I suspected poison? I'd talked to her a few times since Uncle Bob's accident, but I couldn't remember what I'd said. I realized I shouldn't borrow her cell phone unless I was willing to lie to her about who I was calling. And I was tired of lying, at least for now.

"I'm not mad." I smiled at her and headed for the door.

"Didn't you want to talk to me about something?"

"Yeah, but right now I gotta pee like a racehorse. I'll be right back." Okay, that was a lie, but a really little one.

Candy and I occupied one of the chorus dressing rooms, which had no bathroom. Usually I complained about having to go down the hall to pee, but this time I was happy for the excuse. Once outside the bathroom, I looked around. Seeing no one, I dashed down the hall toward Linda's office. I could use her land line to call

Jason. I'd tell him about Edward and get at least part of a load off my mind. The dead girlfriend bit I wanted to address in person.

I'd heard Linda's door was usually unlocked during a show. It was. I slipped into her office and shut the door behind me. I wasted a few precious seconds gawking at her office décor. I don't know what I'd expected, but it wasn't...kittens. Lots of kittens, tumbling on posters, crawling on calendars, even ticking at me in the form of a cat clock with a swinging tail. Huh.

I pulled myself away from the kitties littering her office. I needed to do this quickly. I picked up Linda's phone, then set it down. I needed a phone number for the hospital. I glanced at Linda's computer, thought about booting it up so I could find the number online, and decided it was a bad idea. It'd be too easy for her to figure out someone had used it, and then there'd be questions. Maybe she still had a phone book. I yanked open a large, likely-looking drawer. I tipped up a couple of loose-leaf binders, to look underneath. No phone book. But I found something else.

Something much more intriguing.

# CHAPTER 31

## *Powerful Trouble*

I stared into Linda's big desk drawer. A tackle box was partially hidden under the few binders I'd picked up. It was brown and beat up from years of service, and it was Simon's. His makeup kit. What was it doing here? Didn't Linda say she wasn't going to move his stuff until the show had closed?

I tried to remember when she'd said that. We'd been in my dressing room, with Candy and...Jason. Jason with two black eyes. That needed covering up. With pancake makeup.

Simon's pancake makeup. Jason had used it and ended up in the hospital. Simon had used it and ended up dead. I popped open the top of the tackle box. Makeup brushes and eye pencils filled the niches meant for fish hooks and flies. I dug around in the bottom compartment and unearthed a used tin of pancake makeup. I opened it and sniffed. Smelled like makeup. I shut the lid to the tackle box, rearranged the binders, and closed the drawer with my knee. I put the tin of makeup on Linda's desk next to a Hello Kitty mug and reached for the phone. I still needed to make that call.

I heard the door open. I sat on the desk, covering the tin of makeup with my butt.

"Ivy?" It was Linda.

Damn. It must be intermission. Even so, why was she here? She usually stayed up in the booth.

"Yeah." I smiled brightly at her and, God help me, giggled. I put on my best dumb blonde voice, hoping it would work on her like it had on Edward. "I needed to make a call, and my cell is dead and I couldn't find a payphone. Then I remembered you had a phone and so here I am. Have you noticed there are no pay phones anymore? I mean, what are poor people supposed to do?" This last was a feeble attempt at the art of distraction.

Linda didn't say anything. Her squint had returned, making it difficult to see her eyes, but I swear they flicked toward the drawer that held the makeup. She nodded at the phone.

"Go ahead."

"Oh, it's kind of personal." I smiled again. My cheek muscles were beginning to twitch.

"All right." She sighed and walked toward me, disentangling a wad of keys from a caribiner clipped to her belt loop. "'Scuse me," she said, motioning that she needed to get into the desk I was perched on.

I hopped down, palming the makeup. I slipped my hand behind my back. I couldn't keep my hand there, way too suspicious. I shoved the tin up the leg opening of my leotard so that it rested on the top of my butt. I'm sure it showed—couldn't hide anything in that leotard—but as long as I faced Linda, she wouldn't be able to see it.

She locked the top desk drawer with a small brass key and then tried it to make sure it had locked. I wondered if she was securing the office because I was in it. I wouldn't blame her. I also wondered what else was in that drawer and why she didn't want me to see it.

"Just don't mess up anything, all right?" she said over her shoulder as she walked out of the office, clipping the caribiner back on her belt loop.

"Sure." I waved at her. "By the way, I love your cats."

She stopped and looked at me. Arghh. Why can't I leave well enough alone?

"Your office cats, I mean. Kitties. I love kittens."

I was fond of cats, but mostly on posters, where their silky fur didn't fly off their bodies and straight up my nose.

Linda looked me up and down. It made me nervous, so I sat on the desk again. The makeup tin in my leotard made a soft "thock" as it made contact with the desk.

"Oops," I said. "Excuse me."

I waved the air as if I'd farted. It didn't really sound like a fart, but my ruse worked. Linda crinkled her nose, shook her head, and left.

I jumped off the desk and tried the drawer with the makeup. Definitely locked. Locking the top drawer must have had the effect of locking all of them. Oh well, I had the pancake makeup I needed.

I picked up the phone. Damn. I still needed a phone book, and I needed to make this call now. We witches were on right after intermission. I had about seven minutes before they'd be expecting me to crawl in the cauldron. A quick scan of the room showed no phone books. I went to a bookshelf and moved cat photos and kitty snow globes, hoping that a phone book was hiding behind them. No dice. I looked at Linda's cat clock. Five and a half minutes until showtime.

I ran back to the phone and tried to dial information. I wasn't surprised when a recording said I must first dial one, and then, of course, when I tried it, said I couldn't dial one from that number. I put down the receiver and looked at the phone. There were a bunch of lines, maybe a different one would let me dial out. I punched one. Nope. Another. Nope. Another. Oops. A few seconds too late, I realized I'd punched a button for a line already in use. I started to hang up, when I heard familiar voices on the line.

"So you did talk to her?" It was Edward. My palms started to sweat.

"Yeah. Is there a problem?" It was Jason. They couldn't be talking about me, could they?

"It depends. Just how close are you two?"

"Listen, if you're asking me what I've told her, the answer is nothing. She knows nothing."

"About opening night?" Edward's voice sounded tight, like he wasn't getting enough air.

"That and...the other."

There was an uncomfortable silence on the line. My stomach took the opportunity to emit a loud growl.

"What was that?" said Edward.

"What?" said Jason.

There was another silence, as if they were both listening. I twisted my body so my offending stomach was as far from the mouthpiece as possible. I held my breath for good measure.

"Nothing. Must have been a connection issue," said Edward, finally. "So she doesn't know where you've been these past few days?"

"No."

My still-growling stomach lurched. Where had Jason been?

"What did you say about this recent...incident?"

"I told Ivy it was peanuts."

They were talking about me.

"Was it?"

"I don't think so. I usually react a lot quicker to peanuts."

There was a crackle on the speaker mounted in the corner of the office. I hung up, hopefully soon enough they didn't hear Linda's voice say, "Places, top of Act Four."

Dammit. I really wanted, needed, to hear Jason and Edward's conversation. What did they not want me to know? Why was Edward pissed off that Jason had spoken to me? And when had they gotten so close, anyway? If I could find out what was going on, maybe my stomach would unclench.

But I'd have to think about Jason and Edward later. Right now I had to get in the cauldron. It was clear from Linda's announcement that she was using the sound system, which meant she was back up in the booth where she belonged. Everyone else should be headed to the stage.

I peeked my head out of the office. I waited until the last actor had disappeared, figuring I'd bring up the rear, so I could keep my makeup-tinned ass undiscovered. I could hide the pancake somewhere backstage. I slipped out of the door, pulled it shut, and ran toward backstage.

"Ivy! What's with your butt?" said a voice behind me.

Shit. I'd forgotten that Riley was always, always late.

"It's uh...chew." Wow. Where did I come up with that?

"Chew?" Riley stared at me, his astonished gaze on my ass.

"You know, chewing tobacco."

I leaned into Riley, trying the art of distraction once again. This time it worked. His eyes were now fixed on my breasts. I was glad he was so predictable.

"Please don't tell anyone, okay?" I said.

"That's nasty." Riley's eyes gleamed.

Great. Who would have thought chewing tobacco was a turn on? I considered using this newfound knowledge, but just couldn't go there. I do have some standards.

"It *is*," I said in my most innocent-girl voice. "I'm quitting. Tomorrow. So you won't tell, right?"

"Scout's honor, nasty girl." He grinned and slapped me on the butt where the tin of makeup hid. I began walking backstage. "Hey!" he said. Dang, not off the hook quite yet. "I did a gig at a car show the other day. Ladies' Day."

Where was this going?

"You know," he said, making a muscle man pose, "sat on the hood of a car with my shirt off? Paid pretty good and they gave me NASCAR tickets for doing such a good job. You want to go with me?"

Oh dear God. "I'd love to, but—"

The pre-curtain music began to play. Shit! I left Riley in the dust as I ran toward the stage. I took advantage of the darkness to shove the tin of makeup under a platform and crawled into the cauldron. As soon as I was in, a stagehand hauled us witches into the air.

The Real Witch was so pissed off at my tardiness he wouldn't even look at me. Good. That way he didn't see me sticking my tongue out at him. Candy saw it, though, and giggled. "You fall in or somethin'?" she asked.

My mind raced to remember what I'd told her, but it didn't have to go far. I'd told her I'd gone to the bathroom. I didn't need long to remember, because now I really did have to go. Bad. I nodded at Candy, bit my lip, crossed my legs, and hoped that once onstage, I'd be so into character I'd forget all about it.

Ha. Every time I tumbled out of the cauldron onto the stage, I prayed I wouldn't pee.

I guess my distress helped my performance. "I've never seen you writhe so beautifully," said Edward as he passed by us witches after our scene was over. I nodded my thanks, crawled out of the cauldron with my legs crossed, stood up, and sprinted for the nearest bathroom, as well as I could with my knees together. I felt Edward watching me as I ran.

I made it to the bathroom with only seconds to spare. I sat on the cold toilet seat, my mind spinning. How was I going to get the makeup out of its hiding spot backstage? Had Linda been hiding the makeup on purpose? What was up with Edward and Jason? I didn't even want to think about the dead girlfriend thing. Maybe that was Edward trying to scare me off. But scare me off from what?

I finished my business, left the stall, and nearly ran into Candy, who had slipped silently into the bathroom.

"You scared me!" I said, with an enthusiasm I didn't feel. Had I told Candy that my uncle was poisoned?

"Sorry, darlin'," she said. "Hey, I heard Edward say Jason should be back for the Sunday matinee."

"Thank the gods of theater," I said. "Much more of Edward as Mac, and I would've tried to behead him myself. I think we should toast our good fortune. You going out for a drink after the show?" I wanted to get her talking, see what she knew.

"Nah."

I waited. Candy always cheerfully disclosed information, often way more than anyone wanted to hear. Not this time, though.

"Hot date?" I prompted.

"Nah." I stared at her until she met my eyes. "Just need my beauty sleep. Got a long day tomorrow." I saw her flinch as she said the last sentence, the physical equivalent of "Oops, shouldn't have said that."

"Why so long?" Damn, I'd spoken before thinking and asked a direct question. "Just work," she said, and slid past me into a stall. "Gotta tinkle before curtain call."

Uncle Bob was right. Direct questions didn't net you much.

I shuffled back to the greenroom, mentally crossing Candy off my list of people I could trust. Did I need to cross off Jason, too? I'd promised Uncle Bob to pull away if there was any "funny business." I didn't know what to do. Last night with Jason—had it only been last night?—I'd felt special, chosen. Now, after listening to Edward and Jason's conversation, I felt duped. I thought of the night before, the way he'd touched me, kissed me. My eyes started to fill. I willed them to stop. I couldn't mess up my makeup.

Makeup. Right. No time to mourn lost love. I needed to get that pancake out of its hiding place backstage without being seen. It'd be easier to do it while the show was running. Backstage was always dark during the show.

I trotted back to my dressing room, where I kept a sweater. A lot of us Phoenicians stash sweaters in our cars or offices. It seems weird to newcomers until they've spent their first summer here, going from 110 outside to an overly air-conditioned 65 degrees inside. Then it just seems smart. It seemed especially smart today, as I needed a way to hide the tin of pancake. Inside the dressing room, I grabbed my black sweater from off the back of my chair, tied it around my waist, and headed backstage.

Once there, I found all the soldier/clown actors milling about, waiting for their time in the spotlight. I elbowed past them to the place where I'd hidden the makeup. I knelt down and slid my hand under the back edge of the platform and felt nothing. Nada. I lay down on the floor, thick with sawdust, and extended my arm all the way underneath. I swept it back and forth, finally feeling the cool metal of the makeup tin. I curled my fingers around it and pulled it toward me. Kneeling, I slid the tin up the butt of my leotard, like before. I stood up and readjusted my sweater around my waist, only to see Genevieve watching me. She wore her sleepwalking costume, a filmy white, almost completely see-through negligee. Edward had said she could wear band aids to hide her nipples, but she'd gone without. Modesty was clearly not one of her virtues. Her breasts clearly were. Even in the dark, I could see them plainly. So could all of the soldier actors who made no attempt to pretend they weren't ogling her.

"Witch?" said Genevieve, one eyebrow raised. I brushed the sawdust off me, slowly, trying to come up with a plausible explanation.

"Lost one of my earrings," I said. I hoped the sweater covered my pancake-shaped butt. "Maybe it came off in the dressing room."

Genevieve smiled at me. And screamed.

I jumped about a foot in the air. The soldier actors sniggered. From onstage I heard Edward/Macbeth say, "What was that?"

"It is the cry of women, my good lord," said the actor who played Seyton.

Of course. It had been time for Lady M.'s suicide and the accompanying off-stage shrieks. Candy and I were supposed to scream along with Genevieve, but I'd been preoccupied. I looked around and saw Candy surrounded by a troop of soldiers. She'd obviously remembered.

I smiled "silly me" at Genevieve and the still-chuckling soldiers, and made my way back to my dressing room. I hoped Genevieve had been distracted by my unintentional buffoonery and wouldn't realize my costume didn't include earrings.

I had the dressing room to myself, so it was easy to bury the tin in my duffle bag without anyone noticing. I'd figure out what to do with it later. In the meantime, no one else was going to wear tainted makeup if I could help it.

I shed my sweater, threw on some earrings I found in my bag, and got backstage in time for curtain call. I'd just made it. The actors with the smallest roles, mostly soldier actors, were onstage taking their bows. I stood in the wings beside The Real Witch, and looked around for Candy. I saw her, huddled in conversation with Genevieve. Weird. Candy typically avoided her, claiming Genevieve's "Method" got on her nerves.

Candy's voice floated toward me. Wait, did she say, "Murder?"

I quickly turned away so they wouldn't see me watching them. I strained my ears to hear more of their conversation, but couldn't catch any more. Then Candy was beside me, just in time for our curtain call.

As I bowed, looking into the bright stage lights, I felt my throat constrict and my mind spin. I desperately wanted, needed, to talk to someone I could trust. Candy was out. Jason, out. Uncle Bob, well, he probably didn't need anything else on his mind right now. I made it through bows and got offstage. I stood backstage for a minute watching the next round of actors take their bows, my mind still roiling. I felt like I'd burst if I couldn't talk through my suspicions and feelings. I knew then I needed to go talk to the one person I could trust. My brother.

# CHAPTER 32

## *That Perilous Stuff Which Weighs upon the Heart*

Late the next morning, I set off. The air still wasn't working in my car, but I had a new plan. I wore a cotton tank top and shorts, filled a spray bottle with cool water, and misted myself really good before taking off. Then I rolled down the window on the driver's side, and let the air rush past my damp skin and hair. Voila! My own evap cooling system. I had to spray myself down every five minutes or so, but at least it made the heat bearable. The weather guy said next week we should dip down into the 90s and stay there. I could hardly wait. In the meantime, I stayed damp.

I drove to the semi-gentrified Coronado neighborhood, where beautifully restored Craftsman bungalows sat next to vinyl-sided houses with dead lawns. I steered toward an old cemetery that had a few scattered upright headstones among the flat modern ones. A fresh pile of dirt bordered a newly dug grave. It somehow reminded me of Simon, put to rest without even a funeral. I swallowed hard.

I shook my head, stepped on the gas and drove past the graveyard, a little too fast. I rounded a corner. Shit! I stomped on the brakes hard, and stopped inches from a pigeon who refused to move from the middle of the road. He didn't even notice the car, just continued strutting and cooing in front of the tires that nearly killed him.

I drove on, fuming. Stupid bird. Didn't even know he was in danger. He was nearly a memory of feathers and blood, and still he was going merrily about his day. It wasn't fair. Why should it be my heart that was pounding?

I realized I was at my destination. Must have been on autopilot. Great. I could have run over someone on top of everything else.

I parked on the street in front of a large green house with a wide front porch. A few struggling rose bushes lined a cement path to the front door. The house looked just nice enough that the neighbors wouldn't complain, but it'd never win House Beautiful.

I started to get out of the car, and then spied Simon's tin of makeup on the seat. Dang. I couldn't leave it in the car or it'd melt. My passenger seat still had a Really Rose stain from last summer's lipstick. I'd only had possession of the suspect makeup for a little over twelve hours, but already it felt like an albatross around my neck. One that I needed to do something about.

But not now. I grabbed the tin and shoved it in my front shorts pocket as I walked to the front door. In spite of the sweltering heat, a couple of guys in their twenties sat on the front porch. One of them, a chubby, sweet-faced guy, waved at me as I came up the steps.

"Hi Olive-y." he said, combining my names. He laughed at his own joke. He always did. My bad mood began to lift.

"Hey, Stu," I replied. "Hot enough for you?"

"It's nice on the porch. Come sit," he said, patting a white plastic lawn chair next to him.

"Maybe later." I rang the doorbell.

It was opened immediately, as if someone had been waiting for me. I didn't recognize the guy at the door. He was about my age, tall—maybe six-three—with curly brown hair and glasses. He smiled at me, glanced at my shirt, then reddened and kept his eyes on my face. I suddenly realized that my new form of air conditioning had another consequence—victory nipples. I crossed my arms over my chest and smiled, maintaining eye contact.

"Olive?" he asked.

I nodded. "Or you can call me..."

"Olive-y." He smiled. "Yeah, Stu told me."

My eyes adjusted as he led me into the dark, swamp-cooled foyer, which smelled pleasantly lemony clean.

"Thanks for calling ahead."

We walked into the living room, which was full of easy-care furniture: vinyl couches and chairs, sturdy round tables with no sharp corners.

"Yeah, sure." I always called ahead. "You're new?"

"Oh, yeah. Sorry." He thrust out a hand. "Matt."

Matt needed a haircut. His hair curled down over his collar and around his ears. I took his hand. He had a firm, dry handshake, and he looked directly at me with steady gray eyes. My uncle would have liked him.

"What name do you prefer?" he asked.

"They're all good," I said. "Ivy, Olive-y, or just plain Olive."

"Olive," he said. "I'll be right back."

I looked around after he left the room, found an old National Geographic, and sat in one of the vinyl chairs. Or tried to. The tin of makeup, even in my front shorts pocket, pressed against my hip uncomfortably. I stood up and flipped through the magazine. The pages with bare-breasted tribal women seemed especially worn, but then so did the ones with panda cubs.

"Olive!" said a handsome golden-haired man, bursting into the room. My throat swelled. Was this what people meant when they said their heart leapt to their throat? He rushed to me and hugged me hard. Cody. My beautiful baby brother. Still held in his embrace, I tipped my head up so I could look at him, but he was tall enough that all I could see was a blonde stubbly chin.

I tried to remember the last time I'd seen him. It had to be a couple of months. Guilt washed over me and I stiffened, ending the hug. Cody didn't seem to mind. Guess he was done hugging anyway.

"Do you like my new shirt?" he asked, thrusting out his chest.

It was a South Park T-shirt, with the whole gang of politically incorrect little guys on it. I shot a glance at Matt, who shrugged and grinned. "Your parents had a fit when they saw it. Said it was inappropriate. Couldn't believe I let him watch 'that show.'"

"A fit," Cody agreed.

Matt went on, "But, 'hey,' I said, 'Cody's an adult. He can watch, and wear, whatever he wants.'"

Oh, my parents would really hate that. No one talked back to them. I liked Matt already.

"Where do you want to go today?" I asked Cody. I already knew, but this was part of our ritual. Rituals were important to Cody. Like a lot of folks with his type of brain injury, he had a hard time learning new information, so old information, rituals we could play over and over, helped ground him. They grounded me, too.

"Hmm," said Cody, playing along. "Somewhere shady."

I shook my head sadly. "Not many trees in Phoenix."

"Somewhere with a lake."

"In the desert?"

"Somewhere there's a train."

Out of the corner of my eye, I caught Matt watching us, a smile playing on his lips.

"Too bad they closed the train station." I shook my head sadly.

Cody waited, his eyes shining.

"Wait," I said, "There's always..."

"Encanto!" we both said together.

Encanto Park was the greenest spot in Phoenix, with statuesque trees, man-made waterways that snaked through the park, and a kiddie-land amusement park complete with a small, slow train. It was a little bit of heaven for those of us who weren't desert rats. As we drove there, Cody sang along with his favorite CD, Sergeant Pepper's *Lonely Hearts Club Band*. I always kept it in the car for him.

"Will you still need me? Will you still feed me," sang Cody, slapping a drumbeat on his thighs. "When I'm sixty-four?"

He was so happy to be with me, so happy to go eat hotdogs and feed the buns to the ducks. Why didn't I do this more often?

Cody's drumbeat got faster as we pulled into one of the

parking lots at Encanto. You couldn't always tell what he was feeling by his face (it's called "flat affect" in psycho-speak), but his body often gave him away.

Once we'd parked, I grabbed a tube of sunscreen from the glove compartment (another habit of smart Phoenicians), slathered the car-heated lotion on my face, passed it to Cody, and then squirted down our shirts with my spray bottle, avoiding my breasts this time.

Cody and I had a ritual here, too. First we'd ride the train, then get hotdogs and Cokes and feed the ducks and talk. We tried it the other way around once, lunch first, but I soon learned that food before rides was a bad idea.

We walked toward the "Enchanted Island" section of the park, Cody hardly able to keep from running. My parents hated this, too, the fact that I took him on "kiddie rides." "Inappropriate," they said, their favorite word when it came to anything Cody wanted to do. It made me crazy, no adult pleasures and no childish ones. It made me crazy enough, in fact, that I helped him move out of my folks' home and into a residential program so he could be independent and have a little fun in his life. It didn't exactly endear me to my parents.

At the "station," I paid for two tickets and we climbed aboard the open-air train. Cody sat next to me on the hard bench seat, wobbling a bit as he does when he's excited and not concentrating on his balance. Cody's disability didn't really show outwardly, except for one thing. They call it ataxia, a lack of coordination, but what it looks like is drunkenness. Cody typically looks like an incredibly handsome twenty something-year-old with a couple of beers under his belt.

The teenager who had taken our tickets stared at us, trying to figure out why we were there. I stared back until he looked away.

The train pulled out of the station with a long whistle. Cody nudged me. He loved the whistle.

The train chugged out of Enchanted Island and into the grassy main park. Families, mostly Hispanic, picnicked in shady spots, kids running and laughing and chasing ducks. Older kids pedaled splashing paddleboats around a big palm tree-rimmed lagoon and through the park's canals.

Cody twisted to look at me with a plea in his eyes, as he always did when he saw the paddleboats. And as always, I shook my head. I could hardly stand to cross over the water on a bridge, much less paddle around in some flimsy contraption on top of it.

The train approached a bridge. I could smell the canal, green and funky, like dead, water-logged plants. I held my breath, and hooked a finger through one of Cody's belt loops.

My old therapist, the one they sent me to after Cody's accident, said my fear of water was "perfectly normal." Every time I was around water deeper than a puddle, I flashed back to that terrible moment. Even now, I could see Cody's yellow hair floating around his head as he sank.

I pushed those thoughts out of my head and managed to enjoy the rest of the ride. Once we'd returned to the tiny train station, Cody climbed out ahead of me and raced to our next destination, which he knew by heart. It was way too hot for me to run, so I kept an eye on him as I walked toward the hotdog cart. When I caught up with him, he was reading all of the menu items out loud, even though he always had the same thing. "Two hot dogs with mustard, and a Coke," he said to the vendor. "Please."

The hot dog man smiled at me as I approached. He was a Philippino man, maybe 50 or 60, who always wore a white yacht captain's hat, as a nod to the paddleboats maybe. "And, young lady," he said to me, "I bet you want a hotdog with everything, a Diet Coke, and an extra bun, yes?" I nodded.

"That's amazing," said Cody.

It was pretty impressive, seeing as how we hadn't been there for months.

"Haven't seen you for awhile," said the vendor as he prepared our dogs. I felt a flush creep up my neck as I searched for an explanation that would sound good to Cody. He surprised me by supplying one himself.

"It's hot. Been too hot," said my brother, fanning himself with a napkin. "Aren't you hot?" he asked the vendor.

"Oh, no, I got the best fan." He laughed, pulled out a stack of small bills, and fanned himself with them. "Best fan."

He laughed again. Cody joined him, but the vendor's "fan" just made me nervous. I kept an eye out for whoever might be watching him wave around all that money. Sheesh, I was getting paranoid.

I paid the guy and gave him a dollar tip. He smiled so big I could see a gold tooth near the back of his mouth. I made a mental note to always tip him and followed Cody to our usual shady bench by one of the canals. He settled in quickly, setting his Coke on the gravelly dirt beneath the bench. He took his time unwrapping his hotdogs, his fingers unsure, his balance wavering as he tried to concentrate on the task in front of him. Once he had the waxed paper off, he placed it in his lap like a big napkin. He checked to make sure I was ready to eat, then bit into his hotdog like he was starving.

"Mustard check," I said.

Cody faced me and smiled. This little ritual started off being about cleanliness, but I kept it up as a way to check out Cody without seeming to stare. I loved his face. My brother had sun-yellow blonde hair, sky blue eyes, and a face that seemed slightly younger than it really was, maybe because his default expression was a slight smile. Guileless, that was how I thought of Cody.

"You're good," I said. "Mustard-free."

We sat close enough that I could smell the mustard on Cody's hotdogs. I popped open my can of Diet Coke and took a long drink. The can felt cold against my lips, and the soda fizzed pleasantly on my tongue.

As we ate, we shared the extra bun I'd bought with the ducks that crowded around, watching out for the geese that liked to bite our butts through the back of the bench. We talked about Cody's job at Safeway, about Matt the new guy, and about Star Trek and James Bond. The ducks punctuated our conversation, quacking and flapping and fighting over bread.

I told Cody about the play, about Simon and Jason and Uncle Bob. I left out the gory details. I didn't need answers, just wanted to sort through my thoughts and feelings out loud in the presence of someone who respected me. Who loved me.

"Thanks," I said after spilling my guts. "I needed someone to listen."

Cody nodded solemnly, then said, "Can I come see your play?"

Cody rarely made requests.

"Oh. Wow. It's um, it's Shakespeare. Do you think you'd..."

"I like Shakespeare. To be or not to be!"

Guileless, maybe, but obviously I wasn't giving him enough credit.

"Well, there are only a few more performances..."

Why didn't I want him to come? I wasn't sure, but there it was.

"I know. Matt said he'd take me."

"Yeah. Okay. Great. I'll get some comps for you."

Somehow. I'd given all my complimentary tickets to my neighbors and Olive Garden friends, but didn't want Cody to know he hadn't been first on my list. As he should have been.

I sat back, annoyed with myself. Did I always use Cody as a sounding board without thinking of him, without considering what he wanted? The tin of makeup in my shorts shifted uncomfortably. I took it out of my pocket.

"What's that?" asked Cody.

"Makeup. The old-fashioned kind, where you just smear it on your face."

"Don't you smear the new-fashioned kind, too?"

He had a point.

"Yeah, but this is thicker. They call it pancake."

"*Pancake*." Cody's sweet tooth asserted itself.

"It doesn't have anything to do with pancakes, it's just...Here." I unscrewed the top of the tin and handed it to him.

He sniffed it. "Doesn't smell like pancakes." He was about to dip a finger in it.

"No!" I leapt up, snatching it away from Cody, my heart

beating a mile a minute. What in God's name had I been thinking?

Cody's eyes filled with tears. Shit. I put the lid on the makeup and sat down next to Cody again.

"Sorry. Sorry, hon. It's not about you. I think this makeup may be..." What? What did I think? "Bad."

"Like poison?" Cody's eyes had dried, but a sort of serious excitement shone in them.

"Maybe. I'm not sure."

"Why don't you test it? Like on CSI?"

Of course. Pinkstaff would test it for me, I felt sure.

At that moment I realized I'd underestimated Cody and had for years. I'd yelled at my parents to treat him like an adult, and yet I kept him in the role of baby brother. I resolved to get to know him all over again and to start right then.

"So," I said. "I never knew you liked Shakespeare."

# CHAPTER 33

## *Our Poisoned Chalice*

I called Pinkstaff after my picnic with Cody. We met up the next day for a bedside lunch at Uncle Bob's house. Deli sandwiches for all, courtesy of Pink. In between bites of pastrami on rye, I explained my suspicions.

"And you want me to take taxpayers' money and test this makeup?" Pink put down his half-eaten sandwich and turned to Uncle Bob. "Just last week, Olive wanted me to exhume Simon's body."

I did. C'mon, they did it all the time on TV. And how hard could it be to dig up a freshly dug hole?

Pink picked up a pickle and waggled it for emphasis. "Changed her mind when I asked her to get permission from the widow." Uncle Bob nodded at the pickle and took a ginormous bite of his potent-smelling chopped liver sandwich.

I had been all ready to get a hold of Nuala. Even found her contact info in Ireland. Well, I found her headshot and agent's contact info, but it would have been easy from there.

"*And* to cough up $10,000 for the exhumation." Pinkstaff punctuated this with a bite of pickle.

Yep, that was when I decided it wasn't such a great idea.

"But testing this makeup shouldn't cost much at all," I said. "It's just a teeny tiny tin." It was actually regular size, but I was wheedling.

"Alright, alright." Pink finished his pickle.

I saw—and ignored—the "poor deluded Olive" look he shared with my uncle.

"But I have to tell you, I probably wouldn't do this if you weren't Bob's niece." Pink held his hand out for the tin. "And if you weren't so damn cute." My uncle frowned at his last comment (or maybe his smelly sandwich). I just smiled and handed over Simon's pancake makeup.


Being on my own at Uncle Bob's office on Wednesday gave me the opportunity to research how he might have been poisoned. Helped me not a whit. All I really discovered was that it was possible someone put something in his Big Gulp while he'd left it unattended on the table in the greenroom.

I got to the theater a little early that night, my mind stuck on the problem. I checked on the nail in the cup of Diet Coke that still sat on our dressing room counter. Though the Coke had not dissolved the nail, it did jostle something loose in my brain.

I could recreate the crime scene by putting a Big Gulp on the table where Uncle Bob left his. I wasn't sure how this would help me learn anything new, but I'd seen it in cop shows. The detectives always seemed to make a new discovery when they did it. What did I have to lose?

I ran out of the theater to where Homeless Hank waited in his typical corner. "If I gave you ten bucks, would you run down to the corner and get me a Diet Coke Big Gulp?" I asked.

"I don't know, Miss." He smiled at me, his white teeth (probably dentures) glowing against his sun-baked skin. "That stuff'll kill you."

Sheesh, was there an anti-Diet Coke conspiracy?

I quickly convinced Hank that I didn't want something healthier, gave him the ten dollars, and agreed to meet him outside the stage door at intermission.

Hank was a man of his word. At intermission, I found him outside the stage door with a big, sweating plastic cup of Diet Coke.

I thanked him, told him to keep the change, and walked into the greenroom with my Big Gulp.

"Mmm," I said, trying to draw attention to myself in a room full of buzzing actors. "Gotta love a Big Gulp." Uninspired, I know. I never was great at improvisation. "Except when you drink too much and have to pee," I said loudly.

I really should take an improv class.

I set my drink down on the table and ambled nonchalantly around the corner into the hall where the bathrooms were. I stopped and peeked back around the corner. I could just see the fake blood-stained table where my Big Gulp sat. Jason walked by it. My chest tightened. I hadn't talked to him since overhearing his weird phone call with Edward. I shook my head to clear it. Needed to concentrate on the task at hand.

I was beginning to think I had wasted ten bucks. This was a pretty silly idea. I mean, if someone did something with the Big Gulp now, it would mean they wanted to harm me, right?

Wait, someone had stopped at the table. Though he had his back to me, I could see the black unitard with jagged silver stripes.

Riley.

He looked around to see if anyone was watching, then picked up the Big Gulp and carried it backstage.

Riley? What did he have to do with anything? Hmm. He *had* been really solicitous about my uncle. And he had worked with Simon in Flagstaff.

I was about to follow him backstage when he returned, Big Gulp in hand. He put it back down on the table.

I leapt out of my hiding place and nabbed him. "Hey! Why did you take my Big Gulp?"

"Uh, five second rule?"

"What?"

"You know. You left it there for more than five seconds, so I figured it was fair game." Riley *was* good at improv.

"I'm pretty sure that only applies to food dropped on the floor." I took my drink from him.

"Sorry." He looked like a dog who'd been caught going through the garbage.

"Why did you take it backstage?" Dang. Not only did I need to work on my improv, I needed to improve my indirect questioning skills.

"So I could drink it without anyone seeing."

"But you brought it back."

"It was Diet Coke." He made a face.

For heaven's sake. I started to defend my soft drink of choice, but had another question to ask. "What about Simon?"

"Huh?"

Too indirect that time. "Had you worked with him before?" I knew he had, but I wanted to see what he would say.

Riley now looked like a puzzled dog. "Yeah, in a couple of shows. I do a lot of Shakespeare."

"What did you think of him?"

Riley shrugged. "He was cool."

The loudspeaker squawked. "Places for Act Four."

I went backstage, climbed into the cauldron with my fellow witches, and formulated my next question to them carefully, not sure who I trusted. "I just caught Riley sneaking off with my Big Gulp. Do you think it's okay to drink? I mean, I couldn't catch bedbugs or anything, could I?" Riley had been joking about bedbugs a little too often for some of our tastes.

"I wouldn't drink it," Tyler said as our cauldron rose up into the flyspace.

"Me neither," agreed Candy. "You never know what he put in it."

"You think he'd put something in it?" I asked.

"Maybe a roofie," said Tyler.

I shook my head. Though the date rape drug Rohypnol was pretty easy to get in close-by Mexico, it wasn't Riley's style.

"You know Riley. I'm still mad he put that fake cockroach in my coffee cup." Candy shivered melodramatically. "About swallowed the dang thing."

Most shows have a resident practical joker. Riley was ours. He'd written "Feel my steel" on one side of his broadsword, stuffed his unitard to give himself man-boobs, and posted a fake online review on the greenroom bulletin board, where the supposed critic got him and Jason mixed up and said Riley was "the best Macbeth ever." Everyone thought it was real (including Jason, who was royally pissed) until we noticed that the critic spelled witches "whiches."

"He'd probably just add salt or booze or something, but still," Candy said. "I wouldn't drink it."

Music began, and the lights dimmed. In the minute I had before the cauldron descended to the stage, I thought about Riley. He could've tampered with my Diet Coke. There was no way to be sure unless I asked Pinkstaff to test it, too, and I had the feeling that wouldn't go over well. He could have put something in Uncle Bob's Big Gulp as well. That possibility brought up another question: If it was Riley who put something in my uncle's drink, could the poisoning have been accidental, a practical joke gone wrong? If that was the case, did that mean nothing else was "foul play?"

By the time we touched down onstage, I realized my crime scene reconstruction had been a bust. I wasn't closer to any sort of truth.

# CHAPTER 34

## *Come What May*

Jason paced the stage under the dim work lights. He always arrived at the theater before the rest of the cast to get into character. He'd texted me earlier, asking me to meet him an hour before call. Said he wanted some private time with me. Probably also wanted to know why I'd been avoiding him. It was Thursday night. We hadn't spoken since I overheard Edward and him on the phone on Saturday.

Now I stood in the shadowy wings, behind a velvet curtain like the one Jason and I had wrapped ourselves in on opening night. God, that seemed like a long time ago.

Jason delivered Macbeth's lines to the dark emptiness. "Come, seeling night..."

Falconers used to train their birds by sewing their eyes shut. "Seeling" them.

"Scarf up the tender eye of pitiful day." Macbeth was asking the night to give him strength to murder his best friend. "And with thy bloody and invisible hand, Cancel and tear to pieces that great bond, Which keeps me pale!"

The creepy speech was too much, and Jason delivered it too well. I decided to leave. Maybe we could talk later, in the open, in the sun.

I must have made a noise. Jason turned. He was already in costume, sans boots. He followed my eyes to his bare feet and smiled a slow smile.

"My boots make too much noise," he said. He walked toward me silently, his eyes locked on mine. "I was afraid you weren't going to come."

I stepped out from behind the curtain, but held onto its soft strength with one hand. "Why?" My laugh sounded nervous, even to me.

He continued toward me with that catlike walk. "I thought maybe you were done with me." He watched me for a reaction. I was careful not to give him any.

"I was...busy." I couldn't meet his eyes.

"Yeah, that's what Genevieve said."

He was close now, so close I could smell the woodsy scent of the soap he used.

"She said she saw you with another guy."

"Another guy?"

"Come on, Ivy. She was on some commercial shoot at Encanto, and saw you on a picnic with some blonde guy."

Cody. An involuntary smile must have crossed my face, because Jason's grew dark.

"I don't like to share," he said.

"He's not the reason I didn't return your calls."

"Why then? You haven't talked to me since I was in the hospital."

It was true. I'd ignored his calls, and even managed to avoid him offstage during the shows on Sunday and Wednesday.

"Why?" Jason planted himself inches from me. I could feel the heat from his body along the length of mine. I wanted to touch him so badly. Even now.

"I don't understand why it's such a big deal," I said. "You didn't return my calls for almost a week when Uncle Bob was in the hospital."

"That was different." Jason's voice was husky with some emotion. Anger? Jealousy?

"Yeah?"

"Yeah. That was before we...made love."

He said the words awkwardly, like they didn't quite fit in his mouth. I saw the seducer mask slip from his face, a glimpse of a real connection behind his eye.

Or I wanted to see it. I wanted the Jason I thought I knew. The one I'd trusted enough to get close. Sex to me was never just recreational. My heart always came with the deal.

"Ivy." Jason stood in front of me, glowering. The muscles in his neck were tense, and he looked dangerous. And, God help me, hot.

Down, girl. This is the guy who lies about why he was in the hospital, who shares some weird secret with Edward, who has a dead girlfriend.

"What's going on?" Jason grabbed my shoulders. "Who is this guy?" I could feel his fingers press into the flesh above my shoulder blades. Not hard or hurtful. Strong. Powerful. Compelling.

Ivy. Don't forget the dead girlfriend.

"Who is he?"

I looked Jason in the eye. "Wanna trade secrets?"

# CHAPTER 35

## *Wrought with Things Forgotten*

Backstage areas have lots of places to hide, if you know where to look. Jason seemed to know all of them. "C'mon," he said, grabbing my hand. "Secrets deserve dark places."

A bunch of unused flats created a makeshift wall at one end of the backstage area. Jason led me behind them to a rectangular-shaped space between the flat-created wall and the real concrete block wall, about six feet wide and three deep. My heart pounded in my ears. Work lights shed gray pools of light around the area, but the space itself was deep in shadow. No one would notice it, or anyone in it, unless they were really looking. I cleared my throat, set my jaw, and tried to look tough. "Tell me about your old girlfriend. You know, the one who's dead."

"Girlfriend?" Jason's brow furrowed in concentration.

"How many dead girlfriends do you have?" was on the tip of my tongue and nearly out of my mouth when his eyes widened with understanding. His face crumpled, just sort of caved in on itself. He looked the way I felt whenever I thought about Cody's accident.

Jason, his face still struggling under the weight of some emotion, slid down the wall, and sat on the dusty floor, his back against the cement block wall.

"Danielle," he said.

He didn't ask how I knew. Theater folk tend to gossip during the run of a show.

It was so quiet I could hear us breathe. I sat down next to

Jason, close, our thighs touching. I couldn't help myself.

"It was a couple of years ago," he began. "I'd been seeing this girl, Danielle, for a few months. It was good for awhile, but she started getting needy. She always wanted to know where I was, what I was doing, who I was with. You know."

I did know. I kinda wanted to know his whereabouts, too. I stayed quiet.

"So I broke up with her," said Jason. "I was going to be going away soon anyway. Had a summer theater gig in Montana. She was devastated. Heartbroken. She kept calling, hanging around the theater, trying to talk to me. I hated it, felt like I was being ambushed. I wouldn't take her calls. She used to park outside my apartment, too, so I didn't think too much about it when I saw her sitting in her car outside one night. I didn't even acknowledge her. The next morning, I heard sirens outside my window, saw red and blue revolving lights through my curtains."

He swallowed. "I walked outside. An ambulance and a police car were parked near Danielle's. One of the policemen said, 'Are you Jason?' When I nodded, he said, 'Sorry, man.' He told me Danielle was dead. Overdosed on her roommate's sleeping pills. She'd killed herself right in front of my house. I asked how he knew my name. He handed me a note she'd pinned to herself. It said, 'Tell Jason I was pregnant.'"

I don't know what I'd been expecting, but it wasn't this. I laced my fingers through Jason's and squeezed his hand. His eyes saw me, but looked beyond me at the same time. He slumped against the wall.

What in the world had I been thinking? Jason couldn't hurt anyone. He had to talk to Edward, he was the director. And the allergy thing—all he had said to Edward was that it wasn't peanuts. That didn't mean he lied to me earlier. He was still pretty out of it then. Probably didn't have all the information yet.

The concrete wall felt cold against my back. I'd been dodging his calls because of this? I felt awful. So awful that I took a deep breath and told him my secret.

# CHAPTER 36

## *From the Memory, a Rooted Sorrow*

"Cody—the guy I was with at Encanto—he's my brother." The breath I'd taken felt thick with dust.

"I didn't know you had a brother." From the corner of my eye, I could see that Jason had turned his head to look at me. I didn't look back.

Hardly anyone knew I had a brother. I never talked about Cody. Not to anyone. Cody and the accident were locked tight in a box in my mind.

A warmth crept up my neck. I was already ashamed of myself. Locks were for secrets. That wasn't fair to my brother.

"Cody is three years younger than me. He lives here in Phoenix." I bit my lip and unlocked that box. "In a group home."

I felt Jason's body lean into mine.

"We grew up in Spokane." I stopped, turning to look at Jason. "It's in Washington." I could tell by the look in his eyes that he recognized a feint. His eyes held mine, silently telling me it was okay to go on.

"We all used to live there. Uncle Bob, too." I could see the impossibly blue skies, hear the river, smell the pine trees. "People think of rain when they hear 'Washington,' but Spokane's different than Seattle. Drier, but the weather can be really extreme. It snows a lot in the winter."

Uncle Bob used to come over and make snow forts with us.

Once, when Dad was out of town, Uncle Bob was shoveling our walk and decided to dig a maze for us, squiggly paths all through the front yard, with snow walls taller than Cody. We ran through it whooping with delight, banging into dead ends and falling down laughing. Our faces streamed with tears from the laughter and the brilliant winter sunlight, the water freezing on our faces in the cold.

I shivered. The chill from the concrete floor penetrated through my shorts. The cinder block wall was cold and unforgiving. I hugged myself.

Jason watched my eyes, waiting, but patient.

"It gets really cold, too," I said. "All the little lakes and ponds freeze up, and we'd go ice-skating on them."

I must have shivered again, because Jason put his arm around me and pulled me close. His warmth felt good but inadequate, like half a blanket.

"One day when I was eleven, me and my friends were all going to the park. There was a big duck pond there, where all the kids went to ice skate and hang out."

The pond had these big goldfish. Not koi, just plain goldfish that grew bigger and bigger over the years. Sometimes in the winter you could see a school of them beneath your feet, circling in the unfrozen water far below the ice.

"Cody begged to go along, but I didn't want him to. I was...too cool, I guess. My mom made me take him, though, and promise to watch over him."

Instead, I acted like he wasn't there, like I didn't have a little brother. Dissed by me and my friends, Cody skated away to the other side of the pond. He stayed there, practicing hockey-style speed stops, spraying imaginary foes with arcs of ice.

I heard him shout just once, more of a yelp, really. I looked over to see what he was yelling about this time. But he was gone, a jagged hole in the ice where he'd been a moment before.

I raced toward him, skates scraping over the rough ice. A patch of snow caught me, and I flew, landing with a hard crack as my chin hit ice. I tasted blood, felt the sting of cold on my cheek, but it was

Cody who filled my eyes and mind and soul. I could see him, foggy beneath the surface of the water. His yellow hair floated gently around his head like a halo. He wasn't even moving, just sinking slowly beneath the icy water, eyes closed.

I guess it was because of the cold that he didn't try to swim, the shock of it or something, but it was also the cold that somehow saved his life, slowing down his bodily functions so he basically came back from the dead. Except for his brain. It never came completely back.

"And Cody fell through the ice?" Jason asked in a gentle voice.

Hadn't I said that? No, I guess not.

"He..." My throat closed up. I couldn't even swallow. I nodded.

Jason pulled me onto his lap, curling his arms protectively around me. I buried my face in the safety of his chest.

"I didn't watch over him," I whispered. "I promised, but I didn't."

# CHAPTER 37

## *Dwell in Doubtful Joy*

Jason held me while I wept like my eleven-year-old self. I couldn't tell if I cried for Cody, for myself, or for the accusing silence that had blanketed my family ever since. I just knew Jason had given me a safe place to cry, curled up against his chest. When I finally lifted my face to him, he kissed my eyelids, soft kisses that mingled with my tears. Our lips found each other. Kisses that started out gentle turned hungry, and soon I was glad for the secret place we'd found.

Afterward, Jason admitted he'd already chosen our rendezvous spot after scoping out the backstage area.

"I wanted to seduce you right here in the theater. I thought it would be hot," he said. "I never imagined we'd talk about..."

He stopped, probably because I kissed him. I couldn't help myself. If there was a Cloud Ten, I was on it. I felt buoyant, like I'd left my secret history at the bottom of that icy pond and floated up toward the light. I had told someone about Cody, and he hadn't judged me.

Now, I hummed to myself as I used the theater shower. I couldn't place the tune but knew it was something happy. As I soaped up, trying to keep my hair dry, my mind circled back to Jason. I hummed again. My body hummed, too, with the memory of our recent lovemaking.

One shadow in my sunny day: Jason asked we keep our real relationship to ourselves. He wanted to keep things light and playful in front of others. "I don't want everyone saying it's just a backstage romance," he said, "when it's so much more."

So much more. That's what I chose to focus on.

I stepped out of the shower and dried quickly, shivering in the air-conditioned room. I wrapped a towel around me and listened at the door. Hearing no one, I sprinted the few doors down to our dressing room. I found myself singing out loud: "Zip a dee doo dah." That was the tune I'd been humming. My mom used to sing it when she was happy, a long time ago.

I ran into our dressing room and flipped on the lights, grateful no one had seen (or heard) me. Candy hadn't arrived yet. I saw a piece of paper folded with my name on the front, propped up against my makeup kit on the dressing room counter. I shut the door and grabbed the note, humming again. Jason was so sweet. Yeah, it was annoying we needed to pretend we were just flirting, but the sneaking around was exciting and it led to romantic things like little notes in my dressing room. I felt all warm and gooey as I unfolded the paper and read:

"I am in blood

Stepp'd in so far, that, should I wade no more,

Returning were as tedious as go o'er."

I dropped the note. It felt hot, like it was burning me. I wondered for a moment if it was poisoned, if someone could poison a note.

Candy opened the door. "Naked as a jay bird!" she sang out. I looked down and realized I'd dropped my towel along with the note. I picked up both, keeping the note out of sight from Candy, who began stripping out of the blue scrubs she wore at the nursing home.

In the play, Macbeth delivers the line about being stepp'd in blood after he's killed Duncan and Banquo. He realizes he is too covered in blood to stop killing.

Duncan and Banquo. Simon and Uncle Bob. Did the person who wrote the note kill my friend and poison my uncle? Or was I reading too much into the one line? One thing I was sure of: the note was a warning. Macbeth doesn't stop killing. He goes on to murder innocent people, Macduff's wife and children. Did that mean I was next? Or someone else? I'd been playing at this "investigation" like it was another play, with me in the role of detective. I felt foolish, guilty, and sick to my stomach. I put my head between my knees.

Candy came over and rubbed my back. "You okay, darling?"

"Just a little queasy," I said, bringing my head up. I wished I could trust her enough to show her the note. "Probably something I ate."

"Better hope so," she said with a wink.

I started to roll my eyes, then realized that Jason and I hadn't used protection this last time. My stomach felt even worse.

"Still and all, better get ready," Candy said, tossing her panties on a chair.

When her head was turned, I shoved the note deep into my duffel bag. I caught a glimpse of my cell phone, which displayed a new message from the City of Phoenix. Huh. I picked up my phone and listened.

"Ivy, er...Olive, it's Detective Pinkstaff."

I sat up straight in my chair.

"First of all, Bob says you better not be at that god...Sorry...that GD theater, since you said you'd quit."

I hadn't actually said I would quit, not out loud. I'd kinda hoped Uncle Bob had forgotten about wanting me to quit or that it was his pain medication talking. Still, I hadn't been completely honest with my uncle and I felt guilty about it.

"And secondly," Pinkstaff cleared his throat, "you were right about the makeup. It was tampered with. Give me a call."

I was right. I wasn't poor deluded Olive, I was right. Then the sobering truth hit me. I was right. Someone had deliberately poisoned Simon's makeup. Someone had killed Simon. I suddenly realized all this time I had hoped it wasn't true. Now I knew it was true, and if this note was any indication, the killer was on to me.

I wished I hadn't deceived Uncle Bob. I couldn't show him the note. He'd have Pinkstaff haul my ass out of this theater ASAP. Not only would I not catch the bastard who murdered Simon and drugged Uncle Bob, but that would be the end of my career. Quitting during closing week was unforgivable. No, I was going to have to handle this on my own. But what did that mean?

Candy must have been watching me, because she said, in a serious voice, "Ivy, hon, you okay?"

I decided to go with the "not feeling well" idea. "It was the clinic," I said. "They want me to call." I left it at that. It was a lie, but one I could get out of later by saying I had something innocuous.

I sat still for a moment. My brain squealed with the effort of thinking so hard. Okay, so I was right, someone did kill Simon. With relief, I ruled out Jason, since he was also poisoned. Plus I wanted to rule him out. I didn't believe he could kill anyone, especially after seeing his true self this evening. No, not a suspect.

"Darlin'," Candy said, "you best get your head out of the clouds and onto the moors, or into the circus, in this case." She was already in costume and wig cap, and was putting on makeup.

I stepped into my footless tights. Uncle Bob had said that everyone had opportunity, but who had motive? Linda. She seemed to have a darn good motive, what with Simon stealing the love of her life. And she was hiding the makeup afterwards. Pretty suspicious.

"You did hear we're giving Edward his present tonight, right?" said Candy, pulling on her wig. Like many casts, we had all chipped in to buy our director a thank you gift. "We're all meeting at intermission on the loading dock."

Edward. He certainly hated Simon, thought he was ruining his play. And of course there was the Simon-Pamela thing.

I pulled on my leotard.

But could Edward kill someone? I remembered the secretive phone conversation, the sound of his voice during our "little talk," the hard glint in his eyes when he told me about Jason's dead girlfriend. I added him to the list. Edward and Linda.

"See ya in the circus," Candy said as she left the dressing room, ready for the show. She left the door open, probably to hurry me along. I saw Genevieve catch up with her and whisper something into her ear. Genevieve. Could she have done it? No motive I could see, but she was certainly a bit unhinged. I decided to keep an eye on her, just in case.

Better start doing my makeup, or I'd be late. I reached for my foundation, then stopped. Could the killer have poisoned it, too? I decided to skip it and just use powder, eye makeup, and lipstick. Those seemed like they'd be harder to tamper with. I hoped so.

Bill stuck his head in the dressing room. "Better hurry up," he said, smiling with his bleached teeth. "Or I'll get you, my pretty." He trotted off toward backstage.

Arghh. Bill was always quoting *The Wizard of Oz* to me, trying to make some witchy connection, I guess. Nearly every day when he came in from the heat, he'd catch sight of me and say, "I'm melting!" He was probably quoting *The Wizard of Oz* because he couldn't quote *Macbeth*. I wasn't sure he'd even read the whole thing.

He was so clueless that several times someone had to clap a hand over his mouth to keep him from saying "Macbeth" out loud in the theater. He said it on opening night when he wasn't even in the show.

Omigod. Bill. I hadn't even considered him before. He was an idiot, but an ambitious, vain one. Having to tell everyone he hadn't been cast—on TV yet—must have stung. Oh, he was definitely a suspect. I added Riley to the list, too. The Big Gulp incident was most likely innocent, but I couldn't ignore it.

I pulled on my wig cap and bobby-pinned my wig atop my head.

What to do now? The makeup proved foul play, but how could I prove who had tampered with it? The play closed Saturday night. After that we'd all be scattered. Theater people took out-of-town and traveling gigs all the time. It'd be easy for a killer to slip out of town without looking suspicious.

I couldn't let that happen. Not just for Simon, but for poor poisoned Jason. For Uncle Bob and his smashed-up car. For me, too, when I thought about it. That note had made it clear I was in trouble. The sooner this murderer was caught, the less likely I'd wind up dead or poisoned. But I wasn't a cop, not even a PI. What could I do?

I could act.

I'd seen tons of cop shows, watched hours of BBC mysteries. I knew those characters.

"Places in five." Linda's voice crackled over the speaker in the corner of the room.

I got down to business. I painted my eyes a sparkly gold, drew on dark eyebrows, and decided to pull a Poirot.

# CHAPTER 38

## *Ripe for Shaking*

I loved Agatha Christie's little Belgian detective. I loved his confidence, his neat mustache, and his tidy bowler hat. I even dressed up as Poirot one Halloween. Everyone thought I was Charlie Chaplin. No matter. Tonight I would emulate my fictional hero with a classic Agatha Christie tactic. I'd assemble all the guilty suspects in one room, tell them everything I'd discovered, and the murderer would show his—or her—hand. The intermission get-together to give Edward his present was the perfect Poirot-type set-up—as long as I could act the part.

At intermission, a stream of actors and techies flowed out the door to the loading dock. Everyone wanted to be there. My amped-up pulse beat a warning. I ignored it. I could do this. Of course I could. I am Ivy Meadows and I am an actress!

I got in line behind Edward and stepped out the door. A blast of too-warm air and a rumble of conversation greeted us. The entire cast and crew lined the sides of the loading dock. A few smoked while they had the chance. All the loading dock lights were on, and the ramp was bare of trucks or equipment.

Edward nudged me. "I'm hoping for a bottle of Rémy Martin. I've been hinting."

I stared at him. He had been unusually friendly to me, ever since...when, exactly? After the phone call I'd overheard. Yeah, that was definitely the turning point. I didn't get it.

Edward was hoping for Rémy Martin. That's what he said. A bitter taste crept into my mouth.

"Everybody!" shouted Riley, who had jumped down to the driveway. He had been appointed to buy the present. "Edward told me what he wanted for a present..."

El Director gave me a sideways smile. My mind's eye flashed back to that horrible night, and I saw an empty bottle next to Simon's body. A bottle of Rémy Martin.

"But I couldn't find 'eye of newt and toe of frog,' or 'wool of bat and tongue of dog.' So instead I bought him three other things that might make a tastier gruel for his cauldron. I was pretty sure he'd like carrot juice..." Groans and laughter as Riley presented Edward with a plastic bottle full of orange liquid. "Rémy Martin..." Applause accompanied this gift. "And..." Riley fiddled with something behind his back. "Diet Coke!"

The plastic liter bottle he held out toward Edward erupted in a fountain, showering several of us with warm, sticky liquid.

"Cool, huh?" Riley jumped back up to the edge of the loading dock. "If you drop Mentos—you know, those mint candy things?—into Diet Coke, whoosh! Geysers of Coke, man!"

"Arrrhhh." The strangled noise came from Edward, whose once-white shirt was plastered to his chest.

Riley burst out laughing. "Oh man. You really got it." Then, as he realized his folly, "Oh, hey. Sorry, Edward. Really. I didn't mean to get you all wet."

"Riley," said Edward. "I am going to kill you."

I screwed my courage to the sticking point. "Speaking of murder," I said in my loudest voice.

"Oh, for God's sake," said Edward. "Don't you know an exaggeration when you hear one?"

I persevered. "As some of you know, I've been investigating Simon's death."

A few groans from the crowd, but several cast members kept their eyes on me, Edward included.

"And I am convinced that it was..."

I tried hard not to slip into a Belgian accent.

"Murder."

Any chattering had stopped and all eyes were now on me.

# CHAPTER 39

## *Desire Is Got without Content*

I looked around at the sea of expectant faces, all waiting for me to tell them what happened next. Poirot-like, I examined each one, looking for signs of guilt. This was going to be harder than I thought, and I only had a few minutes before intermission was over.

Shit. Intermission. What would happen to the second half of the show if I did catch a murderer? Not smart, Ivy, not smart. But it was now or never. I couldn't wait. I said a little prayer to the gods of theater and St. Agatha Christie, and played my next card.

"It was the same makeup that sent Jason to the hospital."

I snuck a look at Jason, and was surprised to see his eyes grow wide. He must have suspected, especially since he knew it wasn't peanuts that caused his allergic reaction. Anyway, the important thing was that he couldn't be guilty.

"So, he can't be the guilty party," I said.

"Sure, he could," said The Real Witch. "He could have faked the whole thing and made himself sick. He could have lied."

Before I could point out that I'd seen Jason in the hospital, Bill spoke up. "Yeah," he said. "He's that way. Everyone knows he stuffs his dance belt."

"No, he doesn't."

It just came out. I nearly clapped my hand over my mouth, but stopped so I wouldn't draw too much attention to myself. Too late. Candy hooted, Genevieve scowled, Edward self-consciously cleared his throat, and Jason glared daggers at me (*Macbeth* pun intended). I knew why Jason was pissed—I'd blown our secret—but what was the deal with everyone else? People seemed more interested in me and Jason than Simon's murder. It didn't seem right.

Sweat, or maybe Diet Coke, trickled down my face. I wiped it away and pushed onward.

"But Edward," I began, addressing the buzzing crowd on the loading dock, "Had motive and opportunity." I kept the Rémy Martin card up my sleeve, in case I needed it later.

"Please," he said. "I would have never poisoned Jason."

Was that a slip? Should I ask him about Simon, or stay on the Jason track?

"Why not?" I asked, sticking with the Jason angle.

"Because he's my lead, for God's sake. It would have killed the show. Who else could have stepped in?"

I saw Riley open his mouth to nominate himself as a potential Macbeth stand-in and then shut it. Was that suspicious?

"Speaking of the show," said Linda. "Places in five."

"Or it could have been Linda," I said. "She had motive, she had opportunity, and she kept the poisoned makeup in a drawer in her desk." A hush fell over the cast.

Linda's face was implacable, as always. "Hated Simon," she said, crossing her arms. "Didn't kill him."

"What motive did she have?" asked Kaitlin/Lady Macduff.

"We loved the same woman," Linda said, her face still stony. "And this is all a lot of fun," she looked at her watch, "but you now have places in four." She yanked open the door to backstage and stood there like a doorman, silently commanding the actors to get into places. The cast shuffled toward the door.

This wasn't working. Damn. I should have known better. These were all theater people, they could act innocent. I knew someone was "in blood, Stepp'd in so far." Someone was guilty, and whoever it was, was after me. But what to do? What would Poirot do?

Bill pushed his way toward the door, ahead of everyone. Wait. "Duncan is already dead," I said. "Bill doesn't have to go on. Stop him."

Two burly techies stepped in front of Bill. He didn't turn around, but stayed facing the door. I was onto something.

"Bill definitely had motive," I said. "Out of everyone, he gained the most by Simon's death."

"What about opportunity?" Linda stood at the open door, her face serious.

"He was here opening night," I said. "Don't you remember?"

"Yeah, he brought champagne," Jason said.

"And he said 'Macbeth,'" added Riley.

Bill turned around and thrust out his chest. "I always attend opening night at this theater."

"Not true," said Edward. "And not only were you in attendance that night, you were on hand to make an appearance at the press conference, directly after Simon's death."

"And I saw you at intermission," said Riley.

"All right!" shouted Bill. "I did it. I poisoned Simon's makeup."

Wow. My Agatha Christie scheme had worked. I was stunned into silence.

Linda shut the door to the theater and took a cell phone out of a pocket on her cargo pants.

"Please," said Bill, appealing to Linda. "Wait until the end of the show. It'll be public soon enough." His face crumpled. "Please."

Linda looked to Edward, who nodded.

"All right," she said.

Bill's body sagged. I was afraid he might faint.

"Jason, Riley, and..." she thrust her chin at a few of the soldier actors. "Adam and Kevin. Would you please escort Bill to the Cage?"

The men surrounded Bill, whose face was turning gray. Linda opened the stage door and held it. I pushed my way through the cast so I could follow right behind the guys escorting Bill. The rest of the cast and crew trailed behind.

Our little group proceeded to the Cage. It's not as bad as it sounds, just a large, fenced-in area backstage where expensive equipment—lights, fog machines, stuff like that—is kept. It's also locked. Linda selected a key from among the dozen on her carabineer key ring and unlocked it. We all looked at Bill, standing there in his ridiculous ringmaster's costume. He didn't move.

"Bill," said Linda, "You gotta get in."

Still nothing. Like his shoes were Superglued to the floor.

Linda pulled out her phone again. "You want me to call the police right now?"

Bill shook his head and unstuck his feet. We were all silent as he stepped into the Cage. He stumbled over some equipment, then headed toward a three-foot square space that wasn't filled with equipment. He looked like a dog that had been banished to the basement.

"Jason," said Bill through the Cage's chain link fence, "I'm sorry."

Jason strode off in the direction of the stage, ignoring Bill's apology.

"Places," said Linda to the group. We all turned to go, when we heard a snuffling, choking sound from the Cage.

"I didn't mean to kill him," said Bill, tears streaking his stage makeup.

"Tell that to the police," I said, trying to sound like a detective. I didn't. I didn't sound anything like Poirot.

# CHAPTER 40

## *To Win Us to Our Harm*

I didn't feel like Poirot, either. I expected to feel vindicated, victorious. After all, I'd caught the culprit. But no. My stomach hurt like I'd swallowed a big lump of something indigestible, and my head ached with the idea that someone would actually kill for a role. I felt like I had food poisoning of the soul.

I passed by Jason, who was waiting in the wings for his entrance. "Hey," I said softly.

He wouldn't look at me. I told myself it was the shock of the revelation, maybe anger at Bill. Yes, I'd spilled the beans about our relationship, but it couldn't be that big a deal. Could it?

I tumbled into the cauldron beside Candy and The Real Witch. No chit-chat there either.

The show felt leaden. Everyone's acting seemed forced, unreal. It was as if we were all Lady Macbeth, sleepwalking our way through the show. I could hardly wait for it to be over.

After our last exit, I turned to Candy, who had just crawled out of the cauldron.

"So..." I began.

"I can't believe you didn't tell me." She made a show of stomping off, though it didn't work very well with bare feet.

I passed Genevieve, whose eyes bore into mine, blazing with hate. What did I do to her?

Still looking over my shoulder at Genevieve, I bumped into

Riley, and felt a sort of relief, like when you run into a really stupid Irish Setter who likes everyone. The look he turned on me, though, was anything but Setter-like.

"What?" I said. This was getting ridiculous.

"I waited," he said. "I even bought you a T-shirt."

I waited, too, hoping he'd enlighten me as to what he was talking about.

"No one stands me up," he said and walked away.

I stood him up? Huh? Oh shit. NASCAR. Did I say I'd go? I must have. Shit.

I made my way back to our dressing room. I could wait there for curtain call, maybe phone Pinkstaff. I had to pass through the greenroom on the way there. Tonight it was strangely empty, except for Edward, who paced the length of it, gnawing on a carrot. He stopped when he saw me.

"Bravo," he said, clapping slowly. "You've ruined the show once again."

I opened my mouth to protest.

"Because of you the police will be called to the theater a second time," he continued.

That wasn't fair. I wanted to shout that it was Bill's fault, not mine, but Edward's face stopped me. He looked a little like Hitler with a thinner mustache. And a carrot. I swallowed my indignation.

He went on. "Twice in one show. Do you understand what that means to this theater?"

"Publicity?" I said hopefully.

"Oh." His face lost the crazed despot look. "Well."

He began pacing again, glaring at the tile floor. "Even so," he said, "that doesn't let you off the hook."

Why was he so mad at me?

I started back to our dressing room, leaving him alone with his thoughts. He'd have to realize eventually I was the hero in all of this.

I was nearly to the hall when he said, "Did you plan to audition for my production of *Much Ado*?"

"Yes! I'd—"

"Don't bother," he said, with an evil little sideways smile. "And you did know my wife is the artistic director here, yes? And that she exerts a lot of influence in the community?"

My throat felt tight. It was no fair. I was doing what I needed to do, what anyone should have done. I was the good guy, dammit.

Edward stood, waiting. I nodded, and slid out of the room, with the understanding that my acting career was over.

# CHAPTER 41

## No Teeth for the Present

I decided to get into place for bows a bit earlier than usual. Didn't want to sit alone in my dressing room with only thoughts of my ruined career for company. Riley stood in the wings, close to the stage, waiting to go on for his big fight scene with Macbeth. I walked up to him and touched his shoulder.

"Riley, I'm so sorry. With everything happening, I forgot. I'm really—"

"You know, Ivy," he said, looking me in the eye. "I thought you were cool. You're pretty and you're funny and you seem nice. But you know what? You're not. 'Cause 'nice' means thinking about other people's feelings, and you don't. You just...don't."

He shook my arm off his shoulder like he was shaking off a bad dream.

"Riley, I—"

"That way the noise is!" he shouted as he strode onstage. "Tyrant, show thy face!"

Cold water dripped down my face into my heart. Or at least it felt that way. I slipped into the shadows backstage to wait for my cue. Riley had struck deep. Why in the world did it hurt so much?

Because he was right. Even now, as I followed my castmates onstage for curtain call, I was thinking about me, about how hurt I was. I wasn't thinking about Riley, who had waited for a date who never showed. Or Bill, whose career might be ruined. Or Uncle Bob, who may have been poisoned because of something I asked him to do. For God's sake, I hadn't even remembered to get him a medical bed.

As we witches got into place for bows, I reached for Candy's hand, but she kept it by her side. Normally we three held hands during curtain call. Not tonight.

Candy didn't come back to our dressing room, either. Must have undressed in Genevieve's. I sat there alone, waiting for the police, like Linda had requested.

After what seemed like hours, a knock.

"Olive?"

A familiar voice. Pinkstaff. Finally someone who wouldn't be pissed off at me. Maybe, *maybe* he'd even congratulate me.

"Can you believe it?" I put on a bright face as I opened the door. "I pulled a Poirot and it worked."

I stopped. Pink's eyebrows were drawn so close together they nearly touched.

"Come with me." He jerked his head in the direction of backstage. I followed him dutifully, my heart sinking further with every step, but without knowing why.

Linda, who had been in the hall with Pink, followed too. Most of the cast fell into line behind us, walking with us to the Cage. Waiting to see what would happen next. I waited, too. Pinkstaff hadn't said another word to me.

Bill now sat on the oily floor. When he saw Pinkstaff, recognition flashed in his eyes, and then something else. Fear? He jumped up, tossed off his top hat, tore off his tailcoat, and started rubbing his face with it.

"What the...?" said Pink.

"I can't go to jail like this," Bill said in a whiny voice. "In costume and makeup?" He stopped wiping the makeup off his face and began taking off his skin-tight black satin pants.

"Keep your pants on," said Pinkstaff. "Olive should have kept hers on. Ivy, I mean. Her." He jerked his thumb at me. I wished I knew what he was talking about. No. Scratch that. I really didn't want to know.

"Besides," said Candy, "isn't goin' to jail in your skivvies worse than goin' in costume?"

Bill stopped undressing.

Pink showed Bill his badge. "Detective Pinkstaff, Phoenix PD," he said. "I'd like to talk to you."

"Watch it, Bill," said Riley, "He might be playing 'good cop, bad cop' like they do on TV."

Pink looked at Riley. "You see another cop here?"

"Maybe you're playing both parts."

"Why would I do that?"

"Cutbacks?" asked Bill, who was smoothing his rumpled hair. "Just the other day I reported on city deficits."

"Shut up, Bill." Linda unlocked the Cage with a jangle of keys.

"No reporters?" Bill stepped out of the Cage. "And you came alone? No other police?"

Pinkstaff didn't say a word, just steered Bill down the hall. Linda walked ahead of us, opened the unlocked door to her office, and held it. Pink guided Bill into the room. "Olive, you too," he said, nodding at me. "Everyone else, take off."

Inside Linda's office, Jason sat up straight in a stained burnt orange chair, staring fixedly at nothing. I decided to stand next to Linda's desk, hoping that not taking a seat would somehow make whatever was going to happen, happen quicker. Linda closed the door and Pink guided Bill to the middle of the room, where they both stopped and stood.

The only noise in the room was the ticking of the cat clock with the swinging tail. Pinkstaff looked at Jason. Jason looked at Bill, who looked at the floor. I looked at Jason, who wouldn't look at me. All this looking must have gotten to Bill.

"I didn't mean to kill him," he blurted.

"And you didn't," said Pink.

My mouth opened of its own accord. So did Bill's. I shut mine.

"Ivy here jumped the gun," said Pinkstaff.

"But you said the makeup—" The glare Pink gave me could've stopped a train, much less my runaway mouth.

"The makeup," Pink said to Bill. "It was mixed with what, poison oak?"

Bill nodded. "Some of it grows near my cabin in Oak Creek."

"Poison oak didn't kill Simon," said Pinkstaff.

I had publicly accused an innocent man of murder. "Bill, I'm so sorry." It was all I could say.

"You didn't kill Simon." Pink continued, giving Bill a hard look. "But Jason here had a pretty bad reaction."

"That was poison oak?" I asked. "His swelling and everything?"

"Yeah." Pinkstaff didn't look at me. "It has an oil that usually causes a rash and blisters, but some people are really allergic. Jason must have licked his lips or something and swallowed some." He pointed a finger in Bill's direction, stabbing the air for emphasis. "You could've killed him. If he'd died, you might have been charged with involuntary manslaughter. You could still be charged with assault."

"I never meant..." Bill's voice was whispery and high. "I just hoped the makeup would make Simon sick enough to need an understudy. I never even considered it might hurt anyone else." He squeezed his eyes shut and looked at the floor. "I'm sorry, Jason." He sank into Linda's office chair.

Pinkstaff's hands were stuck deep in his pockets, like he was afraid of what they might do. "Jason," he said. "Should we press charges?"

Jason's face was still puffy and splotchy from the poison oak, and his makeup barely hid the remnant of the shiner Bill had given him. "No." Jason shook his head, like he was disgusted. He pushed himself up out of the chair, then turned on his heel and left, slamming the door.

Bill's face, which had been gray and pinched, regained its color. A small smile of relief played on his lips. Pinkstaff took his hands out of his pockets with a shrug and nodded at him. "You can go."

Bill turned to Linda. "Can I still do the show tomorrow?"

"Yeah," she said, shaking her head at him.

Bill strode toward the door, his smile now all wounded dignity, playing the king already. As he passed by me on the way to the door, he gave me a slight, magnanimous nod. "Pardon me," he said. His newscaster voice was back.

# CHAPTER 42

## *The Harvest Is Your Own*

I went to follow Bill, but Pink stepped in front of the door. "Get your stuff," he said. "You're coming with me."

I turned to look at Linda. No help there, but a kitten clinging to a branch on a yellowed poster shouted, "Hang in there!" I hoped I could.

I grabbed my duffle bag from my dressing room and followed Pink out to his car. I climbed in over what looked to be the same pop cans that rolled around the floor on my last ride, when I was still in favor.

Pink didn't say anything as we pulled out of the theater parking lot, just smoked a cigarette that smelled a little like Vapo Rub.

I didn't say anything, either, until he made a wrong turn.

"Hey," I said, craning my head to look behind us. "The police station is the other direction."

"Uh-huh." He continued going north when he should have been going south.

"You're not taking me to the station?"

Pink sighed and tossed his cigarette stub out the window.

"Taking you somewhere else."

"Where?"

"Someplace where your punishment will fit your crime."

I looked to see if he was kidding. He looked serious. Then he turned onto a palm tree-lined street I knew well. I shut my eyes. "Oh no." I knew what was coming.

"Oh, yes," said Pinkstaff, and I heard the gravel crunch as he pulled into Uncle Bob's drive.

Imagine a very, very angry Santa Claus. That was my uncle when we walked in the door.

"Um, hi Uncle Bob," I said. He was still in his rented medical bed. The room smelled of disinfectant and boiled hotdogs.

No reply, just a steady gaze. I felt like Christmas had been cancelled permanently.

Pinkstaff shut the front door behind us. He nodded to my uncle and walked past us up the two stairs and down the hall. I wanted to follow him, go hide in one of the bedrooms. Instead I sat down in the chair next to Uncle Bob's bed.

I sat. I waited. Damned if I was going to be the first to break the silence. Everything I had done was well-intended. All I wanted to do was exonerate Simon. And catch the person who had hurt Jason. And Uncle Bob.

"I did it for you, too, you know." So much for waiting. And sitting. I was up and pacing the floor before I even knew I was doing it. "I mean, someone had to go after whoever poisoned you and Jason and Simon, who, yes, I'm sure was poisoned. I know I disobeyed you, but I don't know why everyone's so pissed at me when all I did was—"

"Lie," said my uncle with that unwavering gaze.

I felt like he'd socked me in the stomach. I sat down again.

"You know, Olive," he said. "There's a little thing and a big thing. Yeah, I'm pissed that you 'disobeyed' me. I may not be God. I'm not even your dad. But I am your boss and someone who cares about you. I don't give orders lightly."

"That's the little thing?" My leg began to jiggle.

He nodded.

"The big thing, the really big thing, is that you lied to me. If you had told me what you were doing, even if we disagreed, we coulda talked it through, probably avoided this mess you've got yourself into. But instead, you lied to me."

"Not out loud." I already wished I hadn't said it.

"Lots of types of lies," said my uncle. "And they all destroy trust." He finally took his eyes off mine. "Pink!" he shouted. "We're through here."

Pink shuffled out of the hall and toward the front door. I got up and followed him.

"Olive," said my uncle quietly. "I do mean through. I love you, but I can't work with someone I don't trust. You're fired."

# CHAPTER 43

## The Sin of My Ingratitude

The next day I sat on the couch in my stifling apartment and watched my favorite telenovela. The villainess had just lied her way into a hospital so she could poison her stepfather.

I turned it off.

I hadn't meant to lie to Uncle Bob. I didn't even really feel like I had lied, more just ignored him. Denied there was an issue. Wow, like I hadn't heard that phrase about a million times before. Oh shit. I'd forgotten yet another promise to Uncle Bob. I needed to find the name of a good therapist. One who worked really, really cheap.

I'd do it later.

I went to the kitchen and opened the refrigerator. I did it for the cool air, not because I wanted anything to eat. That was a good thing, too, since a quick check showed butter, milk, some cream cheese in a crusty-looking foil wrapper, and a bottle of champagne Simon had given me when he cleaned out his fridge.

Simon. Had I really gone through all of this for him? I suspected not. I suspected I was "denying there was an issue." I suspected this was really about Cody.

Cody. Crap. I'd never gotten him tickets to the show, never even thought about it again.

I called him in the afternoon, as soon as he got off work. He was thrilled. He and Matt would be there closing night.

He was just about to hang up when I said, "Listen, Cody?"

"Yeah?"

"Would you like to spend more time together?"

"Um...yeah?"

I needed to be more concrete. "I was thinking about..." I stopped. I'd been about to say "Suns games," but I couldn't afford the tickets now. And I realized I didn't know enough about Cody to suggest something. "What would you like to do?"

"Go to plays?"

Perfect. I could almost always get into previews for free. "Great. I'll figure it out and we'll make a date for next month. Cool?"

"Cool." He hung up, but not before I understood that Cody knew what I liked to do.

# CHAPTER 44

## *Thy Hope Ends Here*

A few minutes after I hung up with Cody, my phone rang. I ran to pick it up. I had called and texted Jason about a billion times since last night.

I didn't recognize the number. "Hello?" Maybe Jason was calling from somewhere else.

"¿Oye hermano, que pasa?"

I didn't think he was calling from that far away.

"I think you may have the wrong number."

"No esta Pablo?"

"No," I said. "Lo siento." I'm sorry. It was one of the few Spanish phrases I knew.

I hung up and walked over to the thermostat. Ninety degrees. I turned the air conditioning down to seventy-two. A clunk, and then cool air poured out of a vent near the bedroom. I went and stood in front of it for a minute, the sweat cooling and then drying on my skin. Lovely. Then I went back and turned the thermostat back to ninety. The theater would pay me tomorrow for the run, but after that I had no source of income. No day job, no acting work. Nothing. I guess *Macbeth*'s curse didn't just stop at death and poisoning.

I ate a quick dinner of Top Ramen and drove to the theater. I'd be early, but I could cool down and maybe even catch Jason during his prep time.

At 5:30 I climbed the stairs to the loading dock. I didn't want to go through the greenroom. Never know who else might decide to show up early, and my courage, though fortified with carbohydrates, was shaky.

I swung open the heavy door and stepped into the chilled darkness. I closed it quietly so I wouldn't interrupt Jason's preparations, but the latch's soft click seemed to reverberate throughout the cavernous backstage.

No need to worry. Jason's voice boomed out. "We will proceed no further in this business."

He was here. I walked toward the sound, toward the stage, my heart beating a tattoo. "A drum, a drum, Ivy doth come!" sounded over and over in my head. Great, a Shakespearean earworm.

I was walking out from behind the black velvet curtains when the earworm turned itself off. Something wasn't right. I stopped and listened to Jason. Huh. This wasn't one of Macbeth's monologues.

"Was the hope drunk Wherein you dress'd yourself? hath it slept since?" said Genevieve. Yes. This was a scene with the Macbeths. I ducked back behind the curtain.

"And wakes it now, to look so green and pale At what it did so freely?" Genevieve continued. Though her voice was tinged with anger, her overall message was seduction. I felt a stab of envy. How did she do that? Maybe I should look into a Method acting class.

Except that, of course, my acting career was dead. But I couldn't worry about that. I had other important business to take care of. I was here to try to revive my comatose romance.

"Prithee, peace," Jason said to Genevieve in a dangerously soft whisper. "I dare do all that may become a man; Who dares do more is none."

I would wait until the end of the scene. Jason and I would still have plenty of time to talk.

"What beast was't, then, That made you break this enterprise to me?" Genevieve said.

I would quietly announce myself and ask to speak to Jason privately.

"When you durst do it, then you were a man." Genevieve's voice was smoky and smooth, like good liquor. "And, to be more than what you were, you would Be so much more the man."

Silence.

Genevieve never took a pause here. I peeked out from behind my curtain. Genevieve was trailing her hand down Jason's chest. "You would be so much more the man," she repeated, reaching lower. Jason shut his eyes as her hand moved slowly down. He grabbed her by the hair. She arched her neck in pleasure and he fell upon it with a vampire-like hunger.

I drew back into the folds of the curtain. I didn't want to see this. Maybe if I didn't see it, it wasn't really happening.

Soft footsteps came toward me. I inched deeper into the curtain. They passed by, Genevieve leading Jason by the hand. I shut my eyes and tried to think of ways to leave without being seen.

The footsteps stopped suddenly.

"No," I heard Jason say. "Not here."

"Is it because of the little witch?" Genevieve asked.

Had she seen me? I opened my eyes. No, they weren't looking my way. Instead, the Macbeths stood in front of the hiding place where Jason and I had made love, just yesterday. Genevieve knew?

Jason didn't reply. While they were intent on each other, I hotfooted it for the exit to the greenroom as quietly as possible. I was pretty dang focused on making it out of there, but I thought I heard Genevieve say, "Or because of what happened here opening night?"

# CHAPTER 45

## *Foul Is Fair*

I got out of the backstage area without being seen and stumbled into the greenroom. The show passed without incident, and without anyone saying a word to me.

After the show, I was slinging my duffle bag over my shoulder when there was a knock on the dressing room door. My heart leapt, just a little, more of a hop, really. It had to be...

Bill? I opened the door to The Face of Channel 10. He usually knocked as he came in, but tonight he stood awkwardly outside the door.

"Come in," I said, dropping my bag on the counter. Bill looked around before entering, as if to make sure no one was lurking in the corner.

"I wanted to tell you there are no hard feelings," he said.

"Wow. Thanks." I meant it. "Seems like you're the only one."

A mirthless chuckle. "We are not well-liked."

Ouch.

Bill sat in Candy's empty chair. "And I think I know why." He looked into the mirror, wet a finger and ran it over an unruly eyebrow hair.

I thought I knew why, too, but waited anyway.

"It's all about Simon."

I bit my lip in an attempt to be patient. Bill was the only

person speaking to me right now. Maybe soon he'd actually say something.

He met my eyes in the mirror. "I am an investigative reporter, you know. And you are a detective."

"I'm really not—"

"And we've turned over a few stones that have snakes underneath them."

Jason had said that Bill questioned him about his whereabouts on opening night. "I knew you'd talked to a few people," I said, "but I assumed you were making sure no one saw you messing with Simon's makeup."

"Yes. Well, yes." Bill now smoothed both eyebrows, pressing down hard. "But my investigation turned up some very interesting information." He swiveled in his chair to look at me. "Several people have no alibi," he said in his broadcaster's voice.

Uh oh. Was he acting? Goddammit, was everybody acting? I spun away from Bill.

I was suddenly mad at the entire theater world. How could you have relationships with people if you never knew when they were being real?

"Ivy." Bill's real voice. And my name, right for the first time.

"Who?" I turned back to him. "Who has no alibi?"

"Well, most people, actually, except for Riley and some of the soldiers. They were shooting off fireworks on the loading dock."

"Okay, thanks." I picked up my duffle bag.

Bill stood. "I have it on good authority that Edward was nowhere to be seen during intermission."

I put the bag back down. Edward should have been with Pamela in the theater lobby, schmoozing with the audience or at least the board members. I tried to remember if I'd seen him at all that night. I didn't think so.

"Was he giving notes?" I asked. After each rehearsal, a director gave actors feedback on their performances. It was bad form to continue this after a show was on its feet, but every so often a director couldn't let go.

"No." Bill gave a smug little smile, the kind that always made me want to slap him.

I bit my lip again, trying to remember he was my only ally. "Still, that doesn't mean—"

"And someone saw him sneaking into the house from backstage."

"He could have been checking on a set issue."

"Sneaking. Looking around to make sure no one saw him."

"Who said this? Who saw him?"

"Genevieve."

# CHAPTER 46

## All Is Over

There was no way I was going to talk to Genevieve, not after I'd seen her with Jason. Besides, it wasn't enough. I knew Simon wasn't killed by poisoned makeup. Bill's makeup/poison oak concoction caused swelling. Jason's face and throat were classic examples. Pink said only certain substances—narcotics, sedatives, and tranquilizers—could have created the illusion of alcohol poisoning and that Simon most likely drank himself to death.

Bill was wrong, at least where it concerned me. This wasn't all about Simon. It was about the denial of long-buried guilt. I wasn't going to deny that any longer.

I thanked Bill and walked out into the night.

"Want another Diet Coke?" It was Homeless Hank.

"I'm good," I said, and gave him the dollar bill I had in my shorts pocket. I had more Ramen at home.

That was another thing. Even if Uncle Bob's Diet Coke had been tampered with, it was probably one of Riley's jokes taken a little too far.

I had made the facts fit the scenario I wanted. I had even misinterpreted Simon's sobriety tally (the paper taped to the mirror). Simon had crossed off all the numbers representing the days he'd been sober. Except for the last one. No X through number 38, Simon's last day on earth.

I slept through most of the next day, drove to the theater, and sat sweating in the parking lot. It was closing night. Maybe my last closing night. I couldn't believe I'd screwed up so badly. No theater in the Valley would hire me after this. Maybe I could move, start over. No. It had taken me quite awhile to get to this level. In a new town, I'd probably have to work a few years before I could get the professional gigs. I didn't have a few years. Women get cast when they're young and when they're old. I needed to get established while I could still play the ingénue (and the occasional tumbling witch) so I would have a chance for the few roles offered to women between thirty-five and sixty. I'd blown it.

Maybe I should throw in the towel now, not even go in tonight. Edward could fill in for me. I felt the edges of my mouth tug up as I imagined Edward in my iridescent leotard. It'd serve him right. But I couldn't do it. Cody was coming to the show tonight with Matt. I got out of the car, but not before noticing the clock: 7:15. Yikes! I was already late—call was 7:00. I threw my keys into my duffel bag, jumped out and ran to the front of the theater.

I skidded to a stop in front of the glassed-in booth that served as the box office. I'd left a message about tickets for tonight but needed to pay for them. There was only one window open—maybe because it was closing night?—and a line six people deep. I got in line behind all six of them.

"Are these the best seats you have?"

The woman at the front of the line leaned in close to the box office's glass window, wobbling on pointy-toed leopard-skin heels that brought her height up to a full five feet. Her hair was a freshly dyed bright orange, except for an overlooked section in the back where her part showed a streak of white. She peered at the young woman in the fluorescently lit box office. Her hair was dyed flat black, to contrast her kabuki-white makeup and blood red lips.

"Because I've been supporting this theater for years," said Orange.

Black started to chew on a thumbnail (also colored black), then thought better of it. "These are the best seats in the mezzanine level."

"Do you have any in the front couple of rows?"

"Yes. But your season tickets are for the mezzanine. The front rows are orchestra level tickets, which are an additional $15." Black picked at the chipped polish on her thumbnail.

Orange's voice got louder, "But I've been coming to this theater since 1967."

I checked my watch. 7:18. My leg started to jiggle of its own accord.

"I'm sorry, ma'am, but I can't upgrade you without an additional fifteen dollars per seat." Black stared at her thumbnail, as if it might magically whisk her away from the box office.

"Do you know how much money that is to someone like me? I'm on a fixed income, you know, and I've been coming to this theater since—"

I couldn't stand it any longer.

"Sorry, sorry," I said to everyone in line as I pushed ahead of them. "I'm in the show and need to get in costume."

The line broke up to let me through. Orange glared at me as I stepped in front of her, and Black gave me a stony stare through the box office window.

"I need to pay for some tickets you have set aside for Ivy—" I began.

"I know who you are," said Black, flipping through her neatly organized box of tickets, thumbnail forgotten.

She knew me. I smiled at her.

She smiled back at me, showing small vampire-like teeth. "You're Poison Ivy," she said. "We were taking bets on whether you'd show up tonight. Guess I lost."

Poison Ivy.

"Are we in line for the wrong show?" said a voice in line behind me. "There's no Poison Ivy in *Macbeth*, is there?"

I wished there weren't. I would have left right then if it weren't for Cody. I shoved my cash at Black and spun around to go.

Orange must have been right on my heels. When I turned I was nearly on top of her. "About my seats..." she continued, shoving me aside.

"Ouch!" I yelped. A leopard-skin heel had come down on top of my shoe.

"Oops," said Orange, releasing my foot. "Sorry."

I thought I saw Orange and Black smile.

I ran to the backstage door and through the greenroom to our dressing room. Candy wasn't there. She must have already dressed. I sat down in the chair in my place in front of the mirror and took off my shoes, rubbing the foot Orange had stepped on.

Candy's counter space was filled with flowers and goodies, typical closing night presents from other cast members. My space was bare, except for a headshot: "To Ivy, from The Face of Channel 10." At least he got my name right.

I didn't have time to dwell on my lack of friends. I needed to get dressed and to prepare for what was likely my last performance. Stop it, Ivy. No time to dwell on that, either. I pulled my T-shirt over my head, but it snagged on an earring. I heard the door open.

"Candy," I said, head still stuck in my T-shirt. "I'm so sorry I didn't tell you about the makeup and my suspicions, but you were acting suspicious, too, whispering with Genevieve and..."

I heard the door shut. I disentangled my earring and yanked my T-shirt all the way off. The dressing room was empty, but not for long. Candy burst in, brown liquid dripping off her. "Dang. That Riley makes me mad as a wet hen."

She looked like a mad wet hen too, but I didn't want to go there. At least she was speaking to me. I pulled off my shorts and my underwear.

"You'd think he'd have gotten over the whole Mentos-Diet Coke thing, but no." Candy stripped down and threw her leotard in the sink.

I knew it was her one and only leotard. "Do you really want to wash that right now?" I asked, pulling on my tights.

"I'm gonna be wet one way or the other. I'd rather be wet and clean than wet and sticky." She turned on the faucet. The diamondback pattern on her leotard undulated in the water.

"Listen, I meant what I said a minute ago."

"Huh?" said Candy, more interested in wringing out her costume than in me. I stepped into my camel toe leotard for the last time.

"About being sorry," I said. "It was just that you started keeping secrets from me, and it made me—"

"What are you talking about?"

"Just what I said earlier, about you and Genevieve." I slathered foundation over my face and neck.

"Hon, you do realize this is the first time we've talked today?"

I had a bad feeling.

"Did you see someone come out of our dressing room a minute ago?"

"I was too busy taking my Diet Coke shower. Why? Someone come in and poison your makeup?"

Shit. I dropped my makeup sponge like it was a hot biscuit. I sniffed my makeup bottle. It smelled like chemicals and the scents they use to cover up the smell of chemicals. Like makeup.

Candy sighed loudly. "Ivy. Darlin'. You gotta give this up."

In the mirror I could see her struggle into her wet, clinging leotard. I started to work on my eye makeup.

"Everyone knows there hasn't been any murder."

She was right. I knew she was right. I had misplaced my guilt over Cody's accident and made everything a bigger deal than it was. Right?

Candy met my eyes in the mirror. "Simon died. He just died. It wasn't murder and it wasn't your fault."

She put a light, damp hand on my shoulder. "Hon, I know about your brother. Jason told us."

Jason. Told. Us. My hands felt icy. I didn't trust myself to speak.

Candy hugged me from behind. "You can't keep blaming yourself for what happened with your brother, or with Simon. They were accidents. You gotta get over it."

She patted me, the way people do when they're done with you.

"And you gotta get over it now, 'cause—"

"Places." Linda's voice came over the dressing room's loudspeaker.

"We have to be witches," Candy continued. "Okay?"

I nodded, scribbled on some lipstick, and held my own cold hands as we left to go onstage.

# CHAPTER 47

## *Though the Brightest Fell*

I stood in the wings and watched Jason and Genevieve plot murder under the bright stage lights. I wondered if I could kill anyone. Like them. I certainly felt like it. My hands clenched by themselves and I realized they were still icy.

It was nearly intermission. I'd done a presentable job of my first two scenes, but not anything that would have made people jump up out of their seats. Not anything that could save my acting career. I'd torpedoed my own boat, and for what? Everyone knew there hadn't been a murder. That's what Candy said.

Onstage, Jason and Genevieve settled upon killing Duncan after inviting him into their home. "False face must hide what the false heart doth know!" said Macbeth/Jason as he strode offstage, head down. Yeah, he should know. Bastard. I'd told him the Cody story in confidence. He knew that I never told anyone, and that I told him because I thought that he and I...

He passed close by me, so near that I felt the curtains move. He didn't deign to acknowledge me. It'd been only a few days since we'd made love. He'd been so tender. I felt my eyes prickle and leaned into the black velvet curtain to hide my face. As I did, I realized it was the same one Jason had wrapped around us when we kissed on opening night. It felt like years had passed since then.

Now, he went to Genevieve, who waited in the wings. He put a hand on her waist and spoke to her, their faces inches apart. She toyed with his lion tamer's whip. I swear he glanced my way, to see if I was watching. He'd actively avoided me since the whole debacle with Bill. Why was he so pissed at me? I was the one betrayed.

Betrayal. Such a Shakespearean concept. Well, Shakespeare's truths are timeless. I felt like such a fool. Another Shakespearean concept. He wrote about two kinds of fools, though. There were the fools who were really wise, like Lear's fool, and then there were the poor deluded suckers like Duncan who believed in friends who killed them in their sleep. So which one was I?

# CHAPTER 48

## *What's Done Is Done*

I made it through the last witches' scene without incident and without looking at Jason. Quite a feat, since I was supposed to be speaking to him. I focused on the top of his head. That way Jason would know I was pissed too, and I figured it would look pretty witchy.

Afterwards, as we all crouched in the cauldron as it was hauled into the air, Candy said, "Did you forget your contacts or something?"

I don't wear contacts. Guess I didn't look witchy, just myopic.

Back in our dressing room, I tugged down my ever-creeping leotard and waited for curtain call. I wondered if Candy would notice if I ate a chocolate out of the box someone had left her. Probably. I eyed her other closing night stash. Lots of MoonPies, naturally, a few cards, and a red rose. I leaned over to see if I could tell who had signed the card stuck in the bud vase. Of course, that's when Candy walked in.

"You better not have snitched any of my MoonPies," she said. "I counted 'em."

She threw herself into the chair in front of her counter space.

"The rose is from Genevieve, if you must know," said Candy, rearranging the rubber snake in her wig. "Don't know why she picked a red one. Probably had it left over from the bunch she sent to Jason. Guess they're having a thing now."

Whatever camaraderie I'd felt before the show evaporated. I pushed my chair away from the counter and stood. "I'm going backstage to wait for bows."

Something hit me in the back as I was opening the door. I turned. A wrapped MoonPie had bounced off my back and lay at my feet.

"Sorry, I was being a bitch," Candy said. "I hate closing night. Everybody going their own way and me having to figure out what's next." She unwrapped a MoonPie. "Just hate it."

I picked up the marshmallowy peace offering and sat back in my chair.

"I'm sorry, too," I said. "Things got weird. You were hanging around with Genevieve, and it felt like there was something going on I didn't know about."

I took a bite of MoonPie for the sugar courage it gave me. "And I heard you say 'murder' before bows one night. You were probably going to murder Riley or something, but I was afraid you'd told Genevieve about my suspicions."

"I did," she said, digging into her own treat. "Not right then, before. I didn't think it was a big deal. Like I said before, nobody really thinks Simon's death was—"

"But I told you not to."

She sighed. "It was really late, like three in the morning or something, and we were on set and I was dog-tired and..." She stopped and stuffed the rest of the MoonPie in her mouth.

Candy never quit talking if she could help it. It must be a clue.

"Wait a minute, on set? You got that film role?"

She pointed to her mouth full of marshmallow.

I pointed back at her. "Finish. I can wait."

But I couldn't. "You were in a film with Genevieve? How could I, hell, how could the entire cast not know about this? You can't fart around here without everyone knowing."

Candy was taking her time with that MoonPie.

"Why didn't you tell me you were in a film with Genevieve?"

She finally swallowed. "She told me not to."

"Why not?" Oh. The lights went on. "What type of film is it?"

She swallowed. "It's an art film."

"What's it called?"

Candy stuffed another MoonPie in her mouth.

"Not falling for that," I said. "The film?"

"Ish caw Achow-uhnt o Ile," said Candy.

Luckily I spoke MoonPie. "It's called *Accountants Go Wild*? So Genevieve, the great actress, is doing softcore porn. No wonder she didn't want anyone to know."

"It's not porn."

"Okay," I said, sitting back in my chair, "tell me about your costume."

She was silent.

"It's alright, sweetie," I said. "Really. I won't tell."

Linda's voice came through the loudspeaker. "Places for curtain call."

Candy and I heaved ourselves out of our chairs.

"At least I turned down the one where I was eaten by a giant mechanical vagina," Candy said.

"Good for you," I said, and meant it. Then I noticed my cell phone. I had voicemail.

Candy saw my glance. "Later, hon. Bows first."

But, as my Uncle Bob liked to say, if you looked under "curious" in the dictionary they'd have my picture.

"I'll catch up."

Candy shook her head at me and hurried down the hall.

"You have one new message," said the calm voice on my cell. Then I heard a not-so-calm voice. "Ivy, Olive, whatever the hell your name is, it's Pink. Detective Pinkstaff. Pink. Shit." This was new. He was usually pretty direct.

"About Bob, your uncle I mean. The tests came back. He was drugged. I think something's up down there at the theater. Watch your back, okay?"

I hung up my phone and ran toward backstage, my thoughts running alongside me. Could Bill have poisoned Uncle Bob, too?

No, the effects seemed completely different. Uncle Bob didn't swell up like Jason. It had to be a different drug. I doubted if Bill was smart enough to figure out two different ways to poison someone.

I heard the applause just as I skidded into place beside Candy. The entire cast was backstage, waiting in the little groups Edward had assigned for curtain call.

Candy elbowed me. "What was it? Your message?"

"Uncle Bob," I whispered. "The lab test came back."

"Oh my God, was your uncle poisoned?" Candy's voice was so loud the old guy in the front row using the hearing thingy could have heard her.

How could she be so obtuse? I shook my head at her, hoping the cast would see me and take it for a "no," and then ran onstage with her and The Real Witch to take our curtain call. As we linked hands and bowed, I wondered about Candy again. Could she have had anything to do with Simon's murder or my uncle's poisoning? I usually had a pretty good instinct about people, but hell, Jason certainly had me fooled. Maybe I was wrong about Candy, too. I mentally added her to my suspect list, then realized I had a suspect list again. It felt kinda good. Knowing I hadn't been totally off base made me feel vindicated in a weird sort of way. For about two seconds. Then I felt awful. There was probably a murderer loose and I was gloating about being right.

We witches trotted offstage, where we waited in the wings. Edward had choreographed the bows so the entire cast was onstage at the end, which was typical for curtain call. The size of our cast, though, was not typical. Only musicals and Shakespearean plays had such large casts nowadays, thanks to arts budget cuts. Seeing everyone onstage at the same time was pretty impressive, and it usually resulted in thunderous applause. I was ready. I decided to put Uncle Bob out of my mind for now. Who knew when I'd be onstage again? I'd just wasted our witches' bow thinking about Candy, instead of really being in the moment. Applause feels wonderful. During this last bow, which might truly be my final bow, I was going to revel in the adulation.

It came time. I walked onstage and stood in my place, nearly the very edge of stage left. I could feel the heat from the lights on my face. One of the things I love about being onstage is the lights are so blinding they actually hide the audience from you. You feel like you're in your own little world, like you're really a witch speaking with a king. This time, though, I was done with the cast, with the whole stupid circus world of *Macbeth*. I decided to look past the lights, so that my last onstage memory would be of applause.

I didn't have to worry. As I listened to the enthusiastic but genteel applause, two voices stood out, mostly because they were whooping and hollering.

"Olive-y! Yay, Olive-y! Woo-hoo!" I could see Cody's blonde head and Matt's curly one as they stood and cheered. I felt my face flush, not with the heat of the lights, but with love. If I had to leave the theater, this was the way to go.

# CHAPTER 49

## *The Instruments of Darkness*

"Yay, Olive-y!" echoed in my head as I walked back to the greenroom. I kept that echo there on purpose, replaying that one past moment so I wouldn't have to deal with the present. The present sucked. Someone had murdered Simon and poisoned my uncle, who was royally pissed at me with good reason. My supposed boyfriend was now un-supposed. My career was over, and the cast, with whom I'd spent hours laughing and talking and bonding, was not speaking to me. I didn't count Candy. I didn't know what to think of Candy right now.

I walked into the greenroom where Riley was high-fiving all the cast. I held up a hand hopefully, but he went right past me.

Edward, Pamela by his side, was talking to Jason. "So we'll remount the Scottish play next summer in Sedona. We don't have a date yet, as I wanted to make sure you and Genevieve were available. You and she make such a wonderful couple." He looked straight at me as he said it and smiled. "Most of the cast will be joining us," continued Edward, twisting the knife further.

"I got it. I got it," I muttered under my breath.

I was headed toward the dressing rooms, my eyes on the floor so I wouldn't have to face any more rejection, when I ran into a pair of red sneakers planted in my path. I looked up to see the first smiling face I'd seen all evening.

"Nice job, Olive-y," said Matt.

He wore a blue retro dinner jacket over a gray T-shirt, Levis, and the aforementioned sneakers. He noticed me giving him the onceover.

"Don't exactly have formal clothes anymore," he said. "But hey, it's Phoenix, right?" He grinned.

"I think you look delicious," said Candy, who'd come up behind me. "Are you going to introduce us, hon, or keep this fine young gentleman all to yourself?"

She actually batted her eyes at him. He smiled and extended his hand. "Matt Jenkins, at your service."

"At my service? I may just put you to work."

God, she was laying it on thick. I grabbed her arm.

"We'll go change out of these costumes." I looked down at myself, suddenly acutely aware of my flimsy leotard and its accompanying camel toe. I crossed my legs and dropped my hands, hoping to obscure the offending area. "And meet up back here with you and..." I looked around. "Hey, where's Cody?"

"One of the cast members said she'd give him a backstage tour," said Matt.

"Great," I said, tugging on Candy. "We'll be with you in a minute. Then maybe we can go get coffee or something."

"Or something," said Candy with a wink. God.

I manhandled her back into the dressing room and shut the door. She started stripping immediately.

"Lordy, that Matt is cute as a bug's ear," she said.

"Yeah," I said. He was cute. I hadn't noticed before.

"Matt Jenkins..." she sang. I recognized the tune to "Maria" from *West Side Story*, but just barely.

"I just met a boy named Matt Jenkins..."

Oh, what the hell. I joined her, "And suddenly that name will never be the same..."

I did a little pirouette. As I spun, something caught my eye. My cell phone, sitting on the counter, right where I'd left it after listening to Pinkstaff's message.

I stopped mid-spin. This was no time to sing. After tonight, the cast would split up. If I were going to find a killer, it was tonight. Now.

Think, Ivy, think! Suspects: Bill, no.

Linda? Definitely. Motive and opportunity. But God forbid I jump to another wrong conclusion, so I considered the others.

Jason? He was a bastard and a two-timer, but was he a killer? I didn't think so, but there was still the question of what he'd been doing on opening night. And other nights.

Edward could have done it. He'd said, "I wouldn't poison Jason." It seemed he purposely didn't say anything about Simon. And there was Pamela and the Rémy Martin and sneaking around on opening night. Edward had motive.

"Ivy?"

I looked at Candy, who had noticed both my mood change and the fact that I was staring at my cell phone. Smart, Ivy, really smart.

"What happened with your uncle's lab test? Was he poisoned?"

I shook my head and started taking off my costume.

"C'mon, hon. You can tell me."

But could I? Candy didn't have a motive, at least not one I knew about, but she was acting suspicious. And reading my mind, it seemed. "Listen, I am your friend," she said.

I kicked off my tights and bit into my half-eaten MoonPie, employing Candy's own evasion tactic.

"I know you're worried about me and Genevieve, but you oughta give her a break," she said. "She's really a big pussycat."

I must have looked incredulous because she added, "For instance, she was the one who put that wad of cash in the kitty at Simon's memorial." The MoonPie was too sweet. I put it down and pulled on my panties. My always-busy mind was startlingly quiet, like the calm before a storm.

"Which was especially nice," said Candy, "since they weren't exactly friendly any more, if you know what I mean. Getting dumped twice by the same guy had to hurt."

"Dumped by?"

"Simon." Candy made a "duh" face at me. "Once when they

were up in Flagstaff for a summer theater gig—remember Simon dated Lucy, Linda's girlfriend? He dumped Genevieve for her. And then he did it again during rehearsals."

"Our rehearsals?"

"Not exactly dumped—she wanted to get back together. He didn't. But like I was saying, or was trying to say, I thought it was real nice of her to give all that cash in Simon's memory. I guess she's not hurtin', though. She's got a bunch of money from when her mama died."

"How did she die?" I asked as I hooked my bra. My little gray cells started sorting the information.

"She had some sort of nasty painful cancer. I guess it was awful. Genevieve took care of her at the end. She had to keep her so pumped full of morphine that—"

Dumped. Morphine. Genevieve. It all clicked into place. I stood but couldn't move. Something else, something else, something else was wrong.

Matt's face flashed into my head. "One of the cast members said she'd give him a backstage tour."

Cody.

I ran out of the dressing room, Candy flying behind me.

"Ivy!" she yelled.

As I whizzed past startled faces in the greenroom, I realized I was only wearing underwear. It didn't matter.

# CHAPTER 50

## The Taste of Fears

I sprinted toward backstage. As I opened the door, a sea of black-clad techies almost knocked me over. One of them wolf whistled. "Nice underwear!"

"What's going on?" I said, struggling against the current of burly men.

"Free beer in the parking lot," said one of the guys who hauled the cauldron into the air every night. "Closing night present from Edward."

I pushed my way through to backstage and stood for a moment, bouncing on my bare heels. Which way to go? Where would Genevieve take Cody?

I ran toward the hiding space where Jason and I and Jason and Genevieve had...

Empty.

I scrambled toward the loading dock, threw open the door and peered outside.

No one.

As I stopped to listen, I heard a clang—the ring of something against metal. But where was it coming from? The floor was wooden. The set, wooden.

Another clang, followed by a skidding sound. I hadn't heard this noise before, not during the entire run of the show. Why not?

"An outstanding view of the stage don't you agree?" Genevieve's voice. From above me.

Hoping to hell I was wrong, I hid myself in a curtain and looked up. Genevieve and Cody stood on the metal catwalk that ran above the stage, a good thirty-five feet up. Cody was dressed for the theater, from his suit and ties down to his shined shoes. He took a step forward and the heel of his dress shoe rang against the metal. I realized I'd never heard the noise before because no one was foolish enough to wear hard-soled shoes on the catwalk. I suddenly remembered the skidding sound and thought I might be sick.

"We're high," said Cody. He walked slowly along the narrow catwalk, swaying from side to side. I choked down the vomit rising fast in my throat.

"Yes," said Genevieve. "This castle hath a pleasant seat; the air Nimbly and sweetly recommends itself Unto our gentle senses." She placed a hand on the small of his back.

I froze. She wouldn't. Not Cody.

To get to them, I'd have to make it to the ladder, climb up and get out to the middle of the catwalk. No way. I couldn't get up there in time to stop Genevieve from doing whatever she wanted.

"Isn't it a nice view?" she said.

"Yeah." Cody turned to her and nearly threw himself off balance. Genevieve steadied him with an arm.

I was wrong. Genevieve was just giving Cody an ill-advised tour. I could breathe again.

I had started to step out of the curtain when I heard, "It's even better if you go out there." I looked up. Genevieve gestured to an area out over the stage, away from the catwalk.

I melted back into the shadows.

"How?" said my dear gullible brother.

"Just shimmy out on this metal beam." She pointed at a pipe that was part of the lighting grid. It wasn't meant to be climbed on. This was no tour.

"Like this." She threw one leg over the beam, as if straddling a horse. She dismounted. "Now you try."

Cody got on and held on tight with his hands, his thighs pressed against the metal.

Do something, Ivy!

"Now move yourself out over the stage. It's easy."

He started to inch out. I ran toward the ladder to the catwalk, as quietly as possible. I didn't know what I was going to do, but I couldn't do nothing.

"Only look up clear," said Genevieve. Her voice was so low I could barely hear her, but I recognized Lady Macbeth's lines. "To alter favour ever is to fear: Leave all the rest to me." Then louder, to Cody. "Don't worry. I'm right behind you."

She wasn't.

Out of the corner of my eye, I saw Matt come through the backstage door, probably looking for Cody. Yes. Now I knew what to do. I caught Matt's eyes. His mouth twisted in a puzzled smile (the underwear, probably), but I held a finger to my lips before he said anything. I waved him over to my spot by the ladder. When he was near, I pointed to Cody and Genevieve high above us. Matt swallowed visibly.

I put my lips right next to his ear and whispered quieter than I'd thought possible. "You climb up to the catwalk this way," I pointed at the ladder. "I'll go to the other side of the stage and distract Genevieve. Just get yourself in between her and Cody. Push her off if you have to."

His eyes widened. "You think it's that serious?"

"I think she's a murderer."

He nodded, set his jaw, and began to climb the iron rungs set into the concrete block wall of the theater.

I crept around the back of the set, trying not to think about Cody high above me. I made it to the stage left wings and looked up. Cody was nearly four feet out on the beam, facing away from the catwalk. Matt had reached the top rung of the ladder. I couldn't see his face, but I could tell he was waiting for me. I entered stage left.

"The raven himself is hoarse That croaks the fatal entrance of

Duncan Under my battlements," said crazy Genevieve.

"Hey, Genevieve," I yelled, waving at her. "So nice of you to give Cody a tour."

Startled by the shout from down below, Cody whipped his head around. Off balance, his body leaned, too far, out into space. One of his arms shot out like he was a bronco rider trying desperately to stay on his mount. Shit! I hadn't thought this through.

"Hold on, Cody," I yelled. "With both hands. Both hands!"

He put both hands on the beams and steadied himself. He looked down at me. "You're in your underwear." I nearly smiled. He was okay. For now.

Genevieve had turned to watch Cody, but didn't give any indication of seeing Matt, who had plastered himself against a shadow on the wall. "So," I said loudly, to draw back her attention. "I wanted to tell you there's no hard feelings about Jason." She listened to my lie as Matt crept onto the catwalk. His Keds made no sound.

"Macbeth and I were destined to be together," she said with a shrug. Not enough of a distraction: she started to turn back to Cody.

"Then what was up with Simon?" I said frantically. She turned back. "Was it leftover feelings, from when you were both in Flagstaff?"

"Flagstaff." Genevieve looked out beyond the stage, as if she could see her past in the darkness. This might work.

"*A Midsummer Night's Dream?*" I guessed, remembering the photo of Simon with the donkey ears. "When was that exactly?" I tried to channel Uncle Bob, get her talking.

"Ten...yes, ten years ago." She stopped.

Damn. I tried again, with a more open-ended question. "What was it like?" Lame, but my mind was on other things, like Matt, who crept closer to Cody's beam.

"God, what a summer." She was Genevieve now, not Lady Macbeth. "Simon was beautiful and talented and famous. He had just won an Emmy for a TV production of *All's Well*. He was our star."

Cody spied Matt. He opened his mouth, but shut it again quickly when Matt gave him the quiet sign.

"He was your 'star,' too, right?" I had to keep her going.

"I was his fairy queen and he was my Bottom." She drifted a few steps toward me along the metal walkway, keeping her eyes on the past. Behind her, Matt knelt on the catwalk, as close as he could to Cody. "Onstage he was rude, raunchy, and always grabbing at me. Offstage, he was charming, chivalrous, and always grabbing at me." Genevieve's voice grew dreamier. "The perfect man."

Matt inched out so one knee was on the beam. He stretched one arm out like a wing for balance, and the other one toward Cody, touching his back with his fingertips.

Cody started to twist around, his body tilting toward the open air.

"No!" said Matt.

Genevieve turned to them. I held my breath.

"It's okay, Cody. No need to turn around. You can feel my hand, right?" Matt ignored Genevieve, so Cody did too. "Just push yourself back toward me, okay?" Matt said. Cody nodded.

I couldn't see Genevieve's face well, but thought I saw her mouth purse in disappointment. She turned back to me and I definitely saw her raise an eyebrow as if to say, "Oh well."

"But what happened?" I knew we weren't in the clear yet, so I soldiered on. "What happened with Simon?"

"Alcohol clouded his judgment. When I learned he was sober, I thought we had a chance." Her voice hardened. "He said it wasn't the alcohol, though he did apologize for his behavior. 'Making amends,' he called it."

*I'm sorry I caused you pain.* Simon's note. It had been written to Genevieve.

Clang! Cody was off the beam and onto the catwalk, his hard-soled shoes ringing as he and Matt walked quickly to the stage right ladder.

"Ah. I see," said Genevieve, watching them. She walked leisurely toward the ladder on my side of the stage, seemingly unfazed by Matt and Cody's escape.

They all climbed down slowly, large spiders on the concrete walls: Cody and Matt on one side of the stage, Genevieve on the other. Me, I was stuck in the middle, in an emotional web. I wanted to run to my baby brother and I wanted to get Genevieve, to make sure she went to jail for a long, long time.

I made a decision and ran toward Matt and Cody. "Get out," I said in a stage whisper. I pointed to the closest exit, the loading dock. Matt would keep Cody safe.

"But—" said my brother, who had just reached the floor.

"It'll be okay." Matt jumped down. "Let's go." He grabbed Cody by the hand as they ran toward the door. "Olive knows what she's doing."

I ran back toward Genevieve, who was still picking her way down the ladder. I hoped Matt was right.

# CHAPTER 51

## The Sticking Place

Genevieve touched down and turned to me. She was still in costume, that skimpy red leotard, with her dagger slung from a jeweled belt around her hips. She gazed at me levelly, then flicked her eyes up and down my underwear-clad body. She smiled.

"So..." I began, not knowing where I was going next. I was afraid to confront her about Cody. I didn't want her following him. I didn't even want her thinking about him. And I needed a confession. I decided to try Uncle Bob's buddy-buddy approach. "Simon. What a bastard, huh?"

No reaction, except for taking a few steps toward me.

"I can't believe he dumped you."

Her eyes turned cold.

"Twice," I added. I couldn't help myself.

Genevieve walked toward me, her eyes little black holes.

"I'd certainly feel like killing him," I said.

Genevieve's eyes got smaller than I'd thought possible. Something felt wrong. Was I out of my league?

"I'm not petty enough to kill Simon," said Genevieve.

Shit. Did I have it wrong again?

"For revenge." Genevieve continued her slow, spider-like advance toward me. "You are such a fool."

All at once, I realized I was a fool, I was out of my league, and yes, something was very wrong. I remembered the techies rushing out to the parking lot in hopes of free beer: no witnesses backstage. I remembered that when I arrived onstage, Genevieve spoke the line about Duncan's fatal entrance, the one Lady Macbeth says when the king walks into the Macbeths' trap. And I realized Cody's escape was too easy. Much too easy.

It was me she wanted.

"A morphine injection, right?" I wasn't backing down.

"And a Rohypnol in his coffee so he wouldn't struggle." Genevieve drew nearer and nearer.

"But why?"

"I was protecting you," said Genevieve.

My disbelief must've showed on my face, because she said, "It was obvious he was after you, that you'd have to go through the pain that I..." She swallowed and held her head high. "You should be grateful."

Don't say it, don't say it, don't say it.

I said it. "You've got to be kidding." I clapped a hand over my mouth in case it wanted to say anything else stupid.

She advanced on me. "But of course, I mostly did it for Macbeth."

My mouth managed to speak through my hand: "Huh?"

"Simon was stealing my dear husband's thunder. Everyone talked about Simon, wrote about Simon, 'the Shakespearean legend,'" she snorted. Her voice rose. "It was not his show. Duncan dies. The king dies! He dies early on so we can triumph—"

"But you don't triumph." I willed myself to stay put, to stand up to her, even though she was now just inches away. "You both end up dead in the play. You kill yourself."

"No!" she roared in my face. I stumbled backward. Off balance, I fell onto the hard wooden stage.

"Not this time," she continued, standing above me. "We win. I win."

Unsheathing her dagger, she held it high above her head. This couldn't be for real. She must be acting.

She began, "Come you spirits that tend on mortal thoughts..."

Lady Macbeth's monologue. She was acting. Phew.

I stood up, brushed myself off, and headed stage right. In a second, I was down again, a bright light filling my head and pain like hot daggers stabbing through my leg. What the hell? I stared up at Genevieve, trying to piece together what had just happened.

"Unsex me..."

"Genevieve," I yelled her name, trying to pull her back to reality. It seemed to work. She looked at me, clear-eyed. "What the hell was—"

"Martial arts training," she said. "It's turned out to be very useful. I just dislocated your knee."

I tried to stand, but pain flashed red in my eyes as my leg gave out.

"I am sorry about this." Genevieve raised the knife again, in a sacrificial goddess sort of way. "If you'd only known your place, stayed away from us. But no, you wormed your way into our world. Your knowledge seals your fate, as it did your kinsman's."

"So you did poison Uncle Bob."

"Blood will have blood."

"This won't work." I tried to think through the pain taking over my consciousness. "What happened to Simon looked like an accident, but this will look like—"

"Self defense," she said, "once I put your prints on this dagger. You came at me like a crazy woman, I'll say, when all I had done was give your brother a backstage tour. No one trusts you after your last wild accusation. They all think Simon's death unhinged you. I'll just confirm that belief."

She closed her eyes for a moment. When she opened them, I swear her eyes had changed, that I could see some ancient darkness in them.

That I could see the curse of *Macbeth*.

Genevieve took a deep breath and drew the knife across her breast, slicing open the thin material of her costume and the white skin underneath. Blood bloomed black against her red leotard. She dipped her dagger into it and stooped to reach me. "I'll gild the faces of the grooms withal; for it must seem their guilt," she said, smearing her blood on my face.

"Shit! Genevieve!"

"I'm not Genevieve," she said in a calm voice as her blood dripped onto the stage. "I'm Lady Macbeth."

I knew then that I couldn't pull her back to the present. She had lost it. And I was dead. Hoping the pain was distracting her, I scooted backwards, pushing myself stage right. Ow. The passage to the greenroom was that way. Maybe I could yell loud enough to attract some attention. Matt must have told someone what was going on. Another scoot. Ow. Shit, my knee hurt. I couldn't see anyone offstage, just the ropes and pulleys that anchored the flats and the cauldron in the fly space.

"Unsex me here..." Genevieve continued her monologue, slicing a bit of skin above her heart.

I managed another couple of scoots. Ow, ow, ow.

Genevieve stopped me with a stomp to my stomach. I gasped like a soon-to-be-gutted-with-a-jeweled-dagger fish out of water. You'd think all this action would've winded her, too, but no, she kept going, like someone possessed. Like Lady Macbeth.

"And fill me, from the crown to the toes, top-full of direst cruelty..." she intoned.

What would stop Lady Macbeth?

"Double, double, toil, and trouble." I chanted the supposedly real spell.

Genevieve halted. Had it worked?

"Make thick my blood," she said after a moment, her eyes still full of that terrifying darkness. "Stop up the access and passage to remorse..."

Hoping to buy some more time, I continued, "Fire burn and cauldron bubble..." Cauldron. *Cauldron.* I pushed past the pain, turned onto my good side and lunged toward the rope that held the cauldron high above the stage.

I yanked it, too late, just as Genevieve grabbed me by the hair. She dragged me back toward the stage and pulled me up, forcing my weight onto my knees. Pain. Oh God, I thought I was going to pass out. A black hole opened up in my vision. It loomed, big and dark behind Genevieve. The blackness got bigger and bigger and then, bam! It hit Genevieve, knocking her off her feet. She fell across me, unconscious, the dagger skittering out of her hand.

The black witches' cauldron hung, swaying, inches above my head. I had released it from the flyspace. I hadn't been too late.

"Ivy!" shouted a voice from somewhere behind me. Jason ran to me, and unceremoniously pushed the limp Genevieve off of me. He knelt down and cradled me in his arms, his breath in my ear. "You're all right now."

Relief flowed over me. I was all right, and Jason was here. Wait. "Aren't you and Genevieve..."

"Shhh!" He shook his head and pulled my face to his chest, so I couldn't speak. I did anyway. "How did you know I was here?" I mumbled into his chest, then managed to push my face away. "And what took you so long? Where were you?"

Edward appeared from the shadows, brushing invisible dirt from the knees of his pants. "We were in the...ahh...area," said Edward.

Everything clicked into place: Jason's mysterious absences, his reluctance to make our relationship public, his evasion regarding his whereabouts on opening night—and the fact that his zipper was only halfway up. I looked at him. He wouldn't meet my eyes but at least had the good grace to blush.

"Omigod," I said. "You're not an introverted actor. You're gay."

"Bisexual," Jason said.

"This is what you've been trying to hide from me? You let me wonder if you'd murdered someone just because *you're gay*?"

"*Bisexual*. And this is my career, Ivy. I'm a leading man."

"Hello? This is the theater," I said.

"And there's my dad." Jason swallowed.

"Wait." My adrenaline rush over, my brain returned along with the pain. I gritted my teeth. "Were you 'in the area' when Genevieve attacked me? Nearly killed me? And you're just showing up now?"

"They don't use that one spot between the flats any longer," said Linda, emerging from the shadows. "They were probably in the techie bathroom. Hard to hear from in there. Especially when you're concentrating on, ah, something else."

The two men stared at her. "I'm a stage manager," she said. "It's my business to know your business." Linda kneeled down beside me. "But I should have been paying attention to *your* business, Ivy. Should have known something was up before your brother and his friend came flying through the stage door. I'm sorry. I knew something wasn't right, but I couldn't put all the pieces together. It took a good detective to do that."

A good detective. My uncle would be proud.

# CHAPTER 52

## When the Hurlyburly's Done

I lay on the ratty couch in the greenroom, my knee propped up on some pillows, sipping lukewarm café mocha from a paper cup. The drink was courtesy of Jason-the-three-timer. Once out of Edward's earshot, he admitted to bonking Genevieve. Said something about doing it to protect his secret. Right.

"Do you want a refill?" Jason hovered over me like a mosquito, whiny and liable to suck my blood if I gave him the chance. I waved him away.

Matt sat down next to me, carefully avoiding my knee. "Found your cell in your dressing room, like you said," he said, handing the phone to me. "Cody's already in the car. You sure it's all right if I take him back to the house?" I nodded. Cody'd be more comfortable at home, and if the police needed to question him, he'd do better in a familiar environment. "Okay, then," said Matt. "We're off." He got up off the sofa just as Candy MoonPie walked over.

"Bye," she said, waving her fingers at Matt. He smiled at her and headed toward the door.

"I haven't seen this much excitement since the pigs ate my baby brother," said Candy. Then in a lower voice, "Dang, that Matt is fine." She gazed after him wistfully.

"G'head," I said. "Go with them. Say I asked you to make sure they got home okay. We can fill each other in later when you come by my house and bring me chocolate and liquor."

She smiled and lit out after Matt.

"Candy?" I called, sitting upright. "Pigs? Kidding, right?"

She just waggled her eyebrows and left.

I sank back on the sofa. My knee hardly hurt at all anymore. My body felt toasty and liquid-y, like warm syrup ran through my veins. My head was beginning to feel pretty good, too. After stabilizing my knee, the EMTs had given me a shot of something while they took care of Genevieve, who wasn't dead, just badly concussed. Concussed. That was a funny word. I giggled. Yep, my head was definitely feeling fine.

I dialed Uncle Bob on my cell. As soon as he picked up I said, "I'm so sorry. I'll never lie again. I'm really working on not being so selfish, and I'll see a counselor really soon, and Genevieve killed Simon with morphine, and it was a good thing the cauldron was fiberglass so it didn't kill her, and oh!" Pink pushed his way through the throng of actors crowding the greenroom and stood in front of me. "I guess Linda called Detective Pinkstaff. Gotta go." I hung up, setting my phone down on Mrs. Lovett's bloodstained table, but holding onto my mocha.

"You shoulda been here," I said to Pink, hoisting my cup in a toast to myself. "I got the killer."

"Yeah. Nice job," he said, "except for the nearly getting killed part."

I shrugged. "Nearly only counts in jazz and horseshoes." I giggled again.

The detective stared at me. "Maybe I'll talk to you a little later." A buzz sounded from his front shirt pocket. He took out his phone, glanced at the number and said, "Hey, Bob. Yeah, I'm with her right now." Pink looked me up and down, focused on my knee. "Not too bad," he said into the phone. "Yeah, you bet. Later." He put the phone back in his pocket. "Just told your uncle you were fine. You are, right? Your knee gonna be okay?"

"Sure." I waved my cup in the air, sloshing a bit of brown liquid on myself. "I'm indestructible."

A couple of EMTs came through the backstage door to the

greenroom, carrying a stretcher with a blanketed figure on it.

"Genevieve, she's a bit more destructible," I said. "Wait, is that a word? Destructible?"

The EMTs carried Genevieve carefully. She looked pretty bad. Her face was swollen and bruised, and they had her in one of those neck thingies. Cast members made little noises of sympathy as the paramedics carried her to the door.

"Hello?" I said to the room at large. "Killer, remember? K-I-L-L—"

I felt a hand on my shoulder and looked up to see Linda. Good ol' Linda.

"Linda's a hero," I said to Pink. "She protected us from makeup."

Pinkstaff looked to Linda for a translation. "I thought it was fishy when Jason got sick after using Simon's makeup," she said. "So I locked it up. Just watching out for my cast."

"Tell him about your ass," I said to Linda.

She rolled her eyes at me. "Someone put a photo of Simon as Bottom—he's costumed like a donkey—in Ivy's purse, trying to implicate me, I guess."

"It was your photo?" Pinkstaff asked Linda.

"Yeah. It was a publicity photo from when we worked together in Flagstaff."

The holes I'd noticed in the picture were made by darts. Linda had told me she kept the photo tacked to a corkboard inside one of her cupboard doors, using it as a target. Just for stress relief, she said.

"I didn't think anyone knew about it," she said. "When it ended up at Simon's memorial service, I figured Edward had seen it and borrowed it for the service. I thought he wanted people to see a photo of Simon as an ass. Seemed exactly like the passive-aggressive bullshit he's always pulling."

"And when she heard about Simon ending up in my purse—Hey, how did you hear that?" I asked.

"Candy," she said.

"Ah."

"When I heard the photo had been planted," said Linda, "I started to wonder if Ivy was right—"

"I was right," I reminded everyone within earshot.

"And if someone was setting me up to take the fall."

Pinkstaff looked at Linda and waited.

"Everyone knew I hated him," she said. "I even started to feel guilty, 'cause I sure as hell wasn't sad to see him go. I kept an eye out, but..." She thrust her chin at me. "Ivy's the one who figured everything out."

I did. I caught Simon's killer and saved Cody. I felt like Poirot and Wonder Woman.

"I got a few things to clear up," Linda said. "I'll be in my office if you need me." She started to walk down the hall.

"Wait," I said. She stopped. There was one thing *I* wanted to clear up. "Do you think you need glasses?" I asked.

"Glasses?" she said, squinting. "What for?"

Ah. It wasn't bad eyesight, just her thinking face.

"Never mind," I said.

She shook her head at me and ambled off toward her office, the keys on her belt jingling.

Pinkstaff glanced around at the cast, who were hanging out in the greenroom, downing most of the closing night liquor-type presents. When his eye fell on me again, he blushed. Someone had given me a blanket earlier, but it had slipped down. I now sat there like a mermaid in my bra with a green fuzzy blanket for a tail.

"Oops," I said. I pulled up the blanket, which seemed to slip down again immediately. "Oops," I said again, tugging it up to my shoulders.

"Nice job figuring out the situation," said Pinkstaff, keeping his eyes on my face. It was a good thing, too. That was one slippery blanket. "Must share some detecting genes with your uncle or something."

"Or something," I said brightly, inordinately proud of my banter. What were these drugs and how could I get more?

Pinkstaff leaned close. "Your uncle was worried about you."

"Uncle Bob! Awww."

"And said to tell you he loves you." Pink blushed again, then jumped up as a wave of people swept into the room. "What the hell?" he said. "Who called the press?"

Bill Boxer rode the crest of the media wave. Of course.

"I'll go talk to them," said Edward, who had appeared as soon as the press did. Publicity whore.

"No," said Pinkstaff. "Out!" he shouted at the press, flashing his badge.

"Ivy!" yelled a young female TV reporter, teetering in too-high heels. "How does it feel to—"

"*Out!*" Pinkstaff's bulk and authoritative voice pushed the mob back out the stage door. He fumbled with the latch for a minute. "How do I lock this goddamn door?"

Edward jumped up and locked the door. He propped a chair up against it, too, for good measure. I smiled and waved at the photographers I could see pressed against the glass door. Oops. I pulled up the blanket again.

Someone large and angry pounded on the door.

"Let me in!"

It was the largely angry Pamela. Edward ran over to me, but made it look as though he was talking to Pinkstaff.

"Did she forget her keys?" I asked.

The Real Witch started toward the door.

"No!" shouted Edward. The Real Witch jumped back. The rest of the cast stopped carousing for a moment, curious. "As you were," said Edward in an authoritative director-type voice. The actors went back to drinking and laughing. "Ivy," Edward said, his voice strained. "About Jason and I...Pamela mustn't find out."

Ahhh.

"You mean how you've been boffing...Oh!" I said to Jason, who was still hovering, "Does the term 'blackball' mean anything to you?" He looked like he might cry.

"Ivy." Edward was actually down on one knee.

"Let me in! This is my theater!" yelled Pamela from the door, fumbling in her purse.

"Oh, I think she's found her keys," I said.

"Ivy," said Edward, his face a lovely shade of red.

"Hmm," I said. "Aren't you directing *Much Ado* next?"

"Yes, yes. I'm sure I could find a part for you."

"Hero. I want to play Hero," I told him. "She's the second female lead," I explained to Pinkstaff. Back to Edward. "Even if I'm still on crutches."

Bam, bam, bam! "What the hell is going on?" Pamela yelled.

Bet the journalists were getting some good photos.

"Deal?" I said, sticking out my hand. Pinkstaff tried to hide a grin.

"Deal," said Edward. He shook my hand hurriedly and rose, looking at the detective. "That's my wife," he said. "The artistic director of this theater. May I?" he pointed toward the door.

Pinkstaff nodded. "Just her."

Edward loped toward the door, took the chair out of the way, and twisted the lock. Pamela burst in.

"What the hell," she panted.

Edward grabbed her arm and steered her down the hall. "You see, darling, I had to get permission from the detective before I could let you in." Their voices disappeared down the hall.

I happily downed the last of my café mocha and licked the inside of the cup. Never was one to waste chocolate. I held my cup aloft. Jason took it from me. He jogged to the coffee machine, put some change in, and watched the cup fill, keeping one eye on me.

"You know, you did one hell of a job here." Pinkstaff pursed his lips in admiration. "Wanna tell me all about it? Over a drink, maybe?"

I looked at the guy. He was nice. He was also old enough to be my father, wore a rumpled polyester shirt with armpit stains, and had hair growing out of his ears. He was nice, though, so I wanted to let him down gently.

"I'd love to," I said, "but I've got a boyfriend."

Jason nearly ran back with my café mocha.

"Not him still?" Pinkstaff said.

Jason tenderly held the cup up to my lips. I grabbed it from him.

"Nah," I said. "Him." I pointed at the nearest manly-looking back.

Jason started to laugh. "Riley?" he said.

Hearing his name, Riley whipped around and poured a splash of Wild Turkey into my cup, spilling a bit onto my chest. Seizing the moment, I grabbed him around the neck and gave him a big wet one, making it look really juicy. After I'd released him, Riley whooped, Jason looked dazed, and Pinkstaff let out a sigh.

Ha.

I'm Ivy Meadows and I am a great actress.

## Cindy Brown

Cindy Brown has been a theater geek (musician, actor, director, producer, and playwright) since her first professional gig at age 14. Now a full-time writer, she's lucky enough to have garnered several awards (including 3rd place in the 2013 international *Words With Jam* First Page Competition, judged by Sue Grafton!) and is an alumnus of the Squaw Valley Writers Workshop. Though Cindy and her husband now live in Portland, Oregon, she made her home in Phoenix, Arizona, for more than 25 years and knows all the good places to hide dead bodies in both cities.

**Henery Press Mystery Books**

And finally, before you go...
Here are a few other mysteries
you might enjoy:

# THE DEEP END

Julie Mulhern

## A Country Club Murders Mystery

Swimming into the lifeless body of her husband's mistress tends to ruin a woman's day, but becoming a murder suspect can ruin her whole life.

It's 1974 and Ellison Russell's life revolves around her daughter and her art. She's long since stopped caring about her cheating husband, Henry, and the women with whom he entertains himself. That is, until she becomes a suspect in Madeline Harper's death. The murder forces Ellison to confront her husband's proclivities and his crimes—kinky sex, petty cruelties and blackmail.

As the body count approaches par on the seventh hole, Ellison knows she has to catch a killer. But with an interfering mother, an adoring father, a teenage daughter, and a cadre of well-meaning friends demanding her attention, can Ellison find the killer before he finds her?

Available at booksellers nationwide and online

Visit www.henerypress.com for details

# THE AMBITIOUS CARD

John Gaspard

## An Eli Marks Mystery (#1)

The life of a magician isn't all kiddie shows and card tricks. Sometimes it's murder. Especially when magician Eli Marks very publicly debunks a famed psychic, and said psychic ends up dead. The evidence, including a bloody King of Diamonds playing card (one from Eli's own Ambitious Card routine), directs the police right to Eli.

As more psychics are slain, and more King cards rise to the top, Eli can't escape suspicion. Things get really complicated when romance blooms with a beautiful psychic, and Eli discovers she's the next target for murder, and he's scheduled to die with her. Now Eli must use every trick he knows to keep them both alive and reveal the true killer.

Available at booksellers nationwide and online

Visit www.henerypress.com for details

# FRONT PAGE FATALITY

LynDee Walker

## A Headlines in High Heels Mystery (#1)

Crime reporter Nichelle Clarke's days can flip from macabre to comical with a beep of her police scanner. Then an ordinary accident story turns extraordinary when evidence goes missing, a prosecutor vanishes, and a sexy Mafia boss shows up with the headline tip of a lifetime.

As Nichelle gets closer to the truth, her story gets more dangerous. Armed with a notebook, a hunch, and her favorite stilettos, Nichelle races to splash these shady dealings across the front page before this deadline becomes her last.

Available at booksellers nationwide and online

Visit www.henerypress.com for details

# FIT TO BE DEAD

Nancy G. West

## An Aggie Mundeen Mystery (#1)

Aggie Mundeen, single and pushing forty, fears nothing but middle age. When she moves from Chicago to San Antonio, she decides she better shape up before anybody discovers she writes the column, "Stay Young with Aggie." She takes Aspects of Aging at University of the Holy Trinity and plunges into exercise at Fit and Firm.

Rusty at flirting and mechanically inept, she irritates a slew of male exercisers, then stumbles into murder. She'd like to impress the attractive detective with her sleuthing skills. But when the killer comes after her, the health club evacuates semi-clad patrons, and the detective has to stall his investigation to save Aggie's derriere.

Available at booksellers nationwide and online

Visit www.henerypress.com for details

# NUN TOO SOON

Alice Loweecey

## A Giulia Driscoll Mystery (#1)

Giulia Falcone-Driscoll has just taken on her first impossible client: The Silk Tie Killer. He's hired Driscoll Investigations to prove his innocence and they have only thirteen days to accomplish it. Talk about being tried in the media. Everyone in town is sure Roger Fitch strangled his girlfriend with one of his silk neckties. And then there's the local TMZ wannabes—The Scoop—stalking Giulia and her client for sleazy sound bites.

On top of all that, her assistant's first baby is due any second, her scary smart admin still doesn't relate well to humans, and her police detective husband insists her client is guilty. About this marriage thing—it's unknown territory, but it sure beats ten years of living with 150 nuns.

Giulia's ownership of Driscoll Investigations hasn't changed her passion for justice from her convent years. But the more dirt she digs up, the more she's worried her efforts will help a murderer escape. As the client accuses DI of dragging its heels on purpose, Giulia thinks The Silk Tie Killer might be choosing one of his ties for her own neck.

Available at booksellers nationwide and online

Visit www.henerypress.com for details

# ARTIFACT

Gigi Pandian

## A Jaya Jones Treasure Hunt Mystery (#1)

Historian Jaya Jones discovers the secrets of a lost Indian treasure may be hidden in a Scottish legend from the days of the British Raj. But she's not the only one on the trail...

From San Francisco to London to the Highlands of Scotland, Jaya must evade a shadowy stalker as she follows hints from the hastily scrawled note of her dead lover to a remote archaeological dig. Helping her decipher the cryptic clues are her magician best friend, a devastatingly handsome art historian with something to hide, and a charming archaeologist running for his life.

Available at booksellers nationwide and online

Visit www.henerypress.com for details